We had everything together. How could she leave all that behind…leave me?

I ran through the parking garage, after parking my truck in the first spot I saw. It might have been a handicapped spot. I wasn't really sure and, right then, I didn't give a fuck. I bought a ticket so I could get back to the gates. I was rounding the corner when I heard them announce the flight that I knew Kitty was getting on.

I got to the gate, scanning all over but it was nearly empty, the sign above the doorway that lead to the plane was flashing last call. I went to make my way down to the plane, but the ticket lady stopped me. When I looked down the walkway, there at the bottom was Caroline. The large woman still blocking my path, I called to her, "Caroline!"

"Sir, you can't go down there without a proper ticket," the pudgy woman said, taking another step forward to block me.

"I need to get down there!" I said frantically.

"I'm sorry but, no ticket, no plane."

What a bitch.

"Caroline!" I yelled, again.

Kitty stood there, a slight hesitation in her body that I had come to know so well, staring at me. I could have sworn she was going to run back, run to me—that is, until she lifted her chin, fixed the bag on her shoulder, and walked away, taking with her what was left of my heart.

Caroline:

When someone says "Make me stay" in the most dramatic, lovesick kind of way, most people think it sounds desperate, weak, or needy. I, for one, think it sounds like all of the above! I'm not stupid, and I sure as heck am not desperate. In fact, I'm the complete opposite of weak. I've lived my live with a steel trap around my heart, and I don't need anyone—especially a man. So how in the hell did a wannabe rock star get me to say those three words...make me stay?

Kane:

One-woman man? You've got to be joking. I was a rock god...in a bar...in a small town...eh, details. I was getting women like I was their gift from God. I was going to make it big. My band and I were going to bust out of Small Town, USA, and we were going to knock the panties off every woman in sight. So, when I caught some sexy groupie touching my baby...my beautiful guitar, did I want to test those waters? Hell, yes! But did I want to be a one-woman man? Hell, no! But after that, all I knew was that I wanted to make her stay.

KUDOS for *Make Me Stay*

In *Make Me Stay* by ME Gordon, Caroline "Kitty" James is determined not to commit to sexy Kane Lawson, lead singer of the band, One Night Stand. Kane is equally determined to make Kitty his, despite the issues they both face. He woos and wins her, or so he thinks. But when Kitty walks away and breaks Kane's heart, it may be more than they can overcome. With a solid story from both points of view, a strong plot, and lots of steamy sex scenes, this is my kind of book. *~ Taylor Jones, Reviewer*

Make Me Stay by ME Gordon is a steamy romance told from both the heroine and the hero's POV in first person. At first, I wasn't sure it would work, but it did, quite well. Our heroine, Kitty James brings a lot of baggage when she reunites with her father after a four-year estrangement. And it's not physical baggage but mental. Her mother's death has left Kitty unable to commit to relationships. She also has a dream job in New York after her summer in Nowheresville, Maryland, is over. So what if she has to leave the only guy she has every loved behind when she goes? Relationships never work out anyway, right? *Make Me Stay* is a fun, heart-breaking and heart-warming story of love, loss, and forgiveness. Add in the hot love scenes, and you have a story you will want to read again and again. *~ Regan Murphy, Reviewer*

ACKNOWLEDGEMENTS

What can I say? The men of One Night Stand came into my life and stole my heart, each of them with their own stories, their own demons.

You see it all started one night when I was driving down my hometown's historic downtown main street. There's this bar at the end, high above the street, and as I drove by I could see people inside, laughing and listening to music. I wondered what it might be like to go to that bar every week and see the same band play. What kind of music would they be playing? Would they be gentleman, would they be wild and sexy? What would they look like? That night I came home and wrote the first five chapters of *Make Me Stay*.

Make Me Stay was an amazing book to write, and it sure wouldn't be as great as it is now without the help of these awesome people: To Faith, my editor, thank you for not killing me for over using the word "toward." I'm still learning so much from you, and I can't wait to keep learning and working with you. To Lauri, thank you for seeing something in me and getting *Make Me Stay* out there for everyone to read. To Melissa, you are beyond talented. You've taken my ideas and made them not only into amazing book covers but beautiful artwork.

To this next group, I hope you were telling me the truth when you said you loved this book: Dora, Susan, and Jessica, thank you for your support.

A special thank you goes out to my friend April. You were the first person to read *Make Me Stay*, and I was a little terrified I might scare you away so early in our friendship, but I think it just did the opposite. Thank you for encouraging me and helping me.

To my development team person, Meaghan. Thank you for listening to me rant on and on about the people talking in my head and for helping me make sense of it all.

To my children, thank you for being patient with me. I love all four of you equally, with all my heart.

To my husband, thank you for being so supportive and for getting up every morning and working so hard so that I can stay home with our babies and write sexy books about other men. I love you more than you could ever imagine.

It is my hope that everyone who reads this book falls in love with the men of One Night Stand as much as I have.

MAKE

ME

STAY

M E GORDON

A Black Opal Books Publication

GENRE: STEAMY ROMANCE/CONTEMPORARY ROMANCE/CHICK LIT

This is a work of fiction. Names, places, characters and incidents are either the product of the author's imagination or are used fictitiously, and any resemblance to any actual persons, living or dead, businesses, organizations, events or locales is entirely coincidental. All trademarks, service marks, registered trademarks, and registered service marks are the property of their respective owners and are used herein for identification purposes only. The publisher does not have any control over or assume any responsibility for author or third-party websites or their contents.

MAKE ME STAY
Copyright © 2016 by M. E. GORDON
Cover Design by Melissa Stevens
All cover art copyright © 2016
All Rights Reserved
Print ISBN: 978-1-626944-82-4

First Publication: JULY 2016

Published by Black Opal Books **http://www.blackopalbooks.com**

DEDICATION

*To the Upper Deck Bar in
Historic Downtown Mount Airy.
Without you there would be no
One Night Stand*

CHAPTER 1

Caroline

For four years I had managed to keep my distance. I kept myself busy so I wouldn't have to think, or remember. Now I stood in front of the old building. My bags weighed me down, and so I dropped them. Spring was present, the trees all had early buds on them, flowers were poking up through the winter mulch, but there was still a slight chill to the air.

I stood before the large wooden doors, not sure if I really wanted to go through them. This building was my father's way of coping. He bought the place in the middle of his mid-life crisis. He packed up my childhood home—without asking me, I might add—and moved from our beautiful two-story house in our relaxed neighborhood and charming little town that was right outside of New York City. And this, was where he picked...Nowheresville, Maryland.

Okay, it wasn't "nowhere," it was forty-five minutes to Baltimore and an hour to DC but, to me, it was a foreign country. I knew nothing about this place. Glancing from side to side, I took in the surroundings. Surprise, surprise, nothing was to my left and nothing was to my right. It was a beautiful day and I was standing in the middle of an empty main street, one of the two streets that even existed.

If someone was looking for small town USA, it was right here. Although it was quaint, with about a mile or two of shops and eateries lining either side of the street, it was empty, and old, really old. I expected people to be walking up and down the street, holding hands, walking babies in over-dramatic carriages, a kid or two on the playground across the street in the park. My father had totally lied to me.

It was a Sunday afternoon and there wasn't a soul in sight. Craning my neck I took a deep breath and took in the tall three stories of the building. It was an end unit, in a row of attached buildings. An alley way, large enough for maybe a large SUV to fit through, separated the last building, a body shop that looked a little too rundown to actually be functioning.

The sign that hung in the middle of the ground-floor windows was lit up. I shook my head. He could have named it anything in world and all he could come up with was BJ's? My father named a bar, BJ's. It was the letters of his name, Benjamin James, but come on, Dad. BJ's? Really? It didn't help that there was another glowing, flashing sign on the other window that said *BJ's you'll never go home disappointed*. I should have run. I hadn't seen my father in four years, what's one more? I still can't believe that I agreed to work here until I could find a job. What was I thinking?

I was in the middle of planning my escape and excuse, when one of the large doors opened.

My father practically knocked me over in an embrace. "Caroline! You're here!"

There was something about being held tightly by your dad that seemed to take all your cares away. Holding my upper arms, he took a step back to admire me, and I got my first look at my father in the flesh. We had skyped and talked on the phone, but other than that, nothing. He was tall, with broad shoulders, surprisingly fit, his hair more salt than pepper. A few more lines appeared at the corners of his green eyes, but overall he looked good. I was relieved. I had this image of him looking worn and run down, beer gut, and unclean, but he actually appeared to be the complete opposite. His sprit was bright, and he looked happy.

If there was one thing I knew about my father, it was that he did whatever he could to make others happy. He worked his butt off when I was a kid, commuting to the city for a job that paid extremely well, but left him in a day in, day out, state of mind. He took the overtime that was offered and sometimes worked late at night, so my mother and I could have everything we ever needed.

Toward the end of my high school career, I could see my mother and father wearing down. He had moved all the way to the top of his company, but he hated it. My parents had more money than they knew what to do with, yet they were both miserable. So when I got a call, six months after my mother died, that my father had sold the house and moved here, I wasn't too surprised. That doesn't mean I agree with it. I mean, the man could have moved anywhere, the tropics, Europe, a log cabin hidden away. No, not my father. He decided to put roots down in Nowheresville.

"So, what do you think? Is it how you remember it?"

Remember it? What was my father talking about? He must have been getting drunk on his own liquor.

"Dad, I've never been here before, what are you talking about?"

Scratching his head he scrunched his face. "You probably don't remember. You were pretty young."

I nodded.

"Do you remember Uncle Brian at all?" he asked.

The name sounded familiar.

"Well, he's not really your uncle, he's my cousin. We came here a lot when you were little, probably until you were four, maybe five, I can't remember. Anyway, this is where they live. Don't you remember playing with his son JJ?"

I took a moment to search for anything I could on this JJ. A picture, in an old photograph binder we had, came to mind. I could see me sitting on a beach—no, not a beach, a lake. There was a little boy sitting next to me with his arm around my shoulder.

"I think I remember," I said, still trying to recall him.

"It's fine. You'll meet him tonight. In the meantime, I'm sure we have a picture of you two somewhere around. Your mother use to take them all the time—" My father immediately stopped talking. Still standing before me, he seemed to be miles away in a memory. Shaking his head a moment later, he smiled down me.

I felt like I should have said something about her, comforted him, but I didn't, because I didn't talk about it, not to him, not to anyone.

"So, what do you think?" he asked again, showing off the brick building.

Nodding and smiling at him, I said the first thing that came to mind, pointing to the glowing sign in the window. "I guess I'll never leave disappointed." His booming laugh took me by surprise.

"Oh, Caroline, I'm so happy you're here. You're not going to want to leave."

I huffed on the inside. I might have agreed to this for the summer, but I was moving on after that. College degree in hand, I was out of here and back to New York as soon as the summer was up and a job was in line. I needed the city. I needed the noise, people walking down the street, tall buildings. Hell, I even missed the rats in the subway. There was no way I was staying there any longer than I had to.

CHAPTER 2

Kane

W hy did the mornings have to come so fast? I stretched my stiffened arms over my head and hit bare flesh. Tilting my head I saw that I'd hit, a long, slinky leg. I watched as it moved under the covers. Facing the ceiling again, a wolfish grin spread across my face. I didn't know who it was, or what happened last night, but that was just how I liked it.

Soft, warm fingers ran up the inside of my leg and suddenly, I was more than awake. A soft giggle came from under the covers as I sprung even more to life. Resting my hands behind my head, I lay back and enjoyed my morning entertainment.

Tossing the covers off us both, the lucky winner from last night was anxiously licking her chops to get a piece of me—again. I've never had a problem with women. They just flocked to me, I didn't even have to try, really. I was living out every fantasy that I had ever imagined for myself. I spent my days working in construction—which helped with keeping in shape—then at nights, I was free to explore more intimate and sometimes, non-intimate, fantasies.

"Oh, yeah, Sarah that's good, keep going," I called breathily to her.

"My name's Ashley," she said through a full mouth.

"Oh, right, Ashley."

Releasing me she sat up in bed.

Damn it!

"You don't remember my name? What about last night, you said—"

I cut her off before she could finish. "Listen, Ashley, I don't remember anything I said last night, but what I do remember is you doing that amazing thing with your tongue." I gestured to myself, all the while flashing a naughty grin.

She was completely naked. Her small chest was perky and asking for it. Black hair spilled down around her face, making her hazel eyes pop in color. *Damn, I did good last night.*

"But you said—"

Sitting up, I held a finger over her lips. My current situation was begging for her to shut up and finish what she started, so I could "finish" and kick her the hell out. She should know the deal. I had a reputation to uphold, and no woman was going to attach herself to me, except to say that they had an amazing one night stand. Maybe I had a couple girls on rotation, but not this one. This one clearly wanted "more," and I didn't do more. The girls who were frequent visitors knew the rules—no snuggling, no cuddling, and definitely no relationships.

I almost had her reigned back in—my lips were presently making their way down her neck, my hand was cupping her perky breast, when out of nowhere my door flew open.

"Kane, come on. We got to get heading out, we need to practice before tonight, it's already three."

Jumping out of bed Ashley, or so she called herself,

grabbed the covers and wrapped herself up. "Oh my God! Can't you knock?" she yelled across the room at an un-fazed JJ.

He gave her the once over, then turned back to me. "Nice one, dude. She looks good in the daylight too, might have to add her to the rotation."

He wiggled his eye brows, and we started laughing. I watched as Ashley's face turned all red. Holding the cov-er tighter to herself, she widened her eyes at me, begging me to kick JJ out, but that wasn't going to happen.

"Well, you want to be added on?" I asked.

Dropping to the floor, she grabbed her clothes and huffed into the bathroom behind her.

"I guess that's a no. Better luck next time, bro," JJ said. "Can you be ready to leave in thirty?" he asked, fix-ing his spiked up hair in the mirror that was hanging on the wall near the door.

"Yeah, I'll meet you downstairs."

The bathroom door swung open, and Ashley stormed out fully dressed. I on the other hand was still sitting in bed, naked with no covers.

She paused at the end of my bed. "I can't believe I'm doing this, but, here." She tossed me a piece of paper and strutted to the door.

JJ and I both watched as her ass swayed past us and down the hall.

"You are one lucky bastard," JJ called over his shoulder as followed her down the hall.

Unfolding the piece of paper, I found her name, number, and a little parting gift. She had kissed the paper and wrote, *Add me on for Tuesday nights.* Shaking my head, I crumpled the paper and tossed it in the wastebas-ket across the room.

I grabbed some clean clothes from my dresser and headed for the shower. As I waited for the water to heat up I checked myself out in the mirror. My hair was wild with curls and unruly from the previous night's escapades. The hairs on my face needed taking care of and as I lifted my head I noticed little sparkles as the light bounced off them. I'd do my best to get rid of them but they'd just be back tomorrow morning.

CHAPTER 3

Caroline

My first thought was, this place looked awesome. It was not at all what I had expected from the outside. My dad took my bags from me and placed them near one of the many tables.

"Pretty nice huh?" he asked.

There was a bar that traveled along the side and, where it ended, was an arched doorway that looked like it led to pool tables. In the very back was a decent sized stage, littered with drums, guitars, basses, and a key board.

It was your typical bar, but decorated really nicely. My father must have hired someone. There was no way he did this all on his own.

I nodded. "Wow, Dad, I'm impressed."

Smiling in triumph, he took another appreciative look around. "It's not too bad. I got it for practically nothing. Luckily, it came fully staffed. Kara, who you'll meet later, is a godsend. This was all her idea. I just gave her the money to get it done."

Kara? My father had never mentioned her before. Then again, our conversations usually didn't go into too much detail. *Is he dating her? Are they in love? I'm not sure I can handle that.* It had been close to five years since—had he moved on? *He's a good man. He should be happy, and if this Kara makes him happy, then I'm going to have to like her, no questions.*

Just then, the back door, which led to a hallway, opened. It slammed loudly against the wall. The bang of the door hitting, made me jump. "B, can you come give me a hand?" a squeaky female voice called from behind two large boxes.

My father smiled down at me. "I guess you can meet her now."

The female voice dropped the boxes on the ground and brushed her hair out of her face. *Okay, I'm going to have to have a talk with my father.*

Kara was young, or she had an amazing plastic surgeon. She was a petite blonde, who didn't look a day over eighteen. *Great, no wonder my father is happy. He turned into a sugar daddy.*

She had on a cropped top that barely covered her boobs, and her jean shorts looked like she had swiped them from a cheese country music video. Flipping her head down, she grabbed all her hair and tied it up in a big floppy bun on the top of her head. A few loose, blonde strands fell around her face perfectly. *Yup, I'm going to have a talk with my father.*

"Kara, this is Caroline, my daughter."

I tried to smile politely, but I had the most disturbing image in my head.

Kara smiled. "Hey, it's nice to finally meet you. B won't stop talking about you, like ever," she said, reaching over the boxes to shake my hand.

"So, are you guys…" *Great, I'm too embarrassed to even say it.*

She ripped her hand from mine, shook them both at

her sides, and ran in place while shaking her head back and forth. "Ew, you think? That I'm? With?"

I had clearly made a huge mistake.

Kara looked over at my father, clearly confused. "B, what the hell? Why does your daughter think I'm dating you?"

My father turned all sorts of red. "Caroline Ann! I am not involved with her."

Yeah, big mistake. "I'm sorry, I just thought that—"

"Well, you thought wrong, honey. I like him, but not like that," Kara said, laughing.

My father grimaced. "Well, now that we have that all taken care of, I'll give a proper introduction. This is Kara, the manager. She started as soon as I bought the place and had some great ideas, because I was too stuck in the eighties, like this place used to be. Kara sold me on re-modeling and things have been non-stop-busy since the day we re-opened."

Clearly, this girl had some real talent with decorating. Why she was working at a bar was beyond me.

She seemed to squirm a little at his praise. "Well, it wasn't all me—ah, who are we trying to kid? It was all me. This place was a pig pen before I came along," she said, admiring her handy work.

"I'm so sorry. I kind of jumped to conclusions," I said apologetically.

"Its fine. You weren't the first person to think that. Your dad and I have been hot gossip since I started working here."

There was another reason to make sure summer ended with me leaving—small town gossip.

Kara grinned at me. "It was great to finally meet you, but I have to get back to it. It's going to get crazy in here tonight."

Thinking back to the barren streets and closed shops,

I frowned. Right then, I doubted anyone but my father and Kara even lived in this town. "Oh, okay," I said, not believing her at all.

"Tomorrow won't be as bad, so I'll start training you then. Enjoy tonight and welcome." Grabbing the top box, she walked off into the back of the bar.

"Hold on one sec, I'll help you with these," my dad called to Kara. He turned back to me. "I'll show you the rest of the place and your room in a minute. I've got to help Kara with this stuff," he said, taking the other box to follow Kara.

I stood there awkwardly by myself in the unfamiliar room. Light bounced off one of the symbols on the drum kit and caught my eye. I made my way to the stage and stepped up to get a better look. There was a name on the front of the biggest drum, ONS, all done in a cool calligraphy. Under that was the proper name One Night Stand. I guessed it was fitting, since they were playing at a bar called BJs and, apparently, you never left unsatisfied.

I took my time walking around all the instruments. The drums were nice. Tapping a holder for extra sticks, I was so tempted to grab one and go to town, but I held back. The keyboard looked extremely used, but it had more buttons on it than keys. The black, slick, base was propped up on one side of the stage. A guitar was a few steps away from that, and it was a beautiful electric blue color. I walked over to the guitar on the other side of the stage. I seemed drawn to it. The glossy red paint was beckoning me toward it.

I knelt down to get a closer look. Within the glossy red paint were very fine black words. They looked like song lyrics, but the closer I got, I realized that they were girls' names. Appropriate, I thought, for a band named One Night Stand. The eight strings summoned me to run my fingers across them.

My index finger was mere centimeters from the tightly strung wires—

"You break it, you buy it."

A male voice, warm and very close, made me lose my balance. In a rush, I tried to stand, but fell back and into the arms of the man behind me.

Hastily getting to my feet, I turned around to see the guy still flat on his ass. He pulled his knees up and rested his arms on them as he eyed me up and down

"I'm sorry. I didn't mean to touch your guitar," I said apologetically.

Of course, he had to be gorgeous. I wouldn't knock over an average guy. "Well, it sure as hell looked like it," he said, as his lips curled up in a smile.

"I said I was sorry. Won't happen again—trust me." I turned from him and prepared to jump off the stage. *What a jerk!*

"You're not even going to help me up?" he asked.

Four other guys came into view from around the corner. *Must be the rest of them, the One Night Stands.*

Rotating back to him, I held out my hand.

"Such a lady," he said as he took hold of it.

I wanted to let go so he would fall on his ass again, but his grip was too tight. If I tried, we were both going down.

"Anything else?" I asked smartly.

Still holding my hand, he pulled me closer. The sudden intimacy made my stomach do a nervous flip. He was almost a head taller than me, so my eyes were dead even with his lips—plump lips, that were curved up in a wicked smile. This ass knew exactly what he was doing.

Pushing against his chest, I successfully put some space between us. "What's your problem?" I demanded.

"What's *your* problem? You're the first woman to ever jump *off* my lap that fast. You into chicks?"

I can't believe the nerve of this guy. Rustling my hair in frustration, I couldn't believe a human being who looked as good as he did could be so crude. His dark brown hair was wavy, unkempt, and swept off his face, but damn if it didn't beg to be played with. He was tan and lean. He clearly took pride in his body. The cutoff shirt he had on gave him away. I unexpectedly got an image of him playing that beautiful guitar, the muscles in his fore arms and biceps moving under that tan skin, his fingers working the strings rhythmically—

Holy shit! I need to snap out of it. I stared at him. "Not that it's any of your business, but I'm not into 'chicks.'"

His smile reached his blue eyes and I found myself trying to remember why I was mad.

"You know for a fan, you're pretty early. The groupies usually don't start showing up till three hours before B opens," he said, cocking his head.

"Groupies? Do I look like a groupie?"

He took that as an invitation to give me a once over. *Disgusting pig!*

"Well, now that you mention it, you are a little over dressed."

I glanced down at my skinny jeans and flip flops. The T-shirt I had on was thin but it was not see-through, thanks to its dark blue color. It was tight but not clingy, and the neckline was a simple U-shape.

Tucking my wild, curly, blonde hair behind my ears, I glanced over at my father, who was still helping carry large boxes in.

"Oh, I get it," he said crossing his arms. "You like them older."

"You are way off base, plus you're a disgusting pig. Your 'groupies' must all be brain dead, if they follow you around."

Yeah, that's right, Mister Rock-n-Roll, let that sink in for a moment.

"You know what—"

"Kane! Hey, man, you guys are really early," my father said, interrupting him as he made his way over to us. So the jackass had a name.

"B, you should really start locking the doors, some out-of-town trash rolled in."

All I could do was smile. Catching my reaction, this so called "Kane" looked me up and down again before turning to my father, who looked ready to punch him in the face. Good to know my father still had that protective streak in him. "Kane, this is my daughter, Caroline."

Kane's perfect little sneer quickly turned to a stunned, open-mouthed gape.

"Is there a problem?" my father asked skeptically.

I should have totally ratted Kane out. *Look at him trying to bat those baby blues at me. Not going to work. I got a pair of my own, and I know how to use them.*

"Oh no, Daddy, Kane here was just telling me how much he appreciated you. He was even saying how he was going to stay late tonight to help you close up and that he really wants to clean the restrooms. He also offered to carry up all my bags for me. Isn't that sweet of him?" I flashed the most charming smile I could his way and girlishly tossed my hair.

Shaking his head and grinning, Kane couldn't say a word in his defense.

"You really going to do that tonight, man?" my father asked. "We could really use the help."

Still acting coy, I made sure to wink at Kane before turning my attention back to my father.

"Yeah, I'll stay to help you out tonight, so long as she helps," he said, winking back.

That asshole!

CHAPTER 4

Kane

I knew B's daughter was coming to stay for the summer, but I had no idea that the girl I had just tried to hit on was her. I had come around the corner to see some girl up on *our* stage, fingering all our instruments. When she turned to look at my guitar, my baby, I made my way to the stage to confront her. I was only able to take two steps, when I saw her face. She was every bit of a ten in my book. Average height, long legs, made even longer by the tight-ass jeans she was wearing. Her shirt hung low enough when she knelt down, I could see the swell of her delightfully large breasts. I suddenly got the image of my hands full with them, and my mischievous friend began to make an appearance in my jeans.

I moved quickly, but silently up on the stage behind her. The smell of her, tickled my senses. I wanted to run my hands through the mane of wild blonde curls on her head as she screamed my name in ecstasy. I wanted to taste her, feel her—I don't think I've wanted to touch a girl as much. I wanted to experience every inch of her.

Unfortunately, all those scrumptious ideas quickly left my mind when I found out she was B's daughter. I expected his daughter to be short, frumpy, and average. What was currently standing in front of me was anything but. He had shown us all a picture of her five years ago when we started playing regularly here. It was a girl with a flat chest and plump body. Her hair was pulled back in a tight braid and she had glasses on. So of course, I didn't expect this girl to be her.

B slapped me on the back. "Okay, I'll be right back. The delivery truck just pulled up. Let me help Kara, and I'll be right back to show you upstairs, honey. Kane, I can't thank you enough for helping tonight. Caroline has the night off, though, so she won't be helping tonight. Kara's going to train her tomorrow, so having you here will be such a help, and thanks for helping my little girl carry these bags up." Smiling, he slapped my back again and then walked to the back door to find the delivery truck. I didn't know if I should be pissed that I had to stay or delighted that I got to see where this beauty was going to be sleeping, even though I had already seen it.

"You can wipe that stupid grin off your face," she said, tossing that mane of hair again.

"What are you talking about? It's not a grin. You think I want to stay sober tonight to help B clean up after our show. I'm usually knee deep in between some brunette or blonde's legs, so it's not a grin. It's me trying to figure out how I'm going to make you pay for getting me stuck here tonight."

If I knew one thing about women, it's that they couldn't resist me. This girl was a challenge that I was determined to make putty in my hands. I'd come across them once or twice—the girl who played hard to get. They always had a hidden agenda, which usually involved them wanting to date me, but I never let it come to that. They'd say that they wouldn't give it up until I promised to date them exclusively, but ten minutes alone with me in a dark room, and they were usually screaming a different tune.

"You're the one who practically invited me up to your room."

Damn, she looks cute with that scrunched up confusion on her face.

"I did not!" she snapped back.

"'Oh, Daddy, he even said he'd carry my very heavy bags up,'" I teased in a girly voice while I waved my hands dramatically. *Shit!* She socked me. Rubbing my suddenly sore arm, I glared across at her. This girl had a mean punch. I had to remember to keep my face away from her fists.

"Jesus, you don't have to beat me into submission. I'll carry your bags up," I said, reaching down to pick them up.

"Kane, what are you doing? We have to practice. We don't have time for you to fuck the help." Reece's red Mohawk was combed back and not in its usually upright position.

The girl fumed. Placing the bags down, I sat back and enjoyed the show.

"There is no way in hell that I would ever have sex with him," she snapped. "And tonight, I'm not the help, you wanna-be-clown." She cocked her head to the side and studied him a moment. "Bozo wants his hair back by the way."

I think I'm in love. I had never heard anyone talk to Reece like that before. He looked like he was going to cry. Why not put the nail in the coffin?

"Reece, this is Caroline, B's daughter," I said. His mouth hung open. I slapped his back. "Yeah, let that sink in a moment."

"That's not funny, Kane," he said nervously.

"It's fucking hysterical. Caroline, this is Reece."

Stepping up to Reece, she got in his face. I was suddenly aware of their closeness to one another. Weird.

She poked a finger in his chest. "Don't ever assume I'm fucking him. You got it?"

Nodding in agreement, Reece was clearly rendered speechless. Just like me, my fellow band mates weren't use to women putting us in our places.

The rest of the guys walked over and, before I knew it, they were all clamoring around her. I wanted to push them out of the way, hold them off, but I wasn't going to show my cards.

I began to introduce them all, I pointed to Reece, "Reece plays the drums," He was in his usual tight-ass pants—that I'd have sworn he bought from the kids department—and a black T-shirt. I turned to my left. "Aiden is a genius on the piano and does all our lighting and boring stuff."

"Dude, without me no one would be able to hear you. I'm basically the tech guy. These assholes would still be in their mommies' basements if it weren't for me," he said irately. Okay, I'd give him that one. We did need him. Aiden had shoulder-length, jet-black hair, which he kept pulled back. Girls went fucking nuts for that guy's hair.

"Trent here is our bassist," I continued while he held out his hand, clearly the only gentleman of the group, even though he looked like a badass biker on steroids. "And this is—"

"JJ?" she asked, taking the words from my mouth.

"Yeah, that's me," he answered hesitantly.

"Do you remember me?" she asked, hopeful.

Great. Competition with JJ was never good. It usually ended up with both of us having a black eye and busted lip. *Have they hooked up before?*

She smiled at him. "I think we're second, maybe

third cousins? I used to visit your family when I was younger."

Taking a moment, he examined her some more. "I think I'd remember if I had a fucking-hot-ass cousin," he said, shaking his head.

I was pretty sure I would have remembered too. After all, I'd been friends with the guy since grade school, and I would have remembered running into her.

"JJ here is lead guitar," I said, draping my arm around him "Dude, why the hell haven't we met your hot-ass cousin before today?" I asked through gritted teeth.

"I can hear you, you know," she said, crossing her arms.

I flashed her a usually effective winsome smile. She didn't buy it for a second. Caroline smiled. "So I guess that just leaves the oversexed, disrespectful, caveman of a lead singer—I'm only guessing here but, by the looks on all of your faces, I'm right."

The audacity! I am not oversexed, if anything, I'm undersexed today. "Yes, I am the lead singer, and I'm damn well proud."

Throwing her head back, she laughed. Her scent filled the air, her full breasts shook with her laughter and, as much as I wanted to deny it, I was fucking turned on.

"I was going to ask why the name, 'One Night Stand,'" she started to say. "Then I met your lead singer here, and all my questions were magically answered."

All of my so-called friends nodded in agreement.

"Hey, these guys aren't saints, either." I found myself trying to throw them under the bus with me. I couldn't have her thinking I was the only asshole in the bunch. "Aiden once took a girl to traffic court just to get some. Reece, he had sex in that bathroom last night. Trent rented a puppy for a day to get a blowjob, and your cousin over here flirts with being a pedophile. It's not just me, honey, we're a group package."

Taking a careful step back from the five of us, Caroline held her hands up. "I'm going to let you all know something right now! I'm not sleeping with any one of you—ever! I'm here to spend time with my dad, make some money, and leave, once I get a job." She put on a good front, but I had a feeling she was finding it just as hard to keep her true feelings about us under wrap.

"All right, everything is taken care of," B said as he joined us and placed his hands on his hips. "Good, you've already met the guys."

"Oh, I've met them," she said, sounding irritated.

"Get use to them, honey. If these guys weren't playing here, I might have to pack up and find a new hobby."

At least B appreciated us. Now I just had to work on winning over his daughter, for a night at least.

"Let's get you unpacked." Grabbing a bag, B turned and headed for the back of the bar.

"I guess I'll see you guys around," Caroline said, spinning to follow her father.

We all stood there watching her walk away.

"Dude, I have to sleep with her," Reece moaned, bending over in fake pain. The moment he stopped talking, Caroline whipped back around. If she had heard him, I was almost positive she was going to come back over here and slap the shit out of him.

"Kane!" The sound of my name coming off her lips had me going from picturing her slapping the shit out of him, to me, and I didn't even say anything this time. "My bags," she said sweetly, too sweetly.

Huffing over, I grabbed the remaining two bags that were fucking heavy as shit. "What do you got in here, a collection of dead bodies?" I asked, walking up behind her.

"Keep pissing me off, and you'll be one of them," she said, before heading up the stairs that led to B's home.

CHAPTER 5

Caroline

I followed my father up the stairs, our shoes clonking on the hard wood. Glancing behind me, I saw that Kane was dutifully carrying my bags. As we entered the apartment that was above the bar, I moved aside so Kane could get in all the way.

My father gestured around. "This is the living area. Over there is the kitchen. It's small, but we've got the huge one down stairs if you really want to cook anything."

The room was small for both the living area and kitchen, if you could even call it that.

There was one couch and a chair that faced a huge TV. Behind that was a small table with two stools. The kitchen was a sink, two cabinets, and a small refrigerator. On the cramped counter sat a microwave and coffee pot.

"Come on, I'll show you your room," Dad said.

Grabbing both my very heavy bags, Kane followed along behind us silently, for once since I'd met him. I didn't want to, but I watched in total guilty pleasure as his muscles flexed when he picked up my bags. Running my eyes up his arms, I caught him watching me as well.

"Like what you see?" he asked, once my father was down the hall.

"You repulse me, so no," I said, turning on my heel to follow my father.

"What do you think?" Dad asked. "You have your own bathroom, those doors lead to a balcony off the back."

This room is huge! The bed had to be king sized and beautifully made. There was enough room for a love seat and full desk. I walked over to the bathroom, which was completely remodeled and updated. There was a huge soaking tub and glass shower.

Stepping up to the French doors, I couldn't help but smile. The view wasn't what I was used to. It was nothing but farmland and mountains in the distance, but it was breathtaking.

"Dad, this is insanely nice."

Nodding in agreement he draped his arm over my shoulder. "I've been working on it for the past few months, getting it ready for you. You can thank Kara for all the decorations."

I took another glance around. It was like the room was pulled from a magazine.

"B! Get down here. I need you to sign for this." We all heard Kara yell from down stairs.

Kissing my forehead, he hugged me again. "I'm so happy you finally decided to come out here. I've missed you so much."

As he exited from my room I was left standing there, feeling guilty. Why had it taken me this long to come visit him? *I was a horrible daughter, that's why.*

Kane cleared his voice, gaining my attention. I looked over at him. He was still holding my bags.

"I guess just leave them there," I said pointing to the floor. Dropping them, he held out his hand, wiggling his fingers. I sighed. "I'm not tipping you, so you can stop begging."

Reaching out to feel the lushness of the bedding, I didn't notice that he had moved and was now across from me on the other side of the bed.

"I never have to beg," he stated, placing both hands on my new bed. He leaned across it with a downright scrumptious look on his face.

I too leaned farther toward the middle of the bed. He licked his lips seductively the closer I got. I swear I even heard him growl.

"Can I tell you a secret?" I asked, whispering. He nodded. I reached out and ran my hand down his stubbly cheek. "You are—" I paused for a dramatic effect, "— never stepping foot in this room again. You may have tons of 'groupies,' but I'm not one of them, and I'll never be one of them. So get your nasty, womanizing hands off my bed and go clean some toilets," I said, slapping his cheek lightly before I stood up straight.

He did nothing but grin back at me. "You're feisty," he said, still smiling "I like it, and I will be back here, maybe not tonight, but I'll be back."

"You're insane. Now, get the hell out," I yelled.

"I'll see you tonight, front row. I'll make sure there's a spot for you," he said, standing in the doorway.

"Not happening," I called to him as he turned and left my room.

That right there was the cockiest man in the world. I guessed when you looked that good, you could get away with it. Lying in my new bed, I took a moment to breathe. In the last twenty four hours, my life had drastically changed and I needed a moment to just relax.

My internship at J&K Marketing was up, and they hadn't offered me a job yet, so I had to move here, until I could find one. The lease I had on my small studio apartment was also up. After packing everything I owned into a storage unit, I took only the necessities, which fit in three large suitcases.

I stayed in bed, my eyes becoming heavy from traveling all morning. I was on the edge of sleep, that moment where you could feel yourself slipping into a dream. That's when a ridiculously loud guitar riff started echoing up through the floor. I suddenly realized my bedroom was directly over the stage. *Awesome…*

Soon after the guitar started, the rest of the instruments came to life. I tried to lay there and block it out, but it was useless. Groggily I got out of bed, dragged one suitcase over, and heaved it up on the bed. The next one was even heavier.

Opening them both, I started to take out my clothes and place them in drawers. The music coming through the floorboards had a catchy beat, and I soon found myself nodding along to it. It wasn't hard core rock music, it wasn't metal, and it wasn't pop music. It was somewhere in-between. I hated that I was actually tapping my foot along to it.

Forty minutes later, the music stopped and silence filled my room. *Shit, now it's too quiet.* I had finished unpacking just as the music had stopped. Stepping up to the French doors, I turned the handles and opened them both up.

A crisp breeze flowed through my hair, cooling my face, warm from un-packing. It wasn't a large balcony, just enough for two small chairs. The black iron bars looked freshly painted. Stepping out, I leaned over, resting my arms on the iron railing.

I was staring out at the open farm land and rolling hills off in the distance when an unpleasant noise ruined it.

"Look, boys, that beautiful, sexy woman right there

is going to be my wife." Standing below the balcony in the back parking lot, Kane stood with his band mates staring up at me.

"Dream on, Romeo!" I yelled back.

"I don't know, Kane, I think she hates your guts. I'm just going to put that out there," Aiden said as he clasped Kane on the shoulder.

The other guys all stood around laughing. They all had tattoos and wore similar style clothes—jeans and T-shirts, except for Reece. He seemed to have a style all his own. They were a good-looking bunch, I couldn't deny it. Aiden's slicked-back, black hair, honey-colored eyes and striking features were borderline making me want to go back on my previous statement about not sleeping with any of them. He seemed mysterious and smolderingly sexy. Plus he was the only one who didn't hit on me, besides JJ. Trent was scary quiet. He looked like a big bad biker, with his shaved head and dark beady eyes. I wouldn't want to be on his bad side in a dark alley. Although Kane carried top honors for being the sexiest man of the bunch, he was dangerous and probably had an STD.

I stood from the edge of the balcony and started to go back inside. "Kitty, come on, don't leave me so dissatisfied."

Stopping dead in my tracks, I whipped back around. "Don't ever call me that again and, as far as your satisfaction, find one of those groupies who adore you so much."

All the guys "oooed" at Kane and pushed him around. Flipping him off for an added effect, I left the balcony and closed the doors.

I didn't want to smile, but there's something about arguing with that man. *Maybe this summer could be fun, as long as I keep my wits about me, and keep him at arm's length.* I was here to spend time with my father, get to know him again, rebuild what we had lost when—

I just needed to stay focused. It wasn't like I'd be seeing these guys all the time. They had to have day jobs and, as long as I was working, and they were playing up on stage, then there wasn't going to be a problem.

CHAPTER 6

Kane

We drove fifteen minutes to the next town over to get some burgers. Sitting in the cramped booth with my fellow bandmates, I listened as they carried on conversations around me. For some reason, I wasn't into talking. I wasn't really into anything at the moment. Our cute waitress, who barely looked sixteen, came to our table way too many times, asking us if we needed anything.

"Kane," Trent said, hitting my shoulder. "You okay man?" he asked while JJ harmlessly flirted with the waitress.

"I'm good," I answered back.

Nodding, he turned back to the conversation that was going on across the table. I didn't know what put me in such a mood. I was usually really pumped up before we played at BJ's but, tonight, I was anything but. Sitting in the family burger joint, it was hard not to notice all the happy families. We were sticking out like sore thumbs, but that's usually how I liked it.

Most guys my age were well on their way to marriage, having kids, but I had sworn I wasn't going to turn into what everyone expected me to be. My friends and I weren't going to conform to the norm. I knew we were bigger than that, I knew we were good, that one day we'd make it out there and be playing the arenas that I was certain we were destine for.

I was twenty-six and loving life. I had women throwing themselves at me, friends that always had my back, and I knew that sooner or later our band was going to get noticed. People came from all over to hear us. We traveled everywhere we could. It was going to happen for us—we just needed that one break.

During the day, I played my role as construction worker. Although B paid us to play at the bar, it wasn't even close to being enough to survive on. Luckily, my uncle had a construction business. The boys and I all worked for him, so we could pay rent and keep up with our music.

"All right, someone needs to say it, and I'm not ashamed," Reece said, after taking a drink of his beer. "I call dibs on Caroline. I know she's B's daughter and all, but fuck if I don't get hard when she's around."

Aiden shook his head in disbelief. "You can't call dibs on her."

"You fuckers can figure this one out on your own. I'm automatically knocked out. She might be hot, but not enough to bang my own cousin," JJ said, holding his hands up.

Four heads turned to look at me. "She already said she's not shacking up with any of us. I think the odds are against us, boys."

"You're kidding right?" Reece asked.

"What? You heard her," I said, sitting back in the booth.

"Like that's ever stopped you before," Tent added sardonically.

"You want her all for yourself, don't you? You must want her bad, really bad," Reece said, nodding his head and grinning like the Cheshire cat.

"No, I don't want her. She's a seven all day. I can get much better." *I was drowning, fast.*

"Look at you,' all quiet and serious. That girl has you all fucked up," Reece continued.

"Shit, Reece, if you want to fuck her that bad, go for it. Why the hell do you need our permission?" I snapped at him.

"Fine, I will. Wish me luck, boys." Getting up from the table, he went out the front and lit up a cigarette.

What the hell did I just do? Of course, I had my sights set on her, but now I had to play it off, like I didn't care. I had to hope that Caroline wouldn't make the mistake of sleeping with Reece. He was an even bigger womanizer than I was. Who knew what kinds of diseases were festering in him?

CHAPTER 7

Caroline

The music from down stairs grew significantly louder in the last hour. It was 8:30. *Must be getting busy down there.* Closing the door behind me, I headed down the stairs to get my first look of my father's bar in full swing. With every step I took, the louder it got.

I guess people do live in this town. Opening the door that separated the stairs of our living area from the back hallway, I stepped out from its safety and headed toward the bar.

I stood in the doorway in awe. The place was packed, like wall-to-wall packed. Every table was full, every stool had a body on it, and there was nowhere to stand. *I can't work here. How am I going to do this?* You couldn't even move. Add a tray full of beers and a basket full of buffalo wings, and I'd call that my worst nightmare. I'd never waitressed before. I expected there to be maybe twenty people, not 200!

"Caroline!"

I turned around in the hallway as Kara walked up behind me.

"Don't freak out, it's not always this bad," she said, clearly seeing the panic on my face.

"This is insane!" I shrieked. My eyes went back and forth over all the people milling about. Out of the corner of my eye, I saw someone walk by with a pool stick, it's then that I remembered there was a whole other room. Craning my neck, I glanced in. *Shit, it's packed in there too!* "Why are there so many people here?" I asked frantically. "It's a Sunday night."

"It's pretty simple, ONS."

She's got to be joking. "There's no way this many people are here just to hear them," I said.

"Believe it," she said, looking out at the crowd. "It took about a year, but every time they play here, it's packed like this. Those boys have a cult following. You think this is bad, wait till Friday nights,"

Just then the back door opened and the devils themselves walked in. Aiden, with his mysterious features walked by me first. Trent, the big bad biker, politely smiled at me before he headed into the bar, which instantly reacted with cheers and screams. *That man is hot!* Trent was followed by Reece. Blowing me a kiss, he moved on and smacked Kara on the ass as he walked by. She tried to smack him back, but he was swallowed by the crowd before she could get him. I took a step back and tried to become one with the wall.

JJ stopped in front of me. "Hey, Cuz, pretty cool, huh?" he said, tilting his head to the open doorway that I had just back out of.

Was it cool? Were they that good? I mean, I had heard them through the floor and thought their music was catchy. These guys were famous here, living out a rock star fantasy, without the bull crap that usually followed famous musicians. I watched JJ walk through the doorway, holding his hands up in the air as the crowd erupted again. I was in shock and couldn't take my eyes off the now empty doorway.

"Kitty, you came for my performance." Kane said as he stopped in front of me. He pinned me on the wall as he spoke in my ear. "I have a seat front and center with your name on it." He pulled back and winked.

"I'm good right here," I responded, not moving my head from the wall.

Leaning in again, he placed his hand on the wall to keep from falling into me. "Ah, come on, loosen up. There's really a chair up front with your name on it. Your father set it up for you."

Up until this point I'd managed to keep my eyes from his. I was looking at everything but him, until I couldn't not look at him. His blue eyes were sparkling down at me and that stupid grin was plastered across his face.

"Just think. I can't try to hit on you if I'm standing up on stage singing to the masses. You're safe." He winked again.

The crowd started chanting O—N—S, O—N—S over and over, no doubt waiting for the man standing before me.

Locking my eyes back on his, I shrugged. "All right fine, I'll go watch." *I know I'm going to regret this.*

"I guess I'll see you front and center then." He took a few steps, paused, then turned back to me, his lips curling up even more. Taking me off guard, he grabbed my hand and began pulling me out of the hallway and into the crowded room. I covered my ear with my free hand. *Shit, it's loud.*

He tried to pull me behind him, but people were clamoring around us. Kane let go of my hand, and I thought I was going to get trampled, but he wrapped his arm around my shoulders and secured me to his side.

Leaning over, he practically licked my ear as he talked above the crowd. I should have been cringing, but instead a chill ran down my spine, the kind of chill I got when something felt too good, like hot breath tickling my skin.

"Stay close. Wouldn't want you to get trampled by my groupies on your first night here."

That was the first time that I punched him in the ribs. I did, however, choose to stay conveniently close to him, but only because people were making a path for us to walk through, and definitely not because it felt damn good to have him hold me close.

I had just met this guy less than six hours ago but I felt strangely comfortable around him. Sure, he was an ass, but even I had to admit it was fun messing with him.

Pulling out one of the two vacant seats at a table near the front he smiled, "Your seat, my lady," There was a piece of paper on top that said, *Reserved for our new mascot, Kitty.* I went to punch him again, but he had already hopped up on stage. The rest of the guys were all laughing. *Oh forget everything I just said. They have officially started a war.*

Wiggling his eyebrows at me, Kane took his guitar off its stand and slung the strap around his neck, blowing a kiss in my direction. I swear I heard a girl swoon behind me. I sat down, crossed my legs and arms, and then gave him the finger.

Walking up to the microphone, he held it with one hand, the other rested over the neck of his red guitar. He was still in his cut-off shirt, and I had to laugh as I thought back to how I imagined it would be to watch him play that beautiful guitar.

I was right. It wasn't the worst thing I'd ever had to watch. *Fine, whatever, it was sexy as hell to watch him up on stage—there I admitted it.* People behind me had cleared the tables and chairs to make a dance floor. He was really good—his voice was amazing, he didn't miss a note, and never fell off key. The rest of the guys were flawless too. They were really good. If they hadn't been discovered yet, I was sure it was right around the corner.

After a few songs, they took a break. "How's everyone doing out there tonight?" Kane asked. He commanded the crowd and knew exactly where to move and how to make the women swoon. It was no wonder he had groupies. "We have a special guest here tonight," he said, looking directly down at me.

My heart sank to my stomach, the same time his lips curled up. I put a stern look on my face. *He had better not do what I think.*

"Tonight we finally get to meet the one and only—"

Don't you fucking call me Kitty, you bitch, ass—

"—Caroline, the daughter of the man who kept this fine establishment alive and well."

A chorus of hoots, hollers, whistles and claps erupted around me.

"Come on, Caroline, don't be shy," he said, as he knelt down on the edge of the stage and held the microphone in my face.

I ground my jaw and clenched my fists. *I swear, if those people weren't here, I would slap that smug smile off his face.*

"Aww, she's still a little shy, but don't worry, she'll be here all summer, helping B out."

Yup, if he leans down again, I'm going to slap him, I don't care who's looking.

Luckily for him, he kept to entertaining the crowd. I needed a drink. I made my way over to the bar and, thanks to Kane's warm welcome, I was stopped at every other table. Once I made it safely to the bar, I saw my dad, Kara, and two other girls working frantically to serve drinks.

Catching my eye my father walked over and slapped his hand on the bar. "Hey, honey, what do you want?"

"Something strong," I replied.

My father reached under the counter, pulled a shot glass out, and placed it on the worn bar top. "He's not that bad, Caroline. Try to enjoy tonight, meet some people," he said, as he filled up the shot glass with straight bourbon. Holding up my shot, I tapped it on the bar and drank it. "Another one?" he asked. I nodded for more, and he filled it up again. "At least I don't have to worry about you driving home. Remember that time I had to come get you at that party. Your mom was so mad at me for covering for you."

The memory of my mother sitting on the front porch when my dad and I got home still made me anxious. I didn't let myself finish out the memory. It was always too much. Taking the second shot, I simply smiled at my dad.

"You know, you can talk about her. It's okay," he said, filling the drink again.

"Thanks, Dad," I said, after downing the third shot. "I think I'll take a beer now."

My father did as asked and soon there was a tall beer resting on the bar. I took my beer and tried to make good on what my father had suggested. I was going to be here, I might as well meet some new people. I struggled to navigate the crowed room with my filled to the rim beer. I was in search of a table in the back, the way, way back. I wanted to be as far away from the eager fans, and wannabe rock stars looking to get laid, as I possibly could.

CHAPTER 8

Kane

Why did her hand have to feel so fucking good in mine? I was clearly off my game, but thankfully the crowd didn't seem to notice. I kept finding myself looking for her in the crowd of people.

When I stopped her in the hallway, I had all intentions of leaving her there, to greet the fans. My hand was flush with the wall, and a little above her head, I had her pinned, with nowhere to go but through me, and I couldn't fight the urge to get even closer.

That was my first mistake. I wanted to grab her, shove her up against that wall, have her legs wrap around me, fist my hand in her hair, and finally taste her. I settled for whispering in her ear. It might have had something to do with the fact, I wasn't sure if she would knee me in the balls, and I liked my balls, so I held back.

My second mistake was coming back and taking her hand in mine. I expected her to pull away, possibly even smack me, but she didn't, which totally discombobulated me. In the six hours that I had gotten to know this girl, I did not take her for the dutifully following type. When the people around us started getting closer and the women tried to grab onto me and push her away, I made my third mistake of the night.

I pulled her up next to me and let go of her hand. I draped my arm around her, pulling her close to my body. The women seemed to back off enough for us to make our way to the stage. I squeezed her shoulder farther into my side, and talked closely in her ear again.

"Stay close. Wouldn't want you to get trampled by my groupies on your first night here." It wasn't that bad, but I couldn't resist messing with her or having my lips centimeters from her skin again.

Her now-familiar punch to my side was delightfully welcome, even though I knew there was a good chance I'd have a bruise tomorrow. I led her to the table that I had lied about earlier. Her father didn't reserve a table, but the guys and I had. She wasn't quick enough to hit me after reading the reserved paper that sat neatly on it. She made sure to let us know she hated the name Kitty earlier, rookie mistake. *Doesn't she know that's what I'm going to call her from now on, just because she despises it so much?* So now, I was trying my best to engage with the audience, when the only thing I wanted do, was watch her. In between two songs, I went back to the drums to grab my beer. Taking a huge swig, I leaned over to place it back.

"Kane, you all right? That girl got you pussy whipped after one afternoon?" Reece asked, still keeping the beat to the next song going. *Pussy whipped me? Hell no!*

"Not a chance, Reece!" I yelled back over the drums.

"Prove it! See that red head?" he asked, pointing to her with one of his drumsticks. "I want to see her in the morning, doing the walk of shame. I want to know if the carpet matches the curtains." He grinned, wiggling his eye brows.

Taking another sip of beer, I leaned over the drums, "Done," I said before heading back to the microphone. *Hopefully, this will get him off my case.* Eyeing up the red head Reece had pointed out, I realized that it was going to be a piece of cake. That girl was pretty much spreading her legs already. Her top was so sheer you could see her bra, and her skirt was so tight and short it didn't leave much to the imagination.

I let go of the guitar and held the microphone with both hands. My lips touched the intertwined pattern, and just as I was about to start the next song, I caught sight of Caroline, sitting at a table in the back. A man appeared next to her. Placing his drink down, he whispered in her ear, and she gestured for him to sit down. I had missed the count were I was supposed to start singing and the guys thankfully started the intro again for me. I quickly turned around to gain my composure. Reece was shaking his head and whipping his hand at me.

"Kat chow!" he yelled to me.

God damn it, I don't know if I'm going to be able to explain this one. Hearing Reece and the other guys cackling behind me, I knew for sure that whatever cover I thought I had was just blown.

CHAPTER 9

Caroline

I found a table at the back that was empty, since people were clamoring around the stage.

"This seat taken?" a deep voice asked from beside me.

I turned in the direction of the voice to find a guy placing his drink down. He was tall, and well built. Dressed in a T-shirt and khaki shorts, he was clean cut, with a healthy five o'clock shadow on his jaw. His hair was dark and in a short buzz, but still long enough to run his fingers through. His green eyes stared down at me waiting for an answer. This guy was good looking, but not—

I took a chance and caught sight of Kane on stage. *I hate that he's so fucking sexy up there.*

"Yeah, I'm sorry. Go ahead, have a seat," I said, tapping on the stool next to me.

"So, this your first time here?" he asked, leaning closer so he didn't have to yell over the loud music, which seemed to be on repeat.

Didn't they already play this? I glanced up at the stage again to see Kane turned from the crowd. Guess he's not as good as he thought if he forgot his own lyrics. It made me chuckle.

"Do I stick out that much?" I replied. As he smiled down at me, I took notice of his kind face.

"Yeah, you kind of do."

Both laughing, we took a simultaneous sip of our drinks.

"So, what brings you to our small town?" he asked casually.

"I'm spending the summer with my dad. He owns the place."

"Oh, B's daughter. He's been telling everyone about you." Taking another sip of his drink, he stretched on his chair and glanced around the stage area.

"What brings you here tonight? You like One Night Stand?" *Did I really just ask that?* Cringing, I quickly took another sip of my beer.

Chuckling he answered, "They're okay, but I'm here on big-brother duty."

They really needed to change the name of their band—it lead to some pretty awkward conversations.

"My sister is a super fan, I guess you could say, and she wrangled me into bringing her here tonight since she's seventeen and can't get in on her own."

I turned back to the stage and noticed that the row in front of it was all women, scantily dressed. No wonder JJ flirted with the line. These girls were dressed to impress and, my guess, not legal yet.

"I can't believe my dad lets them in underage. Can't he get in trouble?" I asked.

"Your dad has an in with the sheriff. They're allowed to come in only while ONS is playing and they have to have a chaperone. Once their set is over, everyone under eighteen is kicked out," the man clarified for me.

I shook my head in amazement that my father had an "in" with the sheriff.

"How do you know all this?" I asked.

"Because, I'm a cop and I know everything," he said, taking another sip of his beer.

"Oh, you don't look like a cop," I said, smiling over at him.

"Thanks. If I ever decide to go undercover, I guess that's a good thing."

"You must really love your sister to sit here."

"Pretty much. She owes me big time for this. I went to high school with these guys, and let's just say their band's name wasn't a coincidence."

Nodding in agreement, I glanced back up on stage, where Kane was currently singing about all the different ways to catch a girl.

He looked right at me and pointed. Our eyes locked for a brief second when he sang, "I'll make you mine." I shook my head and held up my middle finger proudly. It made the biggest smile spread across his face, as he placed his hand back on the strings of his guitar and continued playing.

"I guess you met Kane already?" my neighbor asked.

"Yes, I had the unfortunate experience of meeting him earlier today."

"Well, not much has changes about him. These guys have been playing together and banging anything that walks since high school." I didn't doubt that either. "I'm Nate, by the way," he said, holding his hand out.

"Caroline," I responded, placing my hand in his.

Downing the last of my drink, I went to stand from the stool, but swayed slightly. *Three shots and a beer had me tipsy?* It had been a long time since I last drank. It might have even been over a year and half ago—hell, maybe two. I had poured everything I had into the internship at J&K and what did I get in return? The boot! I put everything on hold for them, friends—which I had lost over the years, boyfriends, who lost interest because I wasn't around, and even my gold fish Roxy died because of that stupid internship.

"Sit down. I'll go get us another beer," Nate said, standing and taking the glass from my hand.

"Thanks." Sitting back down on the stool, I watched as he walked across the room to where the bar was. I pulled my phone out of pocket to check the time, 9:45. *These guys can't have much longer up there, can they?* They had been playing for over an hour, only breaking to get sips of beer, and tease the girls who were practically crawling on stage with them.

During the next thirty minutes, I chatted with Nate and continued to throw back at least two more beers. When the guys finally told the crowd goodnight, I watched them all jump off the stage and into the throng of women. They were swallowed whole, but I saw them all leave through the hallway that we had all come through earlier—a few extra people leaving with them, all women, of course.

My father got up on the stage and took the microphone in his hand. "All right, another great performance from the one and only ONS! Sorry, but if you don't have a yellow wrist band on, we're going to have to ask you to leave."

A chorus of groans vibrated in the room. Two girls came up to the table that Nate and I were sitting at, and I could tell instantly that this was his sister.

"Can't you pull some strings, I'm going to be eighteen in two weeks. It's ridiculous that I have to leave," she said, pouting.

"Caroline, this is my sister, Piper, and her friend Morgan," Nate said, introducing us.

"You're the girl that Kane was walking in earlier, Caroline. You're B's daughter. You are so lucky. I'd give anything to—"

"Hold it right there, sweetheart. Don't get any absurd ideas about Kane and me."

"So you're not—"

Cringing, I shook my head. "Don't even say it," I said, holding my hand up in her face.

That seemed to put a smile on Nate's face but, unfortunately for him, I wasn't here to date. I was here to work and hang out with my dad.

"Come on, girls. We've got a forty-five-minute drive, better get to it."

A forty-five minute drive? "You came forty-five minutes out of your way, to watch those guys?" I couldn't for the life of me see why…well, that was a bit of a lie. All of them were good looking in their own way, and their music was catchy. I guess I could understand why these teenagers and grown-ass women would clamor around to see them.

"It's not that bad," Nate replied. "I guess I'll be seeing you around. This is the best bar in an hour radius. Don't judge me if you catch me in here more than once a week." Smiling, he stood up from the table.

"I live upstairs, so I'll be here every day."

"You are so lucky. Did I already say that?" his sister said for the second time.

I suppose having some eye candy while I worked the summer away wasn't the worst thing that could happen.

CHAPTER 10

Kane

Backstage—or in our case, out back of the bar—we all grabbed a beer from Kara and sat at the table and chairs. Not the best backstage, but we took what we could get. B always gave us free booze and let us have our own private party back there, under the covered patio. Hell, even if it was snowing, we'd have a fire, warming pots. It might have been below freezing, but our little area was a toasty seventy degrees. Plus the guys could smoke and we could all come down from our high of being rock stars, kind of.

The redhead, sitting on my lap, kept messing with my hair. I hated when girls messed with my hair. Maybe this wasn't going to be as easy as I thought. I was getting over it fast, until Caroline walked outback.

Swaying as she walked, Caroline tossed her arms around her father. "Hey, Dad," she slurred. Her eyes were hooded as she smiled up at her father. The next thing I knew, she was mean mugging me. "You were awesome," she said, pointing in my direction. She was definitely wasted, there's no way she'd openly admit she liked me. "Oh, wait wrong person." Turning to Trent, she swayed across the patio and plopped herself down on his large lap, taking him totally off guard. "You, were amazing. Everyone else sucked, especially that one," she said, pointing at me.

I knew there had to be a catch. "Can you guys keep an eye on her for me?" B asked. "I have to go help out inside, there's still a ton of people."

"Hell, yeah, we'll take good care of her," Reece said, nodding his head and bouncing the blonde who was on his lap.

B shook his head. "No, not you. You stay away from her," B said, before heading back into the bar.

"What the hell? What's his beef with me?"

We all laughed and ignored any further noise coming from Reece. I couldn't help but watch as Caroline made herself familiar on Trent's lap, laying her head gently on his broad shoulder. He took advantage and held her waist tightly.

"You smell really good," she said through glazed-over eyes.

Why won't this bitch stop messing with my hair? Taking her hand in mine, I moved the redhead's hand to her lap for the tenth time. I caught Trent's hand move from Caroline's hip, to the middle of her back, and it kept moving south.

"Kitty," I called to get her attention.

Sitting up, she swatted Trent's hand away. Jumping off his lap, she turned to face him. "I told you not to call me that and stop feeling me up," she spat, laying in on him.

"It wasn't me—" Trent tried to say.

"Save it. I thought you were the gentlemen of the group. Clearly I was wrong."

I couldn't hold in the thunderous laugh that busted out of me.

"And you," she said, turning her rage on me.

I went to stand up, but the bimbo on my lap wouldn't move. So whispering in her ear, I told her exactly what I knew she'd been waiting to hear. "Go get me another drink, then we'll leave this place and head back to mine."

Sucking in her bottom lip, she copped a feel. Finding me halfway put a fire in her eyes that matched her hair. "All right, I'll be right back," she said breathily.

She quickly stood and headed for the door. Little did she know that my "situation" had absolutely nothing to do with her. Caroline was still in front of Trent, when I was free to stand.

"What about me, Kitty?" I challenged.

Her cheeks were flushed from the alcohol but her temper made them redder.

"Don't you ever call me out like that again! And stop calling me Kitty!"

"Okay. Kitty," I said, stretching my back.

Oh shit! Her mane of blonde curls barreled toward me. I had a microsecond to react. Her shoe got caught on the uneven pavement and she was falling to the ground, fast. Taking two huge steps, I reached out and grabbed her up in my arms before she face planted. She was heavier than she looked, but I almost expected that. She had a nasty punch, and muscle like that isn't light.

Her legs were draped over my arm, her arms tightly around my neck. I looked down at her. The blue in her eyes was deep and rich in color. I needed to just sleep with her to get her out of my system. Once that happened, I'd move on to the next one. *I can't be hung up on one girl, that's not what I do.* Maybe once I got that redhead home, I'd be in a better mood. Fucking always put me in a better mood.

"I'm so tired," she grumbled in my chest. "Put me down so I can go to bed, you big jerk."

Her eyes were closed and I could swear I heard her snore.

"Come on, Kitty, I'll take you home," I said, watching her as she tried her hardest to keep her eyes open.

The guys were all preoccupied with the ten or so other girls that were joining us on the patio. I took advantage, snuck back inside, and carried her up the stairs to her and B's living quarters. Her bedroom door was slightly open as I approached it. Kicking it with my foot, I opened it all the way. The door bounced off the wall behind it and closed slightly. Cringing, I glanced down, but Caroline was still passed out in my arms. Yup, she was definitely snoring.

I took her over to the bed and gently laid her down. Deep blue eyes locked on mine as I went to move my hand from behind her neck. As she searched my face, a beam of a smile came across hers. I would have loved to know what was going on in that mind of hers.

Lost in her features, I released my hand from her neck. I had to touch her. I had to know how soft her skin was. I ran a shaking finger down the side of her face. I'd never been so nervous to touch a woman before. I was in knots. I hadn't noticed before, but she had small freckles that ran across the bridge of her nose and under her eyes.

If I wasn't straining against my jeans before, I sure as hell was now. Her hand reached up over my neck. Her fingers glided over my Adams apple and down my exposed skin. Her lips twisted with a gleam of passion. *Fuck yeah, she wanted it as bad as I did.* I climbed on the bed and positioned myself perfectly over her body. I felt like putty as she kept moving her hand up and down my arm.

Oh God, I groaned inwardly. *What the hell is she doing?* Arching off the bed she brushed her breasts against my chest. I tried my damnedest to keep a straight face, but I knew my eyes rolled to the back of my head as her hand curled around my belt. Yanking me closer to her, she closed her eyes and sighed just loud enough for me to hear. Her legs moved under mine, and that sweet hand of hers fisted my belt tighter—

Pain struck me hard and fast. I jumped, or more like fell off of her and the bed. I clutched at my balls and curled into the fetal position. *The bitch kneed me in the fucking balls*! I tried to stand but kept doubling over in pain. *Oh, man, that's not right!*

"Jesus Christ, Kitty!" I cried, clutching my throbbing crotch. Just to be safe I took a few steps back.

She stood from the bed and yelled down at me as I knelt on the floor. "I told you, to never step foot in this room again," Standing a little straighter, I bit my lip as another wave of pain shot from my balls. "I was just helping you, since you can't drink with the big boys," I groaned.

"I was just fine, and you really expect me to believe you over top of me, feeling up my face is helping me? You were trying to take advantage of me. Thankfully, I came to my senses before you could infect me with your whore-dipped dick."

"Whatever, won't happen again. I'll make sure to let you face plant on the asphalt next time." Backing up, I held my side as a wave of nausea came over me. I really hated getting kneed in the balls.

"I'll take my chances with the asphalt," she said, placing her hands on her hips.

"Fine, maybe it will fix that face of yours."

Sucking in a breath, she fought with her hair, pulling it back into a ponytail. "That's it!" she shrieked.

The next thing I knew she was running me at full speed.

CHAPTER 11

Caroline

I'*m going to kill him. There's no questioning it, the headlines will read, woman kills absurdly hot lead singer of popular hometown band.* What was he thinking trying to seduce me with his good looks, amazing smell, and gentle hands? I wasn't falling for it—scratch that, I wasn't falling for it anymore!

He held his hands out in front of him, bracing himself for a collision. I kept running, at him. I was swinging my arms violently. He grabbed them and held them above my head. So I resorted to other means of beating him. I went to knee him again, but he saw it coming that time. Pulling my arms up, I jumped to kick him, but wrapped my legs around his hips instead.

"Will you stop it?" he said, adjusting his grip on my wrists. "Get off me!" he yelled, trying to wiggle from the tight grasp I had on his waist. I crossed my feet, pinning myself even closer to him.

Losing his balance he stumbled.

"Let my hands go, so I can strangle you!" I said through gritted teeth.

"I don't think so, Kitty," he yelled back.

We kept moving around the room, struggling to overpower the other. That is, until we began to fall. He had tripped over the rug, and we were now falling backward. The plush mattress broke our fall, but neither one of us let up. My legs were still around his waist and his hands were still clutching my wrists.

My feet were sore under both our weight, so I uncrossed them but kept them tight so he couldn't wiggle free. He went to sit up but I pushed him back down, trying to free my hands again. I wiggled my fingers, the closer I came to his neck. I was determined that I going to hurt him.

"You're such a jackass—let me go, so I can strangle you," I said struggling against him as I gained a few more centimeters toward my target.

Stretching his hands up, he pulled them over his head, making me have to lean over him. Inches separated us.

"No! You kneed me in the balls. I'm not letting go till you apologize." His voice was even and stern. The pompous ass then flashed that stupid grin of his.

"You were taking advantage of me. I had to do something to get you to back the fuck off!"

Tugging my arms, he was able to pin me closer to him. "Apologize!"

"No!"

It was only then that I felt the tension between us. Not the angry, fighting tension. I had felt that all along, since I first met him, eight hours ago. This was different. This was feral, heavy, sexual tension. It was as if he felt it the same moment I did, because he let go of my hands and gripped the back of my neck, the exact moment I loosed my legs and ground my hips into his. His face came up off the bed, his lips crashed onto mine, or maybe I crashed onto his, either way it was fucking amazing.

He sat up, hand still holding my neck while the other wrapped around my hips, pulling me even tighter into him. Taking a hand full of his hair, I pull his head back, dragging my fingers along his exposed neck and face. All the while his hand griped my ass tighter. His velvet tongue snuck between my lips, and for the love of all that's right, I let him assault my mouth. He tasted too good not to let him in.

My body took over. I had no control as I arched into him, for real this time. Loving the way my breasts flattened against his hard chest, I pushed harder. Yup, my brain had lost all control as we admittedly gave in to desire. So when he began to pull away, leaving soft little kisses on my lips, I had a moment of realization.

What the hell were we doing? I am repulsed by this guy, he is a womanizer. I was so dense that I hadn't realized I was being used. I was exactly where he wanted me. *Hell if I was going to let him continue to mess with my head!* I jumped up off his lap, and he carefully took his hands from me. I stood at the foot of my bed where he was sitting, wrapped my arms around my midsection, and shook my head no.

I know there was a blaze behind my eyes when I was finally able to look at him. "Get out!"

I made sure my words were icy, with no sign of banter in them. He didn't say anything back, he just stood in front of my bed.

"This was a mistake, and one I intend to never let happen again."

He took a step toward me as I took one away from him. "You're a fucking tease," he said, pointing to me.

"And you're an asshole. Now that we have that cleared up, get the fuck out of my room." I pointed at the door and stepped out of his way as he stormed out. I heard the door to our living quarters slam shut.

I can't believe I just let that happen. I had been here less than twelve hours and this place had me wishing the summer away, so I could get the hell out of here. I was going to have to take extra precautions around Kane. He was clearly more clever than I expected. I didn't easily get caught up like that. I usually kept my wits about me, but there was something about him that sacred me and made me feel things. I wasn't ready to feel anything. Previous guys only had me thinking about sex and nothing else. When Kane and I kissed, I felt a future that I had sworn off when my mother—

Nope, not going there. I don't do happily ever after. I do right now, a hook up here and there, but not the future. When I kissed him, I saw it all, marriage, white picket fence, kids, a dog. I didn't want that life for myself, not since Mom.

CHAPTER 12

Kane

I slammed the door closed, stomping my way down the stairs. I couldn't believe that tease. She was a real piece of work. I was ready to finish what *she* had started, get her out of my system, cross her off the list, and worry about the consequences later. I was even willing to put *my* ego aside, just to get her out of my mind.

There was no way one girl should have had all that clout over me. Standing in the doorway that led to the covered patio/outdoor bar, the red head I was slated to take home and examine had two beers in her hand, nervously looking around for me.

The crowd had grown by at least twenty. I wasn't the least bit surprised. We usually got about a half hour before someone found us and told their friend, who told their friend, and before you knew it, there was fifty-plus people milling around. The women would all be fighting for our attention, while whatever men were hanging around were waiting for our leftovers.

"She realized your dick is the size of a two-year-old's?" Reece asked, jumping on my back.

Shaking him off, I pushed him back against the wall,

not really in the mood to put up with his fucking antics.

"Well, don't hold out on me, bro, how was she?" he asked, straightening from the wall.

"A tease," I said, crossing my arms and continuing to look out at the patio.

"Maybe she's just not into you, maybe she prefers a man with style and devilishly handsome good looks."

Inhaling deeply, I turned my body toward him. "Whatever, dude. She's not worth it. That redhead over there better be ready, because I'm going to screw the shit out of her."

"Damn, Kitty has you all sorts of messed up." Clapping his hand on my shoulder, he squeezed it, his way of showing compassion.

Nodding, I turned to look at him. "If you're going to try, make sure you wear a cup."

With that, I left him standing there, mulling over what I had just said. Out of the corner of my eye, I saw him finally get it—holding is hand over his balls as he scrunched his face, and then shook his head before jogging after me.

An hour later, I found B and let him know that I wasn't going to stay to help out tonight. I told him I wasn't feeling up to it, but I'd come back tomorrow afternoon and help out before they opened.

"Is Caroline okay?" he asked, looking around the patio. "I don't see her."

"She was tired and went up to bed an hour or so ago, haven't seen her since." As much as I wanted to let B know his daughter was a fucking tease and ball buster, I held back. He was ecstatic she was here and I wasn't going to ruin that for him.

I wasn't sure what happened between the two of them four years ago, before he came here, and I really didn't care, but B was like a second father to us guys, and

I wasn't going to hurt his feelings. If it wasn't for him, we wouldn't have had a place to play or the huge cult following we had.

"I'll be down here around noon to unlock the door for you, that too early?" he asked, before taking a swig of beer.

"Nah, noon is good, I'll see you then," I said before, heading for the parking lot. My conquest was already sitting in the passenger's seat waiting for me, when I got there.

⌀ↄ∾

It was eleven and I was fully awake. What am I saying? I never went to sleep. After finding out the carpet and curtains didn't match, I rolled over and tried to fall asleep, but it wasn't happening. I grabbed my acoustic baby and headed downstairs to sit on the huge porch that encompassed our house. The guys and I rented a five-bedroom farmhouse from a couple who had moved Down South. Rent was cheap and the privacy was even better.

We had struck a deal with the couple that we'd fix up the house, if they'd cut the rent in half. We'd usually work on it in between construction jobs that my uncle had us doing. We had even done B's whole upstairs for him, three months ago. He had anticipated having his daughter visit for the summer, so we demolished the upstairs, made the living area minuscule and her bedroom huge, adding the large bathroom and closet.

We all specialized in something different. I did most of the woodwork with JJ, Aiden was good at all the electrical, Trent had a knack for plumbing, and Reece was our demo guy. Together we were the total package—not only could we sing your panties off, we could also fix your house while we did it.

I was on my second cup of coffee and hundredth re-run of last night. Although I enjoyed exploring the interi-or decorations of the woman who was still sleeping in my bed, I wasn't into it as much as I usually was, and that was all Caroline James's fault. Glancing outside, I no-ticed a van with a taxi sign on top of it. The next thing I see is the redhead, two blondes, and a brunette walking past.

They didn't say anything to me as they did. They just headed to the door to leave.

JJ came down the hall next. Grabbing a cup of cof-fee, he joined me at the table. "I'm so glad we have off this morning. I don't think I could lift a nail," he said, gulping down his coffee.

Nodding in agreement, I sat there silent.

"Kane, what's going on?" he asked.

"Your cousin, that's what's going on. She's found a way to fuck up my head, playing hard to get."

Chuckling, JJ took another gulp of coffee. "That bad? Why not sweet talk your way in? It's worked before for you."

"I'm done with her. I just have to get out of my own head. I guess I can't win them all. Plus, I don't want to make things weird with B. She's only staying for the summer then moving on." I was trying to convince my-self of everything I just said and it might have been work-ing, a little.

The next to join us at the table was Aiden, followed by Reece. "So...carpet...curtains?" Reece asked, wig-gling his eyebrows.

"Nope, not a match, but a pretty good lay," I added, standing from the table.

"Gentleman, you're now looking at the very proud, very exhausted, only male involved in a foursome, which happened after you assholes passed out last night, before boning the ladies *you* brought home. Thank you!" Trent said, as he strutted into the kitchen.

Reece called his bluff from the other side of the table. "You're lying,"

"Not even a bit. Next time, make sure you fuckers take your ladies to your room before you pass out."

"Nice," I said, before setting my cup in the sink.

Grabbing my keys, I headed for the back door.

"Where the hell are you going?" Reece asked.

"BJ's. I told B that I'd help him out before they open tonight."

"If you see Kitty, grab her ass for me," he called while grabbing the air.

"I don't think so. That girl's got issues, and I don't want to get involved with them."

"I said grab her ass, not play psychologist," Reece replied.

"I'm not going within an arm's length of her. I got bruises, blue balls, and I'd really like to keep my face from getting smacked. So, I'm not going anywhere near that feral kitty."

Turning from their stunned faces, because I had never let a woman get to me like that, I left.

CHAPTER 13

Caroline

S o there was one good thing about not getting the job at J&K—sleeping in. Rolling over, I glanced at the clock, feeling well rested. That was the first night I had slept that soundly since I started my internship. The alcohol might have had something to do with the sound slumber I had just enjoyed.

I had totally missed the whole morning—*Guess there's no point in making breakfast.* Glancing at the small kitchen, I headed straight for the refrigerator. Nothing. There wasn't even ketchup, just vitamin water and OJ. How was my father surviving off of vitamin water and OJ? Then it hit me, the kitchen in the back of the bar. Slipping on my flip flops, I headed down stairs in a tight tank top, and my comfy flannel PJ pants that hung low on my hips, making them extra comfy. *Another perk of not working at J&K, comfy clothes, all day!*

I walked into the back kitchen to find my father prepping food for the night. Even though it was a bar, my father offered some really good bar food.

"Hey, Dad," I said as I walked around to the prep station.

He was cutting potatoes into fries, a hug tub of already cut potatoes sat at on the floor next to the table.
"Hey, sleepyhead. You hungry?" he asked.

"Starving," I replied.

Dropping what he was doing, he went to the huge in-
dustrial fridge and pulled out lunchmeat and cheese. Taking a loaf of bread off the shelf, he walked back to the
prep station and proceeded to make me a sandwich. It
was the best sandwich I had ever had. The moment he put
it in front of me, I quickly scarfed it down.

I sat back on the stool and held my delightfully full
stomach. "That was so good, Dad, thank you,"

"How are you doing, honey? You like your room?
Are you finding everything you need?" he asked with a
twinge of nervousness to his voice.

I knew my father wanted me to be happy, and he really wanted to make me stay. I was finding it hard to tell
him I wasn't planning on staying longer than summer. So
I chickened out. He had no clue I was hell bent on leaving. He thought I was going to work here, love it, and
never want to leave. I didn't have the heart to tell him
because, as much as he wanted me to be happy, I wanted
him to be just as happy. If I told him I was counting down
the days till I left, he'd be crushed.

"Everything is great, Dad, I love my room, you did a
great job—" I was going to go on about how much I liked
the bar and how nice everyone was, but—

"I'm glad you like it, Kitty. It was a bitch laying that
lovely hardwood floor that your father just had to have in
there."

I turned around to see Kane standing behind me, a
bucket of cleaning supplies in one hand and a mop in the
other.

I don't know what shocked me more, the fact that he
had actually cleaned something or the fact that he was in

my room before I was. Smiling that stupid grin of his, he winked at me then moved to place the cleaning stuff in a nearby closet.

"Bathrooms are done B. You need help with anything else?" he asked, a few feet from us.

I wanted to ignore it, but I could feel the tension between us. It was intense and dripping with anger, with only a hint of sexual desire. And that might have just been me because—*Shit, he looks sexy as hell*. He was in mesh shorts and a white wife-beater, which showed off his muscular arms that I was starting to really enjoy looking at.

My eyes drifted on their own, running up his body, as if I'd never let them look at a man before. His arms crossed, making his chest puff up and the muscles in his arms bulge in a delightful way. For a split second, I forgot why I hated the man. I forgot why I shouldn't be running toward him, to be engulfed in those mesmerizing arms. Pulling my mind out of a daydream and back to reality, I made myself remember that not even twenty minutes after we had…whatever we had…he was feeling up and kissing some redhead that kept running her hand over the balls I'd kneed back into his body.

"Caroline, I forgot to tell you, the boys—JJ, Trent, Aiden, Reece, and Kane—they're all contractors. They rebuilt your room and the living area. I had them working like dogs for the past three months." My father chuckled to himself, no doubt remembering all the shenanigans of having four rowdy musicians working on his house.

I turned from my father to eye Kane up again. That stupid grin was plastered even bigger on his face.

"Didn't they do an awesome job?" Dad continued, seemingly oblivious to the tension. "Hold on—let me run upstairs, I took a bunch of before pictures. You won't believe what it looked it before they got a hold of it." Without another word, my father exited from the kitchen and went in search of the photos.

Rocking on his feet, Kane turned to leave the kitchen as well. *Yeah, he should leave, I don't have anything to say to him, and he sure didn't have anything to say to me.* I think we said it all the night before. So why couldn't I help the stupid pit that was in my stomach as I watched him leave. *Oh, this is ridiculous.*

"I saw your night got interesting. That redhead give you what you wanted?" The moment the words left my lips, I wanted to run and hide, I should have just let it go, let *him* go.

Stopping in his tracks, he threw his head back and laughed loudly. "Let's just say, she knew the right way to handle my balls," he said, turning back to me.

"You deserved it," I called back. I moved anxiously on the stool, his brisk walk across the room was putting me seriously on edge.

"Why do you even care? You made it perfectly clear last night that you want nothing to do with this or my balls," he said, gesturing at his body.

I stood from the stool, "I don't care," I clipped back. He was still an arm's length away and as I was standing there, I caught a whiff of his cologne—*Amazing.* "Why do you sleep with so many women, can't find one that can stand to be in your presence for more than one night?" I asked, crossing my arms.

"Kitty, drop it. You want me to leave you alone, fine, but it works both ways," he said, maintaining his distance.

"I don't want you to leave me alone—" *Aw dammit, not like that.* "Listen, I'm going to be here. I live upstairs, and we're going to run into each other. I'll try to be civil, but we can't let what happened last night happen again. For some reason, my father loves you boys, and if we're constantly fighting, then it's going to put stress on him, and that's the last thing I want."

I meant that, all of it. I knew he was bad news and the way I felt last night while we kissed was terrifying, but we had to coexist. My father loved those boys like they were his long lost sons, or so he'd told me over lunch.

"I agree. But you have to realize, women love me. You can't walk around jealous of them then take it out on my poor defenseless body. I bruise easily," he said, smiling.

"What a baby," I said, as I closed the distance between us so I could punch his arm.

Rubbing his arm, he scrunched up his face in pain. "What the fuck, Kitty? I just said I bruise."

"Found them!" my father yelled, walking back into the kitchen.

He had an album of photos under his arm. Setting it down on the work station, I started flipping through them, Kane by my side. He talked me through all that they had done to get my room ready for me. I caught myself leaning in closer to him, taking in his unique smell. His voice drifted to my ear as he talked, almost lulling me to a state of clam, peacefulness. As long as I kept things to myself and kept up a hard exterior, I thought, I was going to make it through the summer.

Turning the page to the next set of pictures, I did a double take. It was not pictures of my transformed bedroom; it was pictures from my childhood. The first was just me, maybe three years old, my blonde crazy curls in pigtails. I was sitting on top of a slide, ready to go down. The next was me on a swing. There was one of my father and me outside of the only home I ever knew. The last picture on the page was my mother.

I stared at it. I hadn't looked at a picture of her since

I had moved away, four years ago. My way of coping was to pretend she never existed. If she wasn't in my memory, then it didn't hurt. So I took on the painful task of un-remembering every moment with her. I was mad at her. *I'm still mad at her.*

CHAPTER 14

Kane

I expected to run into Caroline. I had planned on keeping my distance. I did not expect to find her in her PJs in the back kitchen. I came around the corner to see her sitting on a stool, talking to her father. She had her mane of curls down, falling on her back, almost touching the bottom of her shirt. Her flannel pants were low on her waist. The dimples that were just above her ass were in full sight. Her tank top was tight and, even though I was standing behind her, I could tell it was above her navel.

I nearly dropped to my knees when she stood up from the stool, and I got my first full on glimpse of her. Her tank top was thin and, as she stood up, her breasts bounced just enough. *Fuck, I'm hard.* Her nipples showed through the sheer shirt and I nearly fainted. I had to cross my arms to keep my hands from reaching to feel how hard and strained they were against the fabric.

I was good. I kept my distance—arm's length, like I had told myself—but as we spoke and resolved how we were going to coexist, she took that step and punched me! I guess if I wasn't going to be able to have her, I was going to have to settle for what I could. I agreed with her, that staying mad at one another was going to put stress on B. He was eventually going to figure it out, that we had issues, and that was the last thing I wanted to do, stress him out.

I wasn't going to stop being who I was, and she was going to have to keep her opinions to herself. If she wasn't going to give it to me, then I was going somewhere else. I had one hell of a libido, and I made sure to keep it happy.

In the middle of explaining how we transformed the whole second floor, she practically froze. Instead of a picture of Aiden messing with some wires, which was what I expected to be next, it was pictures from her childhood, her past. B never spoke about his past, only of Caroline. No one ever asked him about the mother or why he left. B could be very standoffish when he wanted to. He was a tall man with wide shoulders. Since he had moved here he had lost a considerable amount of excess fat and started lifting weights. For someone who was knocking on fifty, he was in great shape, and the ladies loved him as much as us, although he attracted a more mature audience.

"Dad, I'm going to go shower and get ready for my training. Kara said she'd meet me at the bar at two, so I'm going to head upstairs."

B simply nodded. A sad look washed across his face, the same time as it did on Caroline's. Clearly something was up, and I had a feeling it had to do with her mother.

"Kane," Kitty said, turning to look up at me. "Thank you for making my room as amazing as you did. Don't let your head get too big, or I'm never saying anything nice about you again."

"I'll try to keep it contained," I replied, leaning back against the table, crossing my arms again so I didn't reach out for her taut nipples.

"I guess I'll see you the next time you play here."

"Oh, you mean in two hours when we practice." I paused for a moment and let that sink in.

"You practice here every day, don't you?" she asked, smiling back.

"Get used to it, Kitty, I practically live here. See you in a few hours," I said smugly, before she sighed and walked out the door. "What was that about B?" I asked once she'd walked out of the room.

"Nothing, she's just—she hasn't dealt with it yet," he said, closing the photo album.

"Hasn't dealt with what?" I asked, digging a little deeper than I ever had with him.

"It's nothing, Kane, just let her be. She might put on a good front, but she's got some serious things to deal with and, until she does, she's never going to be truly happy."

I stared across at him, not wanting to intrude anymore, so I dropped it. I sat on the edge of the stage, my baby on my lap. I started strumming the tune I had started last night on the porch. It was a new song, slow and serious. I didn't have words to it, but the melody flowed enticingly around me, and I couldn't seem to stop playing it over and over again. While I played, I couldn't get the image of Caroline out of my head, not the one of her breasts, or the dimples above her ass. It was the image of her looking up at me, before she kneed me in the balls. She could deny it all she wanted, but that look was real. No one had ever looked at me that way before, like she could see all of me.

I had my own reasons for staying single and most of them were selfish and egotistical. To put it plainly, I wanted the freedom to love 'em and leave 'em, to come and go as I pleased. You can't do that with a stage five clinger, trust me, I've tried. Kitty though—I had a feeling, the reason she had a stone wall up had more to do with her mother, than not being attracted to me.

The guys arrived right when Kara was starting to train Caroline. Since we had the day off, we took advantage and put in a good long practice. We worked on a horde of new songs, but I kept that one to myself. I wasn't ready to share it, just like I wasn't willing to share her. Not like I had a choice in the matter, but I'd do my damnedest to keep her from anyone else, at least until I got her out of my system.

Three hours in, Kara had us pretending to be customers. We each sat at a different table, placing orders and giving our little Kitty one hell of a time. If she could get through serving us, she'd have no problem in the future.

Reece shrugged. "I said, I wanted this medium, it's too over done."

"I don't care anymore, Reece! I'm not taking it back again! Just eat your fucking food and shut up," she yelled back down at him, smacking his red mohawked head for added humph.

I was almost crying, because I was laughing so hard.

"Caroline, you can't do that. What if he was a real customer?" Kara called from behind the bar, trying to hold in her own chuckles.

"Well, he's not. He's a pain in my ass," she yelled back, turning to Kara and slamming her hands down on her hips.

"You're damn right, I'm a pain in the ass," Reece said as he tried to swat at hers.

With sonic speed, she turned around and took his food from him.

"You're not eating now. I'm kicking you out. Leave," she said, walking away from his table and toward mine.

She was headed in my direction and I tried really hard to control myself. If she caught me still laughing, I had a feeling it was going to end in a new black and blue bruise.

"What are you laughing at?" she asked, glairing down at me. "Nothing. Can I get another beer? Mine's gone," I said, holding up my empty beer bottle.

"No! We're out of beer, and I'm done playing around. I get it. Bring on the real customers that actually have some manners," she said, snatching the empty beer bottle from my hand.

I watched along with the rest of the guys as her fine ass walked away and into the kitchen.

"Kane, what the hell? I need her to practice," Kara called from behind the bar.

"It wasn't me. I just asked for another beer. Reece is the one who pissed her off," I pleaded in my own defense.

"You're the ring leader, so you automatically get blamed," Kara said, before leaving the bar to go after Caroline.

CHAPTER 15

Caroline

My first night was a piece of cake. The guys had stayed, but since they weren't slated to play, the bar was not at all like it was the previous night. I found my way around and things were going perfect. The guys were giving me a hard time, but I eventually got a little revenge.

A group of women walked in, clearly having a girl's night. They sat down and I proceeded to get their drink order and appetizers. I couldn't help but notice that every time I walked by, they would be whispering and giggling about the guys. I stood back, leaning against the bar, watching the woman openly observe ONS as they sat around a table drinking and having a good time.

I kept looking from one table to the other, when Kane caught me. Leaning back on his chair, so he was away from the table, he beckoned me with a finger and a devilish grin. I shook my head and mouthed the word "No." His face fell, his mouth twisted, and he really looked like he was going to cry. His usual grin turned upside down, his eyes got all big and round. *He's ridiculous.*

I stood from the bar and made my way over to their table. Stopping in front of him, I sat back on my hip and crossed my arms. "What do you want?" I asked, looking down at him.

"Kitty, the guys and I wanted to ask you something."

Rolling my eyes, I switched hips to show my frustration. "What pray-tell do you want to ask me? And I swear to god, Kane, if you ask me to have an orgy with you all, I'm going to punch you in the face." I held my fist up for added flare.

"Calm down, calm down. We weren't going to ask you that, although…"

"Kane," I seethed, taking a step closer to him and pulling my fist up.

"Whoa, calm down, Kitty," he said, holding his hands up.

"What's you type Kitty, what makes you purr?" Reece asked from the other side of me.

Whipping my head toward him, I felt my jaw drop. "You'll never know, Reece, because it sure as hell isn't you!"

The door to the bar opened just then and we all turned to see a man walk in. My eyes stayed on the person a little longer than the guys' did. It was Nate from the other night. He stood by the door while Emily, another girl who worked at the bar, grabbed him a menu and took him to a seat in my section.

The wicked smile speared across my face as I watched him pull the chair out and sit down. Catching my eye, he held his hand up and gave a little smile and wave. He was in casual clothes, jeans and a T-shirt with a leather jacket. His hair was slightly messy but still off his face. He was every bit my type, my go to when I was living in New York.

Rotating back to the table of playboy rock stars, I

smiled down at them. They were oblivious, except Kane. He was attentively watching me watch Nate.

"That right there boys, is my type—a man." Shrugging my shoulders, I cheerfully smiled at them. "Anything else?"

"Nate Rodgers, is your type?" Kane asked in disbelief.

"Yeah, but don't worry, one day when you grow up, you all might become men too. Reece, you might become a woman, if you keep wearing those tight-ass pants."

"That's harsh, Kitty. Do we have to cut your claws?" Reece asked.

"Yeah, come on, Kitty, you don't have to be mean to us all. I haven't even made a play for you," Aiden added.

"I only speak the truth boys." I went to walk away but Kane reached for my hand, pulling me back to the table.

"Don't lie," he breathed, standing from his chair and getting in my face. "That's not really you're type. You keep that wall up if you want, but I know you felt something last night and Nate Rodgers didn't have a damn thing to do with that."

I thought that we had squashed this, this morning. "Kane, we talked about this. Last night was—"

"It was real," he said, before I could finish.

"No, it wasn't. I have to go," I said, trying to back away.

"Caroline, take the wall down," was all he said before letting me turn to leave.

I glanced back once I got to the bar. But Kane wasn't looking. He was laughing and smiling with his friends.

Why did he have to do that? It was bad enough I had to pretend I was in a straightjacket so I didn't reach out and grab a hand full of that hair of his, or caress his tatted-up, cut arms. What I did feel, for a moment last night with him, was enough for me to scare myself straight. Nate was my type because, he was simple, average, easy to let go. If I kept up what I was doing last night with Kane, it would have gotten difficult, because he's not average and I didn't trust myself not to let go. So the best thing to do was exactly what I did. Put that wall up and keep him at bay.

I walked over to the table of women. "I couldn't help but over hear you girls," I said, kneeling down by the table.

The five women turned their heads my way. They weren't the prettiest bunch, but they seemed nice. I smiled wickedly at the guys, as they watched me talk to the women. Their faces scrunched in confusion before I turned back.

"The guys over, they were wondering if you would join them? They've had their eyes on you girls all night."

All five women stared at me, a look of disbelief on their faces.

"How do you know that?" the girl with the round face and glasses asked.

"I'm friends with them. I was just talking to them, and they'd really like to meet you ladies," I said, smiling.

The women looked at one another before standing from the table. They grabbed their drinks and followed me over.

The guys were all talking and didn't notice the horde of women coming their way. I stood in front of Kane and tapped his shoulder. Rotating around in his chair, he looked up at me then behind me to the five women, who these guys would never give the time of day to.

"Kane, guys, here are the girls," I said with a huge smile. Their faces were priceless. "I was just telling the girls how much you were begging me to bring them over here. Ladies, these guys might be studs on the stage, but in real life, they get a little shy around women." I glanced down to see Kane shaking his head and laughing. I held his shoulder and pinched the muscle tightly. His smile fell as he withered in pain. I then reached over to Reece and did the same thing. He didn't say ouch, but his mouth opened wide in pain. I leaned over in between their heads and spoke softly. "You fuckers better be nice to these women. They are your fans too. If I see you being mean or rude to any one of them, I'm going to hunt you down and put your balls in a vice grip. Kitty has her claws out, so you better behave, you got me?"

They all nodded to me and I think Trent even clutched his balls. *Good my point was made.*

Smacking their backs, I stood and faced the women. "They're all yours, ladies, enjoy your night. ONS is paying your tab."

CHAPTER 16

Kane

I can't believe she just did that. Elbows on the table, I rubbed my eyes then ran my fingers back through my hair. Our Kitty was clever, there was no doubting that. We all shook our heads and tried to make the best of it. I, for one, wasn't going to mess with these women. The idea of Kitty with my balls in a vice grip was enough to make me do almost anything, including entreating these women. We all stood from the table and grabbed a chair for them.

Once we were all settled around two tables, they began asking us questions. I felt like we were being interrogated.

"We're really big fans," one said nervously. She was sitting next to me and Reece was on my other side.

"I can see that," Reece said. I knew exactly what he meant by that, and I was hoping like hell that these women didn't catch on. I turned to him, eyes wide with warning before I stepped on his foot. "Damn it, Kane, watch your fucking feet," Reece yelled.

Just then, Caroline walked back over. Standing between Reece and me again, she grabbed our shoulders. I tried really hard not to make a pained face. Reece did the same.

"Is there a problem? Everything going okay?" she asked through a gritted smile.

"We're fine, Kitty," JJ said, coming to Reece's and my rescue.

"Good! You ladies be nice. These guys are family," she added, winking at JJ.

I didn't know why, but hearing her say that made me smile.

We had kept our word, we were as proper as we could be. These women were fans, the real kind. They loved our music, they weren't just here to jump us or become one of our conquests. Most of them were married. One was even six months pregnant. What we thought was going to be torture, ended up being a good time. Go figure. Kitty's plan backfired. But we weren't going to let her know that. We were grateful to meet with fans who actually appreciated us for our music and not just how we could please them in bed.

I caught Caroline chatting with Nate. It would be Nate. He graduated a year before us and was jealous as hell that we'd get so much tail. I didn't see what she saw in him. I sure as hell didn't believe that he was her type. He was boring and complacent—he was basically the complete opposite of me. *Whatever, my Monday night was most likely waiting on our front porch. I'd get over Kitty one way or another.*

 භභභ

A week had turned into a month. Not much had changed. We played every Friday night at BJ's, picked up a few other gigs. We worked construction during the day, and we practiced as often as we could. The only thing that was different was I'd get a fucking hard on every time I'd see Caroline. *Seriously, someone is going to start noticing.*

Our banter was going strong and the practical jokes were getting borderline dangerous—for us, that is. It started with Reece. He was making a thrusting motion behind Caroline as she walked by, but the dumb ass forgot that there was a mirror and she had seen the whole thing. Kitty immediately turned around and kicked him in the shin, hard. The next night we had to play, and he was missing beats because he was in so much pain.

Next was JJ. He had found a photo of Caroline when they were little, in the bathtub, together. He showed us all. Now, JJ will think twice before showing any other photos like that, because she went to his mom and got a picture of him when he was twelve in a zip up PJ, a horrible haircut, and full head gear. She blew the picture up and hung it on the wall near where he stood, so everyone would see while he played.

Aiden had finally gotten the balls to make a move on Kitty. He was trying to sweet talk her at the bar one night while she was making drinks. I don't know what was said and he swore never to tell us, but her face went from smiling to serial killer in a split second. Reaching below the bar, she emerged with the soda hose and proceeded to spray him in the face. Two days later, he had a nasty eye infection. Red and swollen. He didn't get laid for a week after that. She was so proud of herself.

Trent was lucky *he* didn't lose a nipple. One night after our show, we were all sitting around out back. Kitty had plopped down on Trent's lap, which had become routine. I hated it. *What the hell was wrong with my lap?* It had to be the big bad biker/protector vibe he put off. Women went fucking nuts for that.

Resting her feet, from running around all night, she

would snuggle up and rest her head on his shoulder.

I didn't know why, but he always got away with feeling her up. Either she would be too tired to notice or, hell, maybe she liked it. This one particular night, he took it a bit too far and paid for it. She swatted his hand away, hit his shoulder, and when he was still laughing about it, she scrunched her face up and went right for his nipple, pinching it hard and then twisting with ferocity. He screeched like a girl, jumped up, but she wouldn't release him. Kitty had her claws in him and she wasn't letting go.

"I like you Trent," she had said. "But if you touch me like that again, you are going to lose this!" she said, twisting his left nipple a little more.

Of course, my pranks were the worst and every day I added at least one new bruise to my sore body. I ran the gambit. I had put a fake snake in her bed, that gained me a bruise on the left arm. I had jumped out of the closet in the back while she was cleaning up one night, which got me a punch in the gut. One of my favorites was when I told her B needed to speak with her in the walk in freezer. I watched her walk in then closed and locked the door behind her. She was in there for a good ten minutes. When I let her out, her teeth were chattering while she was swinging her arms at me. The only reason she got me right in the jaw was because I was hunched over, laughing so hard.

Now, she wasn't a saint either. She was just as nasty with us. She had ordered thirty pizzas one night and sent them to our house. Two hundred and some odd dollars later, we had pizza for a week and a half. Then there was the group of guys who were under the impression that we swung their way. Our Kitty had managed to make sure no women were allowed on the patio, thus we were surrounded by dudes with disturbing ideas about us. That was a long and very uncomfortable night.

The worst happened last night. We were just getting ready to go on. Kitty was standing in her usual corner just before the door to the open bar. I was trying to ignore her because she had practically broken my hand. It didn't matter that she had bent my hand back for trying to smack her ass. When she grabbed me by the arm and hulled me back so I was flush against her, I was more than surprised.

"Kane," she breathed, running her fucking, soft hands all up and down my shirtless arm.

Swallowing the huge lump in my throat I looked down at her.

"I want to try something with you. When you're done playing, I'm really embarrassed to admit it, but I can't hold back any more." She kept running her hand up and down my arm, then she bit her lip nervously.

Fuck! I prayed that she didn't see the raging hard on I was sporting. That would have totally given me away. I needed to play cool, like I didn't care, but who the fuck was I trying to kid? "What do you have in mind, Kitty?" I asked leaning into her, her body was flush with mine, and fuck if I couldn't feel her nipples through her thin shirt. *Shit!* I looked down, and she wasn't even wearing a fucking bra.

"I want it to be special, just us," she said, chewing on her finger.

Holy shit balls! I was ready to cancel the show, tell the guys to fuck off, and rush her up to her room.

"After," was all she said as she pushed me back and pointed up to the stage.

I kept it just to the songs, no drinks, no flirty banter with the crowd, I just wanted it over. The guys kept giving me looks, but I didn't care, I still had chub just thinking about all the naughty things I was going to do to my little kitty. When we finished, I raced straight out the back, only to find Kara. She handed me a note, I opened it and felt my jaw go slack as I read the words that were so beautifully written. *Meet me down by the river. I'll be in the water, waiting...naked...*

There just so happened to be a large river that ran behind Main Street, It was great to wade in and float down and Caroline James was naked in it, waiting for me. She had finally taken that fucking wall down and was ready to give in.

I was standing on the edge of the water after walking up and down the edge trying to find her, and then I spotted her clothes, all of them! I searched the water. Lucky for me, the moon was bright, which made it painfully obvious where she was. Coming up from under the water, she pushed her hair out of her face.

"Kane, hurry up and get out here, I don't know how much longer I can wait."

I couldn't speak. I just stripped as fast as I could. As I pulled off my boxers and tossed then into the pile of clothes, I realized just how much I liked seeing our clothes mixed up on the ground together.

I looked back out to the water when Caroline yelled "Now!"

I watched as she stood up in a bathing suit from the water that was at her thighs. That's when a huge flood light turned on illuminating the whole side of the river. It's then, that I noticed all the people standing around laughing. *That sneaky little bitch*! Everyone from the bar, the guys, B, women of all ages, stood around admiring me in all my glory. Usually, I wouldn't mind. But as I glanced around with a huge smile on my face my eyes landed on my mom! *She fucking called my mom*!

I ran into the water at full speed. "You're going to pay for this Kitty!" I yelled as I made my way in the cold water. When I caught up to her, I pushed her head under the water. "If you wanted to see the package that bad, Kitty, you should have just asked," I said when she reemerged from under the water.

"Wasn't that impressive," she called and then pushed me down in the water.

"Oh, Kitty, when will you just admit, you want me?"

"Keep dreaming, Kane," she said as she swam away.

CHAPTER 17

Caroline

I was sitting on my balcony, drinking a beer. It was close to three in the afternoon, and I was killing time before I had to help Dad prep for the night. There was another band coming to play. The guys were friends with them and were helping them gain a bigger audience. *I guess these rock guys stick together.* The boys had promoted them last night, telling the audience that they'd be here to watch and that everyone should come and join them.

I sat, thinking about the previous night. I still couldn't believe I pulled it off. After the shock wore off that Kane was buck-ass naked, everyone stripped to their underwear and jumped into the river. It ended up being a really fun time. When I was planning it, I didn't think too far in advance. I had seen Kane—all of Kane and it was making things—difficult. I'd never let on that it was, but now, I didn't think I'd be able to look at him with a straight face, because all I'd see was that glorious package of his, that I had straight-up lied to his face about.

Sitting up a little from my chair, I heard, then saw, Kane's red pickup truck pull up. His truck was a beautiful red color, just like his precious guitar that he called baby. It had chrome in all the right places, it was high off the ground with big tires, and it looked hot. I didn't see him as a truck-kind-of guy. I saw him more as an older muscle car guy at first. I thought it went better with the whole rocker thing. Suddenly, my mind wandered and I got an image of me in cowboy boots and daisy dukes, jumping out of the truck and into his arms. Shaking my head quickly, I got the picture out of my mind before I could elaborate on it.

It was getting hotter by the day and, as he jumped out of his truck, I nearly dropped my beer on my lap. He was a sweaty mess, no shirt, cargo shorts, backward hat, and glistening body. *Fuck, Caroline, get it together*. He stood next to his truck, his arms hanging over the bed. The other guys pulled in next. Trent was also driving his truck, which was black like his bass. Aiden, Reese, and Trent all got out of his truck, looking just as yummy as Kane. None of them had shirts on. Their tatted-up bodies had a glorious mix of dirt and sweat coating their muscular frames. This was clearly the best perk of me being here. Them not talking to me, and me just getting to watch them in all their sexy glory. I wouldn't be surprised if women hired them to fix their houses, just so they could get this view every day.

JJ was the last to pull up. He did have a muscle car— a blue 1969 Dodge Challenger. It was a sexy beast. I had gotten to ride in it twice since I had moved in. Once to the grocery store and once to his mom's house for dinner. As the boys would say, it made me purr like the kitten they thought I was. As much as I hated it in the beginning, that stupid name had grown on me. Looking back, if you would have told me I'd be working in my father's bar, be surrounded by a hunky pack of rock stars who referred to me as their mascot Kitty, I'd have laughed in your face. *Yet here I am, and I don't hate it—that much.*

I couldn't help myself. "Don't you guys think you should go clean up before you make your groupies sit on your laps tonight? You fucking reek! I can smell you all the way up here!"

All five heads turned my way. Reece raised his hand and saluted me with the middle finger.

"Oh shut up, drink your beer, and enjoy the view," Kane said, while flexing his arms, in a bodybuilder way.

Oh, why did he have to do that? I stood from my chair and leaned over the railing. "Why are you guys even here?" I asked.

"We're meeting our friends from Fallen, plus we got to pack our stuff up so they can set up for tonight's show." Aiden replied, while re-doing his shoulder-length black hair into a man bun atop his head.

I knew nothing about this band Fallen, but the crowd last night seemed to know exactly who they were. I guess I'd be meeting them soon.

"I'm coming up to use your bathroom," Kane said, as he walked from his truck.

"I don't think so. Use the one in the bar. I don't need your smelly ass in my house. It's bad enough its wafting up here," I said this as he kept walking under the patio and finally out of sight. *That asshole!* I stood there for a second, eyeing the rest of the guys in guilty pleasure, drank the rest of my beer, then left the balcony. *I'll be damned if he was going to use my bathroom, I don't need his ass anywhere near my toilet.*

I strode across my room and ran smack into Kane, sweaty, dirty, and fucking sexy as hell.

"I don't think so Kane," I said, pointing a finger at his chest.

"Kitty, move, I helped put this bathroom together, I've used it before, and I'm going to use it now!"

Ew, he had used it before! Like recently?

"Yeah, let that sink in. While you're down there serving drinks all night, I come up here and use your bathroom. I can really relax in there. It must be the lavender candles that you have."

Clenching my fists at my sides, I ground my jaw. "Get out of my room."

He stood there looming over me, his hat still on backward holding his mess of curls back. His raw scent tickled my senses and I had to do everything I could to keep my hands at my sides. He didn't have a lot of tattoos, but the ones he did have were delightful to look at. He had some colorful design over his left peck, which led all the way over to his shoulder, and down to his elbow. He didn't say anything, just turned from me and headed toward *my* bathroom. I was shell shocked, not only that he was actually going to use my bathroom, but at the tattoo that ran across his shoulder blades.

That wonderful scent that was coming off of him had disappeared, replaced by something foul. *That fucker farted in my room! Hell if I'm going to let him blow my bathroom up!* I ran straight at him and jumped on his back. I slipped on his slick damp skin but that didn't stop me, it only slowed me down, I was out for blood. Clearly, I had taken him off guard. He stumbled forward to gain his balance back and as he did, I laced my arms around his neck and my legs around his waist, so I wouldn't slip again. "You are not going to take a shit in my bathroom, Kane!"

He stood still, his arms dropping to his sides. His head hung down and he was shaking, while I clung to his back.

"Woman, don't think I won't go in there with you on my back to get my business done." I quickly jumped off his back. Rotating toward me, he cocked his head. "You can't keep your hands off me, can you?" He stood there, crossing his arms and looking all sexy.

"You're insane. Whatever. Use the bathroom," I said, throwing my hands up in defeat. Right now I just wanted him to get it over with and leave. He was too fucking sexy standing there and I didn't know how much longer I could hold out.

"Oh, I'm not insane. You saw something you liked last night in that river and now you want more," he said, taking a step toward me. "I *know* I saw something I liked. You just got to get out of your head and let me in."

"I don't have to do shit, Kane. I'm not in my head. I just don't like you," I said back, my hands on my hips.

"You see, I don't believe you. I believe that you're doing everything in your power not to reach out and get another taste. I know this, because I'm in the same boat. I don't know what it is about you. Maybe it's because you're holding out on me, but fuck if I don't want to shove you up against that wall and have my way with you."

I hadn't noticed, but I was backing up and hit the wall behind me. Kane was toe to toe with me, hovering over me as he spoke.

I knew he had ideas that involved getting in my pants, but this seemed a little different. I don't like different. Different is dangerous. His lips came millimeters away from mine. I should have pushed back. My brain knew that, but my body was frozen. When I didn't move, he took that as go ahead. *Damn it!* I reached up, grabbed the back of his neck, and pulled him the rest of the way so our lips finally touched. His hat fell off his head and hit the floor as my hands ran up the back of his head. It wasn't a nice kiss—it was a fucking amazing kiss.

CHAPTER 18

Kane

S hit, she tastes good. It had been a long month since the last time I kissed her. I had tried to use other women to get over that scrumptious taste, but they never seem to be as good as her. I fisted her hair at the back of her neck, pushing my body into hers, farther against the wall. Her hand left my neck and came up my face, tossing my hat off. She fisted my hair, pulling me closer to her. I usually hated when women played with my hair, but fuck if it didn't send goose bumps down my arms.

I was lost in her, and I was loving it. That is, until I got pushed back.

"Kane, I can't do this, we can't do this," she said, holding her hand over her mouth, as if to keep from kissing me again.

She looked close to tears and I didn't have a clue why. *It felt right with her. Why does she keep pushing me away?*

"Caroline, what's the problem?" I asked, squatting a little so I could get eye to eye with her.

She looked up at me, tears filling her eyes, but not

spilling over. "My dad—I work here. It's just—I can't," she said.

I didn't believe her. "B won't give a shit. You know that. You're a grown-ass woman, you can do what you want. Who cares if you work here? All the better, I said, in a sad attempt to make a joke.

"I don't like you."

"Are you asking me or telling me, because it sounds like you're trying to convince *yourself*." I stood straight, running my hands through my sweaty hair

"Just use the bathroom," she said, tossing her hands up as she turned away from me.

"Caroline, I don't get it. You kiss me like you never want to let go then push me away and say you don't like it. That's fucked up."

Her hair fanned out as she spun back around. "What do you want me to say Kane? I don't want to be another notch on your belt. I let this go further, it might be great, or hell, you might be horrible—"

I quickly cut her off. "I'm not horrible. For the record, I've been told I'm amazing."

"Doesn't matter, Kane, I'm not going to be that girl. You're not going to sleep with me today and then someone else the next. I *don't* do that, you *do,* so it's never going to happen. Now use the bathroom and get the hell out."

I stared down at her deep blue eyes. *Nope, still don't believe that.* "You're going to crack and tell me what the hell is going on, eventually, because that shit you just said doesn't make any sense. You've had one night stands, I know it. I also know you watch my every move. I know this because I watch yours. You're a game changer, Kitty. I'm not against cutting it down to just you, if that's really your issue, but I know it's not."

Shock came across her face and mine the moment

those words left my lips. *I can't believe I just said I'd give up my amazing sex life to sleep with her.*

"Stop! Just shut up, Kane, you don't mean that," she said, shaking her head.

I stood there, looking at the most beautiful girl I had ever seen, and I did. I meant it. *Holy shit!* I was falling hard for Kitty, and not merely in a sexual way. "I do. I will fucking give it up for you."

The tears she had kept in her eyes finally spilled over. She shook her head no, the same time I was nodding yes.

"No! No, you don't. Kane, you and I can't be together, ever. I'm done talking about this. I slipped up, and it won't happen again. I won't let it happen again."

She sounded like she was talking to herself and not me.

"Caroline, you do get what I'm telling you, right? I'm saying that I will stop sleeping with other women, to be with you. Holy crap, I can't believe I just said that out loud." I scratched my head, still amazed that I felt this strongly about her.

"I get it, Kane, but it doesn't matter. It's not you. It's…well, it is you. I like you. I like hanging out with you, I like our banter, but I can't do more than that with you."

She straightened up, wiped away the few tears that were still under her eyes, and I knew that I wasn't going to make any progress now. She had that fucking wall back up and, apparently, she was not going to let me over it anytime soon. So I took a step back from her, putting a few feet between us. "I'll do it, Caroline. I'll do it because for the first time in…well, ever, I don't want to stick my dick in anyone unless it's you. That kind of pisses me off, now that I think about it. You fucked me up, big time," I said, pointing to her.

"Save it, Kane. I'm sure you'll be balls deep in some girl tonight, and I know for damn sure it won't be me!"

Popping her hip to the side she crossed her arms again, while throwing me a dirty look.

"I swear to you, Kitty, if you have ruined sex for me, I'm...I'm going to..."

"What, Kane, what are you going to do to me? Lock me the freezer again?"

Fuck her! I kept walking until I had her backed up against the wall again. "I'm not going to stop next time. I'm going to make sure you know all that you're missing. Your little 'No, Kane, I can't,' won't mean shit, because I have a feeling you really want to say 'Yes, Kane, don't listen to me and fucking ram me hard!'"

I didn't touch her, I didn't kiss her, I didn't let her have another word. I just turned around, grabbed my hat from the floor, and walked into the bathroom, slamming the door behind me. When I came back out, she was no-where to be seen. I left her room and headed down to the bar. The guys and me had to move our stuff to the back, so that we could help Fallen set up. I went out the back and grabbed my guitar case from the cab of my truck. The guys were still standing around having a beer.

"Kane, man, you all right?" JJ asked, coming to stand next to me as I pulled the case out all the way.

"Your fucking cousin is ruing me," I said, getting in his face.

"What the fuck! I have nothing to do with her. She's a breed all her own. Must get it from her mom's side," JJ said, pushing me back.

That was when it hit me—her mom. This all had to do with her mom. The way she'd been acting, something was making her hold back from me, and I had a feeling it was her mom, but how could her dead mom keep her from fucking me? I knew I didn't have the best track record with moms, but I couldn't even begin to figure out how to schmooze a dead one.

"I'm sorry, man," I said, clapping his shoulder.

"It's fine, bro. I'd just leave her alone. There's going to be new tail here tonight, and if Kitty isn't giving it up to you, may as well find someone who will."

ᑫᓄᑫᓄ

Fallen had arrived. The four piece band was good. They weren't as good as us, but they were good. They had their own following from the city and made sure to bring the best of the bunch with them. Which included their lead singer Chloe. I had a tendency to wander down that all-too-familiar path every time we hung out. She was a knock out, and unlike our fans, the band had a good deal of men following them just because of her. Chloe and her twin brother Collin had started the group. They were good on their own, but with the help of Hunter and Levi, they were amazing.

Caroline had made herself scarce since our incident in her room. It was nearly time for Fallen to go on, and I hadn't seen her all night. I knew she was working tonight. One of the other girls was off for a wedding, so B needed her to be here. I scanned the room and even walked into the pool hall, but she was nowhere.

I ignored and kept my distance from, the long-legged, dark-haired, tatted-up beauty that was Chloe. As stupid and fucking love sick as it sounded, I didn't want Caroline to see me with her because, I knew Chloe, and she'd be all over me. I couldn't hide forever, though.

"Kane, sexy-ass Lawson. Where the hell have you been hiding all day? You trying to avoid me?" Chloe's sultry voice, swirled around my ear, as her hands ran up my chest from behind.

I turned in her hands, and we ended up nose to nose. She was an Amazon and fuck if those green eyes weren't begging for it.

"I've been busy," I said back, keeping my hands at my sides.

"Not as busy as you're going to be later on tonight. I didn't take the hour drive out here just to sing."

When she tried to bite at my lip, I thought about backing up, pushing her away. Then I decided fuck it. If Caroline was going to be a bitch about things, I may as well try to move on. So I let her take my bottom lip between her teeth, then I let her suck on it, because *I'm a man, after all.*

"Chloe, come on. Stop sucking face with Kane and get onstage," Collin, her twin brother said, walking up behind her, he grabbed her arm, and pulled her toward the stage.

Saved by the brother. Never thought I hear myself say something like that. I walked up to the table where the guys were sitting. It was crowded and people kept clamoring around us. I sat down and tried to act casual. I had just came into a conversation, so I sat back and listened.

"I don't get it. What does he have, a golden cock or something?" Reece asked. "I can't believe we just walked by and let it happen, I feel like we should have stopped it," Aiden added.

"I haven't punched anyone in a while. Maybe I should go back out there," Trent said, cracking his knuckles.

"What are you guys talking about?" I finally asked, since I couldn't for the life of me figure it out.

"Dude, it's Kitty," Reece said.

"What about her?"

"When we came in from outside, we...well, we're

pretty sure she was fucking Nate Rodg—"

JJ couldn't even finish his sentence before I was up and out of my chair. The music had started and people were dancing. I made my way around them, determined to get out back and fucking punch that asshole in the face. If I couldn't have Kitty, then no one was. I got all the way to the door when I ran into Caroline.

"Jesus, Kane! You scared the shit out of me," she said, clutching at her chest.

"Nate Rodgers! You're shitting me right?" I watched as her jovial smile was replaced with irritation. "Not four hours ago, you tell me you can't even kiss me, and I got to hear it from the guys that they saw you fucking Nate Rodgers out back!"

Grabbing my arm, she pulled me back outside.

Once there she dropped my arm. "Jesus, Kitty." I cringed as I kept walking. I needed to put some space between us. I was frustrated as fuck! I spun back around and saw her standing there like she didn't know what the hell was going on. "Did you? Did you fuck him?"

I'd walked all the way to the other side of the patio, but I still saw the disgust and anger on her face before she stomped her feet in my direction. "No, Kane. Not that it's any of your business, but no I didn't *fuck* him. Will you quiet down?"

Relief washed over me. *Why did I care so much? I shouldn't care this much.*

Nate was a regular, but ever since the first night he came and talked with Caroline, he was always hanging around, waiting for her to come talk, looming around out back. I guess I underestimated him.

"Good."

"Good? Kane, I don't know what you think this is, but if I want to fuck Nate as you so blatantly put it, I'm going to fuck Nate. I'm human, I get horny, and if he's willing, it's going to happen. There isn't a damn thing you can do about it to stop me. You don't see me running after you every night, while you suck face with every Heather, Jane, and Sally."

She had a point.

"A little heads up would be nice. I just told you I'd give up all that for you. You think I wouldn't care if someone was fucking you in a parking lot? You're fucking insane. I'm fucking insane for ever thinking you were worth it. Fuck who you want, Kitty, 'cause I sure am."

I was furious. Nope, I was beyond furious, if there even was such a thing.

"Kane, stop being so dramatic."

I had walked away from her, even farther, to the edge of the parking lot that backed up to the woods.

"You okay, Kitty?" Trent asked, walking up next to her.

I turned around to see not only Trent, but the rest of the guys surrounding her. She didn't look at them, her eyes were fixed on mine, and, for a split second, I saw the girl that I had laid down in her bed that first night. The girl who could see me, see through the rock star, the playboy, the asshole. She was seeing me, Kane Lawson.

CHAPTER 19

Caroline

I *see him, right now I see Kane Lawson.* Not the wanna be rock star, the playboy or the pain in my ass. Just like that first night when he carried me to bed, I saw him, nervous and kind. Tonight he was honoring my virtue, as absurd as that sounded. He was being vulnerable for the second time tonight. It had taken everything in me to walk away and say the things I had said up in my room. Thanks to his smart-ass mouth, I was able to get back in the right frame of mind. The frame of mind that avoided the type of feelings that Kane was bringing to the surface. Hearing him say he'd give up his lifestyle for me, that's not what I wanted, but was it romantic as hell? *Yes. Did he have me rethinking everything? Fuck, yes.* But I didn't want him to be remorseful of having to give up a part of himself. That's what happened with my parents, and I would not make the same mistakes.

I was not turning into her. I was not going to let that happen. I cared too much about my dad and myself to let that happen. She was weak, and I'd be damned if I was going to walk down that path. I was a strong, independent woman. I'd keep fighting these feeling I had for Kane, because I knew that, in the end, neither one of us was going to be happy. I just needed to keep telling myself that.

"Kitty?" Trent said, pulling me out of my own thoughts. I turned and looked up into his brown eyes, as he held on to my shoulder. "You okay?" he asked again.

"She's fine," Kane said, walking up behind us. "She just had a lapse in judgment, realized that Nate wasn't the man she thought he was. Game on, boys, Kitty's frisky and looking for a tomcat to play with."

There it was, typical asshole Kane.

"Kane's right, Trent," I said, looking up at him, "Tonight's your lucky night. I'm giving out kisses for free." I grabbed a fist full of his shirt and pulled his large frame down, pressing my lips against his. I gave him one hell of a kiss, a kiss I knew he'd been dreaming about.

The loud hoots and hollers came from all the guys, except Kane. I wanted there to be something behind that kiss, just like I wanted there to be something behind the kiss I had with Nate, but there was nothing. This was usually good. This meant I could shag 'em and leave 'em. Sure, it was a nice kiss, but there wasn't a spark, or sense of future, like the one I had with Kane. It was just a kiss. I was glad, but this only made things worse, because kissing Kane and having the feelings I did, just justified that I needed to stay away, and deep down I didn't want to stay away. I was going to have to endure lack-luster kisses for the rest of my life. *Fuck you, Kane Lawson!*

"Well," I said, after pulling back from Trent and fixing my hair by tossing it around. "I have to get back to work. See you guys later." Before I turned to walk back to the bar, I smiled and winked at Kane, only to see that wicked grin of his spread across his face as he shook his head, chuckling. *Good, he doesn't hate me.*

I could live with our banter, but I'd be lying if I said it wouldn't bother me if he hated me.

"Dude, I saw her tongue in your mouth!" I heard Reece say, as I walked back through the door.

As much as they were a pain in my ass, I loved One Night Stand.

⚜

Another month went by and summer was here in full force. It was the Fourth of July weekend and the county fair was in full swing. I was currently helping my dad carry boxes to the tent that was set up for the bar, away from the bar. Friday night and as always the boys were slated to play, but not at BJ's. The fair had a huge stage. While my father and a couple of the other girls helped unpack, the boys were busy setting up for their big concert. They were the closing act to the fair and the whole town was on edge, getting ready for the hundreds—hell, maybe even thousands of people who would be coming to see them. Roads had been blocked and extra security had been called in. I was told by my father that last year they only got two songs off before people started going crazy. Hence, all the security and refurbished stage.

Things had gone back to normal, as normal as they could get. Since I had kissed Trent, I had also made the mistake of kissing Aiden and god help me my lips touched Reece's too that night. So I might have only kissed Reece to piss Kane off because he kept deliberately palming Chloe's ass, and I knew he was doing it on purpose, because he wouldn't even touch her unless I was looking. Either way, I hadn't been able to live it down since.

I was keeping my distance from Kane and he was doing the same. I made sure not to put myself in a situation where we were left alone, simply because I didn't trust myself.

Things with Nate took a step up, after I had kissed him the night Fallen had come to play at the bar. He was sweet and I didn't have the heart to tell him it wasn't going to go anywhere, but he was a good kisser, and if I couldn't have Kane, I guessed I'd have to settle for Nate. He was meeting me later on in the evening.

I had stopped moving boxes and leaned over the impromptu bar we had set up. Resting my elbows on the laminate bar and propping my head up on my hands, I guiltily watched the boys practice for tonight.

Kane had jeans on, with a black tee, and his hair was a sexy mess. His guitar was slung over his body, the beautiful red color glistened when the sun hit it. He was going to break so many hearts once they made it big, and I was going to be able to say that I had spent a whole summer with him. My future friends wouldn't believe me, but I'd know the truth.

"I told you, they'd grow on you," my father said, leaning next to me.

"Yeah, they're pretty great," I said, smiling at him.

"I know it's none of my business, but I see the way he looks at you," My father added, nodding at Kane.

He can't be serious. "Dad, I—it's not like that," I said, trying to play it off.

"Caroline, I'm not dumb. I know you have commitment issues. You've never introduced me to any of your boyfriends, and you never talk about a future, getting married, or having kids. I know you don't want to be like your mother. You can still have all that if—"

I cut him off quickly. I didn't want to hear this.

"Dad, I'm fine, that's not the kind of future I want. Not everyone wants the big house, white picket fence, and 2.5 kids." I hated lying to him, I did want those things. I was just terrified I'd end up like her. He was absolutely right.

That man up on stage was the first person to ever make me really want those things since my mother died. Catching my eye, he kept his on me as his fingers skillfully worked the strings on his guitar. We were far away from the stage, but I could see the way his muscles moved in his arms, as if he was standing right in front of me.

"Kane's a good guy. I wouldn't be upset if you two—"

"Dad!" I said, breaking eye contact with Kane. "You're really giving me your blessing to get it on with Kane, the same Kane that you watch leave every other night with a different girl. You been drinking top shelf again before work?"

A loud, haughty laugh left my father as he patted my back. "Oh, Caroline, haven't you noticed, he hasn't left with anyone in a long time? I know because I have to kick the girls out of the bar when he leaves without them."

I didn't believe it. There was no way he'd kept it in his pants that long. Not Kane, the self-proclaimed playboy, who had a different girl for every day of the week. I glanced back up at the stage as he began singing one of their slow songs. Holding the microphone in one hand, while the other held the stand, he looked at me again then closed his eyes as he sang.

Why does he have to be so sexy up there?

Kissing my wild hair my dad whispered, "Give him a chance."

CHAPTER 20

Kane

I sat backstage, which was actually a backstage and not a parking lot. The crowd was so loud it felt like the walls were shaking. This was going to be the biggest venue we had ever performed at. After last year, the county had upped their game, demolishing the old rickety stage and putting in a brand new one. It was huge, had lights and an amazing sound system. I knew that they didn't do it just because of us. They were hoping to have bigger-named acts come and perform there.

"We're gonna get fucked up after this show tonight! I don't want to be able to walk tomorrow," Reece said, banging his drumsticks on the back of his chair.

The room that we were in was a moderate size. We had water and snacks. There were two couches, a few chairs, and a bathroom around the corner. *I could get use to this.*

"Did you see Kitty while we were practicing? She looked fucking hot in that dress," Aiden added.

I couldn't disagree with that. She had a sundress on that didn't have a back, which meant she didn't have a bra on, which meant, side boob, and a lot of it. It was tight up top then flowed softly down around her legs. Her wild, long curls were down and blowing in the hot July air. I couldn't stop looking at her while we practiced earlier.

I hated that I hadn't been able to...perform, since the incident in her room. It was as if ever since I said that I'd give up other women, my dick was on strike until it got what it wanted—her. I tried that night to bang Chloe, but nothing, I blamed it on being drunk and dead-dog tired, but I knew the real reason. *Fucking Kitty had ruined me!* I was close to getting a prescription for Viagra. Yes, it was that bad.

It was also painfully obvious that she was avoiding me. So I gave her space, watched her from afar. But every night was the same. I'd dream about her on top of me, her long curls falling around my face, her smile, everything. I'd dream about it all and have to wake up and take a cold-ass shower or attempt to rub one out, but it never worked. I'd fucking get a cramp from trying so hard, I'd always end up under the ice cold water.

∽∾∽

This is amazing. There was a sea of people cheering for us as we walked out on stage. A thousand or so for sure, all screaming for us. *Yeah, I can get use to this.* To the side of the stage and up the hill, there were people sitting on blankets, but to the front of the stage, no one was sitting and everyone was pushed up against the railing that separated the stage from the crowd. There was enough room between the two for a bunch of guys in "security" shirts to stand. I looked to my right at the people sitting on blankets, and fuck if my eye didn't go straight to Kitty, who was huddled up next to Nate fucking Rodgers. I really hated that guy. I didn't know why I just got a weird vibe from him, always had. Something about a cop just gave me the willies.

The whole hour and a half that we played, the screaming never stopped. It had died down while we flirted with the crowd and introduced ourselves, but other than that, I was surprised people could even hear us. We were getting ready to leave the stage, when I glanced over at Caroline, for the millionth time. She was gazing up at Nate, while he said something to her. His hand cupped her face, and his lips found hers in a tender kiss. She wrapped her hand around the arm that was holding her face and kissed him back.

"Get your fucking hands off her, Rodgers!" I roared, completely forgetting that I was still standing in front of my microphone, that was clearly still on. The whole place went silent. If I could have, I would have shot lasers out my eyes and split Rodgers in two. I had succeeded in getting him to back the fuck off, but now everyone was following my gaze and looking at kitty and Nate. Something in me had snapped. Actually seeing her kiss him had taken me over the edge. Thankfully, the guys came up next to me. I knew how much they cared for her too, and we all stood staring at them.

"Kitty, come on. You're our mascot not his," Reece added.

"I thought you loved me," Trent put in, sounding disheartened.

She stood from her blanket and stalked away, clearly pissed. Nate just sat there, looking like the tool that he was.

"Come on, lover boys," JJ said to us all, pushing us off the stage.

We took a moment to run back and wave to the fans one last time before we made our way to the backstage area.

"What the hell is with that guy? He's such a tool," Reece said, slumping down in a chair.

"She said she loved me," Trent added, sitting next to Reece in disbelief.

"She doesn't love you, Trent. She's a fucking whore just like the rest of them. She's using you as a chair, getting her kicks from Rodgers and who the fuck knows who else she's using?" Finishing the rest of my beer, I turned to toss it in the trash can, and that's when I saw her, eyes a blaze, her mane of hair, wild from blowing in the warm breeze all night.

She walked right up to me. I didn't move. I was disgusted. She was screwing with me, with all of us, and she didn't give a fuck. She got toe to toe with me then slapped me across the face. *Fuck, that stings.*

"You're an asshole, Kane Lawson." That was all she said, before she turned and stalked out of the room.

I stood there silent, like the rest of the guys. *That ungrateful bitch.* Hell, if I was going to let her just leave after slapping the shit out of me. I ran out of the room and down the hall after her. I passed a group of girls going into our room and heard the door slam shut. I didn't care how many women were freely giving themselves up, I had my sights set and nothing not even a parade of beautiful women were going to stop me. I caught up with her in a dimly lit hallway that ended up being a dead end. I reached for her, needing to explain myself. As my fingers wrapped around her arm I pulled her back to me. "I don't think so."

Her face was wet and splotchy, her eyes red. "Go away, Kane! *This* whore is trying to find her way out of here," she said, shoving my chest with her balled up fists.

"Shit, Kitty, I didn't mean that. I was just—"

"You were what, Kane, jealous? You're so selfish. Thanks to you this whole fucking town is speculating what the hell is going on between us," she ranted, wiping her eyes in frustration.

"I don't give a fuck what they think, because there sure as hell isn't *anything* going on between us. You've made sure of that," I said through a snicker.

"You think this is funny. You think this isn't hard. Fuck, Kane, I wanted to give into you that first night. I wanted to lose myself in you. I wanted to feel you pressed up against me. You think that all just disappeared, vanished? I've been going out of my mind trying to stay away from you," she said, while pushing her hair out of her face.

"Then don't, don't stay away," I challenged her.

She bit her lip, the back of her hand resting on her forehead, as she shook away her feelings. She wouldn't look at me.

I closed the space between us in that barren hallway. I grabbed her face with my hands and gazed into her dark-blue eyes. Her hands wrapped around my wrists on either side of her face. She bit her bottom lip again and shook her head with a worried frown.

"Fuck it." She ripped my hands from her face and grabbed my shirt, pulling me down to her with a force that told me she had finally given in.

CHAPTER 21

Caroline

I couldn't take it anymore. I crashed my lips to his, with a need so strong, it nearly took my breath away. His tongue entered my mouth the same time his hands cupped my ass. He was sweaty from singing on stage for the past hour or so, but I didn't care. The salty taste of him, mixed with the sweetness of his mouth, was downright wrong. I ran my hands through his hair, loving the way my fingers got lost in its thickness. He was moaning, I was moaning. Everything felt good. His hands explored my body, cupping my breasts. His thumb ran over my hardened nipple. My head fell back in delight. His mouth found my exposed neck. Taking full advantage, he kissed along it and under my ear, sending shivers down my spine.

When he found my mouth again, I reached down and grabbed the hem of his shirt, pulling it up and off in a hurry. He backed me against the wall, framing me with his bare chest and a hand at either side of my face. Reaching out, I ran my hands carefully down his cut chest and over the ripples of his stomach. I pulled on his belt, bringing him closer to me, the grunts and noises he made as we—I—gave in, was music to my ears, my body. I looked up into his blue eyes and saw him, just Kane Lawson.

I worked on his belt as he stood there, watching me. We were both panting heavily by then. I had it undone and was shoving his jeans down around his ankles. As I rose back up, I let my hand graze his thigh. Stopping over his protruding boxers, I slipped my hand inside and grabbed him, before shoving his boxers down as well.

"Fuck, Kitty, you have no idea," he said, grabbing my dress and hiking it up around my waist in a hurry.

I shimmied out of my underwear, grabbed him around his neck, and jumped up into his arms.

No foreplay needed. He was ready. I was ready. Hell, I had been ready for three months. I slid down on him, hissing in pleasure. Adjusting me against the wall, he thrust into me. Holding onto him for dear life, I sank my teeth into his shoulder to keep from screaming in pleasure.

It wasn't sensual, it wasn't graceful, but it was fucking hot, and it was exactly what I needed. Before I knew it, I was ready to combust. The tightening started before I could stop it.

"Kane," I panted. "Don't stop, please don't stop," I begged, whispering in his ear.

He didn't stop. If anything, it made him work harder. My hands splayed down his back, feeling his muscles move as he gave me what I asked for.

I squeezed him tighter, as I fell apart around him.

"Fuck, Kitty, I can't hold on," he panted as he thrust into me.

Growling in my ear, he leaned me against the wall and moved his hand down between us, rubbing me with every thrust.

I didn't know how he did it, and I really didn't care.

All I knew was, I found myself growling right along with him as we came together.

We stood there, my arms still tight around him, my lips to his neck, his hand still between us, the other wrapped tightly around my waist, and him still deep within me. I didn't want to let go. I didn't want to move, and it seemed he didn't either. If I moved from this spot, if he withdrew from me, it would be over. That was too intense, too good. All those things added up to danger in my book. It was better than I ever thought it could be and, again, like all the other times, I felt things, saw things, that I still wasn't ready for. My only hope was that he'd get over it, me.

I finally let him have sex with me. Hopefully, that would be enough in his book. He'd cross me off his list and move on. I needed the asshole Kane back fast, so I could snap back to reality.

With whatever strength he had left, he lifted me up with his hands around my rib cage and off of him. Releasing my tight hold, I let my hands slide down his chest as he placed me on the ground. My dress fell back into place around my legs. He let me go and pulled his boxers and pants back up, only buttoning them, the belt hung to either side and his fly was still down. More sweat escaped his body, putting off a scent that was intoxicatingly delicious. We stood across from one another, silent. *What do you say after something like that?*

"Kane, I think we should just…cherish this and move on. It was great but—"

"Shut the fuck up, Kitty. We're not going to forget this. We *will* cherish it, and we're going to do it again and again and again," he said as that wicked grin came across his face.

Why can't he be an ass about this? I guess I'm going to have to do it. "No we're not. I can't do this with you,

Kane," I said, reaching down to grab my underwear and put them back on.

"What is your problem? You need to tell me, so I can understand, because you're acting like a lunatic. Are you psychotic or something? You got two personalities, one that hates me and one that wants to fuck my brains out. I don't get it."

Grabbing my hair in frustration, I pulled it back out of my face and into a ponytail, resting my hands on my hips when I was done. Then I took a deep breath.

"Hello, anyone in there?" Kane demanded. "We just had fucking amazing sex against a wall, in a hallway and I'd like to know that I'm going to get it again."

"Kane, I can't," I said softly.

"Kitty, I swear to god, if you don't start talking to me—"

"My mother committed suicide, all right?" I yelled at him to shut him up. I hadn't said that out loud in over four years. It was still fucking awful.

He stilled and stared at me. "That sucks but what the hell does it have to do with me?" he demanded.

"I don't want to be like her. I don't want to follow her path, and I want to do the complete opposite," I croaked.

"Caroline, you're not her—"

"Yes, Kane, if I allow myself to go down this road with you, then I'm just like her. I'll give up everything that makes me, me, and I'll follow you. I'll be miserable, you'll be an ass. I'm terrified of turning into her so much, that I'm walking away from what could possibly be best thing for me. She ruined me. She acted like everything was fine, but she wasn't, and instead of doing something to change it, she copped the fuck out and took the easy way out, leaving my father and me to pick up the pieces."

"Are you listening to yourself right now? You. Are.

Not your mother, but you *are* copping out—you're just doing it in a different way." He was trying to convince me, but I had blinders up and wasn't paying any attention. "You're not even going to give this a chance, are you?" he asked, straightening up.

I shook my head. "Give what a chance, Kane? I'm leaving in a month and a half. I have an interview back in New York next week. *You* can't keep it in your pants. *I* have commitment issues. We're a fucking mess."

As I spoke, his face looked like I had tossed a brick at his gut. "You're leaving? You can't leave. B needs you here," he bellowed.

"I haven't told him yet. Please don't say anything. I don't belong here, in a small town. I miss my home. New York is my home. Since my mom betrayed me, it's been home, and I want to go back."

"You're a fucking liar. You're going to stand there and preach to me about taking the easy way out. New York isn't your home. It's where you used to live. Your home—" He paused, taking a step toward me, his hand cupping the back of my neck over my hair. "Your home is here, with B, with the guys, with me. You can deny it all you want, but you know I'm right."

"I care about you. Is that what you want to hear? Do you want to hear me say that you're right about everything? 'Cause you are. Let's give Kane a trophy because he's figured me out. It doesn't matter what you say. I'm not changing my mind about this. When I'm kissing you, I see it all—" I paused momentarily, not sure if I even wanted him to know this. It was just going to make things harder. "I just want to have a good time while I'm here. When I move back to New York, you're not even going to miss me."

He dropped his hand from around my neck and took a step back.

I hate this.
"All right," he finally said, crossing his arms.

CHAPTER 22

Kane

No matter what I say, I'm not going to convince you. I don't want to ruin whatever it is that we have, so I'm going to back off."

That tasted so fucking sour.

"Okay, I think this is the best for both of us. We got all the sexual tension out of the way and we can move on." She was lying again—fuck if she wasn't a horrible liar. Her nose always scrunched up right after she did. "Will you answer one question, before we put this all behind us?" She bit her bottom lip, her eyes stayed glued to the floor.

"Shoot, Kitty," I replied.

"Did you really stop sleeping around?" she asked, scrunching her face up.

That question could go one of two ways. The first, I could say yes. I could tell her the truth that I couldn't get it up for anyone but her. Now, if I answered yes, *she* could react in one of two ways. The first, hopeful that maybe we could make this work. The second, it could frighten her to the point where she didn't even want to talk to me, and I couldn't have that.

My second option, lie my ass off. If I did this, it might make her decision to keep her distance, easier for her. She could also be disappointed that I had said I would give it up and basically, I would be proving her point of why we'd never work.

I'd never fallen for a girl before, not like this, not like her. For the first time, I didn't want to be selfish. I wasn't thinking about what I'd get in the end. I wanted to make this easier on her. I'd eventually get over her, but I couldn't take having her upset and terrified that she was like her mother, whether I thought it was crazy or not. So, I did what I thought she wanted me to do, I was that ass-hole she was always accusing me of, and I lied.

"Come on, Kitty, you believe that?" I asked, winking at her.

Her face brightened as she looked up at me. "I knew he was full of it," she replied.

"Who told you I was being celibate? Trent, or was it JJ?" I asked.

"It was my father, to be honest."

I snickered to myself. "No shit."

"We need to keep this quiet. I don't want anyone to know that, we...umm...keep your mouth shut, Kane, or I'm going to grease up my vice clips. Get my drift?" she said, clearly threatening my precious balls.

"Loud and clear, Kitty." I bent over to fix my belt and zip up my jeans. I retrieved my shirt, putting my arms through the holes. I paused before putting my head through. "All right, you can't do that," I said, taking her off guard.

"Can't do what? I'm not doing anything," she shrieked, clearly embarrassed that I had just called her out.

"You can't look at me like that anymore, like you're trying to decide which part of my body you want to lick first. That can't happen, because *this* happens when you do that," I said, gesturing to the bulge in my pants, after I pulled my shirt all the way on. My cock was straining against my jeans again. This was going to be a long fucking month and a half.

ఌఌఌ

"It's got to be 100 degrees out here," JJ said wiping the sweat off his brow.

We had just finished up working for the day and were packing up when JJ's phone rang.

"It's Kitty," he said, looking over at me. "What's up, Cuz?' he asked. "Yeah, I know where that is…You want us to come?…Oh yeah, she is…Count us in. I'll be by to pick you up in twenty, that good?…All right, see ya."

I stared at him from across the truck. His face had lit up like a freaking light bulb. "What was that about?" I asked, dumping a bottle of water over my face.

"Kitty wants us to take her to the lake. You up for it?"

Hell, yeah, I was up for it. Sitting back in a chair, watching her fine ass frolic along the shoreline? Wouldn't miss it for the world. "Yeah man, I'm all about watching her walk around in a bathing suit, dripping wet," I replied, running my hand through my soaked hair.

"Bad news, Nate's meeting her there for a date, with his sister and her friends. Supposedly, they are big fans and just turned my favorite kind of eighteen."

She would do that, go on a date with him, and drag us along?

"Whatever. Doesn't mean I can't look." I jumped in my truck. JJ did the same. He called the rest of the guys, telling them to meet us there. We headed for the bar to pick up Kitty, so we could escort her on a date.

The weeks that had followed our sex-capade in the hallway were pretty normal. We went right back to the way things were. She never brought it up and neither did I—because I liked my balls. She was gone for two days, for her interview. B didn't take it too well. He was in a pissy mood from the moment she told him she was still leaving at the end of summer. She came back, hopeful and rejuvenated, so it must have gone well. She informed us that they'd be calling her in the next week or two. It was now the second week and her perky disposition had deflated—big time. I was currently sporting a new bruise on my shoulder and poor Reece almost got his ear ripped off.

I still didn't understand why she thought being with me was going to make her think she was her mother. From what I had learned from JJ in casual conversation, her mother had given up her career to raise Caroline. B was working late nights and was always tired, and they drifted apart. By the time anyone started noticing, Caroline's mother was already on loads of meds. One night she made a lethal decision and put herself to sleep. No one saw it coming, not B, not Caroline, not even her mom's close friends. Total blindside.

For this reason, and this alone, I could see why Caroline was so pissed. But to disappear for four years, not even visit her father, and from what I could tell, she acted like her mother never existed. She wasn't dealing with it the right way, but I was not a fucking psychiatrist, so who the fuck knew?

"You really got a thing for her, don't you?" JJ asked, pulling me out of my thoughts and back into the cab of my truck. His out of the blue question put me on edge.

"Nah, man, I just hate that she won't give it up."

JJ adjusted himself in his seat, so he could get a good look at me. "You're my best friend. I know you, and I know you're fucking into her. It's painfully obvious. You're constantly watching her. You get in a pissy mood if you don't see her, and I swear I hear you calling her name in your sleep, unless of course, you know someone else by the name of Kitty."

Shit, I'd been had. "It's not—ah fuck, it is. She's got me by the fucking balls, dude. Do the other guys think the same?" I asked, secretly praying they didn't. I didn't need Reece knowing and giving me shit for the rest of my life.

"Secret's safe with me. They don't have a clue. Have you even gotten close?" he asked.

I wanted to shout it from the roof, that yes I had, and yes it was fucking amazing, but I didn't, because, again, I liked my balls. "Kissed her twice, but she's holding out on me still, felt up her ti—"

"Enough!" he shouted, cutting me off. "I don't need to know anymore. Go easy on her. She's been through a lot of shit."

Sadly, I knew that already.

We stopped by the house, got our swimming shorts, chairs, and a cooler filled with beer. When we pulled up to the back of the bar, Caroline was sitting under the patio waiting for us. She was wearing the same dress she had on the night she finally let me in, in more ways than one. Stopping the truck, we both jumped out, slamming the doors closed behind us.

"So you have us chaperoning now? What the hell is that about?" I asked, with a snicker to my voice.

"I just didn't want to go alone. You guys are like brothers and I'd like to have you there for backup."

Backup? What the hell does she mean by that? What the fuck does she mean by brothers? If that's the case, and she thinks of me like a brother, then we have committed a disgusting crime, and I still want to fuck my sister.

"What do you mean by backup?" JJ asked, taking the words out of my mouth.

"Nothing. I just want you guys to come and have a good time, plus he's bringing his sister and her friends." *There she goes again scrunching her nose up—liar.*

"Whatever, I gotta piss, then we can go," JJ said, walking in the bar and leaving us standing there alone.

"So, what's really going on? I know you're lying about why you want us there. Is Nate bothering you?" I asked.

I had ignored it as much as I could, but she was hanging out with Nate a lot. Seeing them kiss the Fourth of July had nearly given me an aneurism. I hated the guy and I hated the fact that he was free to date her and kiss her, but I wasn't. I was one jealous SOB.

She was gathering her book and towel in her hands as I spoke. An anxious looked washed over her face, and I thought that she was going to be honest with me, but she quickly recovered and hid behind her wall. I'll say it again.

I never liked Nate Rodgers. He was a year older than us and was creepy as hell with his whole I'm-a-cop-you-can-trust-me act.

"Kane, it's fine. Nate's a guy, and just like you, he's looking for *more*. I'm not going down that road with him, so things have been a little awkward. I just want to go, have a good time, and get my mind off everything."

"Okay, don't be surprised if I'm sporting a raging hard on while you prance around in a bikini, I'm warning you now. Try to contain yourself," I said, wiggling my eyebrows.

Her laugh was music to my ears, and her vicious punch to my already sore arm was painfully pleasurable.

"All right, you ready?" We turned to JJ and nodded, smiles plastered on both our faces.

"I'm going to grab some wood for a fire," I said, turning to do just that.

"Shot gun!" she yelled, running to the truck, passing JJ and hopping in the front seat.

"Fuck no, Kitty, get out! In the back with you," JJ said leaning through the open window.

"Aww, please," I heard her beg.

I glanced over at the truck, JJ was talking quietly to her. Her smile faded. She opened the door, jumped out, and got in the back.

Tossing some wood in the truck bed, I jumped in. Peeking in the rear view mirror, I saw that Kitty was sitting in the middle, her arms crossed, and a confused look on her face. JJ must have said something to the effect that he knew about us, that's the only thing I could think of. She didn't say a word the whole way there, seeming deep in thought. I'd glance in the mirror every so often and caught her quickly adverting her eyes.

This whole situation was fucked up. She clearly had issues, but to completely shut me out, just because she didn't want to turn into her mother, was fucking ridiculous. The past three weeks she flirted with the guys, snuggled up with Trent—she'd do anything to put me out of her mind, that even included stringing along Robo-Cop. I hadn't *fully* gone back to my ways, but every night I saw her, I'd come home horny as hell, and if there happened to be an extra laying around, I'd indulge. Was it good? Fuck no—it was just enough to get me off, cure a little itch to a big fucking rash.

As I pulled up, I saw Nate's car and Trent's truck. They had a bunch of chairs set up around a fire pit that had yet to be lit. About six girls in barely there bikinis were splashing in the water.

"Jesus Christ, these girls are here to get laid and I might have to indulge. You sure they are all eighteen?" I asked, leaning closer to the window to get a better look.

"Christ, I hope so," JJ added, grinning in pleasure.

"You guys are fucking gross," she yelled, getting out of the truck.

She slammed the door closed. I watched as she stalked over to Nate, wrapping her arms around his neck. She practically swallowed his face. I knew exactly what she was doing, and it wasn't going to work. *She thinks she's going to make me jealous. She's playing with fire.* By the end of tonight, she was going to wish she hadn't started this war with me.

CHAPTER 23

Caroline

Third beer, in thirty minutes. If I kept that up, I wasn't going to be able to walk to the car. Under the cover of my black sunglasses, I sat on the beach, watching as Kane and the other guys made asses of themselves. They were chasing these barely there eighteen-year-olds up and down the beach and through the water. Nate was sitting next to me, our chairs butting up to one another's. His fingers were playing with mine, and I was about one second away from ripping them away, when I caught Kane grabbing one of the girl's ass.

Clenching my fists, I narrowed my eyes on him, still shielded by my sunglasses. He looked right at me while he did it, a stupid grin spread across his face. I instantly unclenched my fists and stood from my chair. I turned to face Nate, knowing my ass was facing the water, and knowing full well that Kane still had his eyes glued to me. I bent over painfully slow, leaning over Nate and resting my hands on the arms of his chair. I kissed his nose, wiggled my ass, then stood back up. Turning to the side so I could get a peek at Kane, I stretched my arms over my head, pushed my chest out, and arched my back.

I heard a huge splash in the water and turned to it. Kane stood back up from under the water, his hands covering what I knew was his violent erection. *Don't mess with the Queen, because you'll lose.*

The night was winding down. We grilled some hot dogs, roasted some marshmallows, and just hung out. I knew I shouldn't have cared, that I said it wouldn't bother me, but fuck! Did he have to have her sit on his lap? It was painfully obvious she was grinding her ass on his dick. I squeezed Nate's hand a little tighter, I was sitting in-between his legs on a blanket, as I watched Kane kiss on some brunette who was giggling all over herself. I finished my sixth, or was it seventh beer. I went to stand, using Nate's knees to help myself up. I stood then stumbled forward, almost falling into the fire. Thanks to Nate's quick reaction, he managed to grab me around the waist, before I set myself on fire.

When I gained my balance and looked up, all the guys had tossed their new lap ornaments to help me. All but JJ, he was still snuggled up with Piper, Nate's younger sister.

Kane brushed off the brunette. "Kitty, you all right?" he asked, truly concerned as he walked around the fire and closer to me.

My head spun, my legs felt like rubber, and I couldn't see straight. No, I wasn't all right, but I sure as hell wasn't going to tell him.

"She's fine," Nate answered for me, pulling me tighter to him.

Blinking my eyes a few times, I shook my head, which wasn't the smartest idea, and finally looked up at Kane.

"I wasn't asking you, Rodgers," Kane said with loathing from beside me. "Kitty. Look at me. You all right?"

Was I all right? I had a lot of beers but I had built up my stamina since working at a bar where the drinks were free.

Nate's hand held the back of my neck, rubbing it soothingly. I again focused on Kane. I also focused on the brunette walking up next to him. Slipping her hand in his, she tugged him closer and I nearly vomited. Reaching up on her toes, she nibbled at his ear. It was that precise moment that it went from repulsion to me wanting to fucking slap her, then slap him. But honestly I wanted to slap, Nate for fucking touching me right then.

"I'm fine Kane. You can go put your pretty ornament back on your lap." I shook off Nate's hand, turned from the camp fire, and started walking down the beach.

"What's your problem, Kane? Back off. She doesn't want you. Hasn't she made that perfectly clear?"

I heard Nate provoking Kane behind me and realized that I had to get out of there. Kane was right. I was leading Nate on, and I needed to let him know where I stood.

Swaying as I walked down the beach, I turned and headed to the thick line of trees that lead back to the state park. I broke through the edge of the woods and stumbled my way back, deeper into the dark trails. My vision was going in and out and things started getting fuzzy. The crack of a branch behind me stilled my movements. Squinting my eyes, I tried to find the culprit of the noise. Hearing and seeing nothing more, I continued on and quickly realized that I had gone off the path. *Fuck! I don't need this right now.*

On top of being lost in the woods, everyday it was getting harder to watch Kane. It was getting harder to remember his taste, to remember how it felt to be in his arms, and of course it was making me rethink *things*. I was banking on the job interview that I had over two weeks ago. I was praying that I'd get it and that I'd soon be on my way out of this fucking town, but they hadn't called yet. Maybe they weren't ever going to call. I needed to come up with another plan. The only way I was going to get over Kane was distance, out of sight out of mind...just like my mother.

Fuck! I squealed to myself as another branch broke. "Hello? Who the hell's out there?" I said into the darkness. I could see a light off in the distance, a large lantern in someone's hand maybe? "Kane? Nate?" I asked taking a cautious step toward the light.

"It's me, it's Nate."

Relief washed over me. *Thank god, it isn't an axe murderer.*

My eyes still fuzzy, and my head still sloshing around, I smiled as Nate came closer. I reached out for his outstretched hand, thankful that he was going to take me back to the camp fire and the guys. Yanking me closer to him, he crashed his face down on mine, forcing a kiss on me. I pulled my head back and tried to back away from him, but he had dropped the lantern and was using both hands to hold me to him.

"Nate, what the fuck? Get off me!" I yelled, while still struggling in his arms.

My adrenalin kicked in as I realized that this wasn't good. *This isn't right.* He was being rough and forceful. I tried pushing back again, hitting his chest, but he kept coming at me.

More dizziness set in and I found my legs becoming weaker. *What the hell is going on?* Panic stricken, I hit him harder and yelled.

"You've been stringing me along for over four months, Caroline. You're not getting away tonight."

He let me go a little, as I swayed even more. *Has he drugged me? That's got to be it.* There was no other explanation for why I felt the way I did.

This fucker drugged my beers.

"Nate—don't touch—me," I slurred, while holding my hand up to keep him back.

I told my body to run, to run like hell, but it wasn't listening. I fell to my knees, my hands pressed into the forest floor. With whatever strength I had, I turned my head to watch him unfold a blanket down next to the lantern.

No, this can't be happening. He can't do this. He's a cop—he's a cop. No one is going to believe me. Dread filled me as I realized that I was about to be raped, and I couldn't do a damn thing about it.

He grabbed my arms and pulled me back to my feet. My body was limp. I had little, if any, control.

"Don't do this," I begged.

"Oh, Caroline," he said, stroking my face with his hand. He let his fingers comb though my long hair.

I turned my face from his and closed my eyes. *Out of sight, out of mind, that's the only way I'm going to get through this.*

His strong hand grabbed my chin, forcefully turning my face to his. "Open your eyes!" His enraged words scared the living shit out of me, so I opened my eyes quickly. "There you are. What is it that he calls you?…oh, right, Kitty," he said, touching my face again. "Well, you're not his kitty anymore." There was an evil sneer to his voice that made my toes curl.

"Why are you doing this? If you're trying to get back at Kane, it's not going to work," I pleaded again.

"Don't you fucking say his name! After tonight, I don't even want you to look at him. You're mine, and this isn't my first rodeo, Caroline. Nothing you say is going to change what's about to happen right over there on that nice blanket."

I had made a fatal mistake, thinking that spending

my time with a cop, the supposedly good guy, would be safer than going down that road I was so terrified about with Kane. I was wrong, so wrong.

Nate dragged me over to the blanket. My weakened body lay on the fabric next to the lantern. I turned my head so I wouldn't have to look at him. I stared straight into the light, even though it hurt my eyes to do so. I tried to take myself to another place, a safe place. I had changed out of the dress I had on and was in a tube top cover all, which came to my mid thighs when I stood. My bikini was still on under it. I sensed him kneeling by my feet, his hands ran up the length of my legs, spreading them as he moved up my body. He settled himself between my weak legs. His hands moved the cover up, exposing my midriff.

Sucking in a breath, I felt a tear roll down the side of my face and fall into my ear. His lips touched my belly button and I trembled when his hand cupped my breasts. I closed my eyes, praying that it would just end, that I'd pass out and not have to live every waking moment of it. Lost in my head, I squeezed my eye tighter. I heard a rustling noise coming closer. I turned my groggy gaze the opposite way, and it was as if I was seeing my guardian angel coming to rescue me from the devil himself. Kane was running—running right for us.

CHAPTER 24

Kane

It had been over thirty minutes since Kitty had stalked off, and twenty since Nate had left. I stood up from my chair. The brunette on my lap, didn't look happy, but I didn't give a fuck. Something was up with Caroline. She was acting drunk, but I knew she hadn't had enough to make her almost fall into the fire.

"I'll be back," I said to no one in particular.

I headed down the beach in the direction that Kitty had walked. When her foot prints made a sharp left back up to the line of trees, I assumed that she walked in and got lost. I pulled my cell phone out and turned on the light so I could see. A few steps in, I heard her voice, faint, but I heard her. I walked in the direction of where I thought the voice was coming from, until I saw a light. I stopped and turned mine off so I could follow it more easily but, the closer I got, the more pissed off I became.

I came up on them and nearly went axe murder on Nate fucking Rodgers. Kitty was laying on a blanket, her head turned to me, a tear rolling down her cheek, and she was shaking.

"Kane," I heard her say weakly.

Nate's head lifted from her stomach. Leaning over her, he slapped her across the face.

"I said don't fucking say his name."

"Fuck you," I heard her say.

Good girl, Kitty.

"Kane," she yelled again as I ran to her.

I plowed into Nate, taking him off guard. We rolled together, me landing on top of him, I punched him in the face. He got his wits about him and pushed me off. We both stood, ready for a fight.

I took a chance and looked at Caroline, still unmoving on the blanket. Nate being well trained took that opportunity to punch me. *Fuck that hurt!*

"What the fuck are you doing, Nate?" I asked, while I figured out my next move.

"Just trying to get what I deserve, one way or another," he said, wiping the blood from his lip.

That's it! Over the line, I'm fucking furious now. I charged him again, hitting him over and over again. He fell to the ground, but I kept hitting him. "Don't you fucking touch my woman again, you hear me, you mother fucker!" I yelled, grabbing his shirt and slamming his head into the ground over and over again.

"She doesn't care about you, you idiot," he said through a frighteningly psychotic chuckle.

"The fuck, she doesn't. Whose name was she just yelling? You're a sick fuck, Rodgers," I spat, punching his face again.

"Kane, please," I heard her say from a few feet away.

I slammed his head down onto the ground again, which was enough to get him to pass the fuck out. I wiped my nose. Blood covered the top of my hand so I wiped in on the back of my shirt.

I knelt down next to her, "Kitty, are you okay?" I asked in a hurry. I didn't want to touch her, if she was hurt. I didn't want to make it worse. So my hands levitated over her face and body.

"Kane, please, get me out of here. Please," she begged through a sob.

"Yeah, I'll get you out of here. Come here."

I got her to sit up, wrapped her in my arms like I had that first night she arrived, and I carried her away from Nate fucking Rodgers. I walked her back to the beach, her head resting on my shoulder, her arms were so tight around my neck, I found myself having to take deep breaths. Her body was still shaking in my arms.

"I was wrong, I was so wrong. Kane, I'm so sorry," she said, as she griped my shirt tighter in her hands.

"Shh, it's okay. You have nothing to be sorry about. I'm going to get you back home, get you into your bed. It's all going to be—"

Her head shot up from my chest, she looked at me panic stricken. "I don't want to go home. Please don't take me home. Take me anywhere but home. Kane, I can't—I—please." She was trembling as she spoke.

I stopped walking and set her feet on the sand. Her arms still wrapped around my neck, she wouldn't let go.

"Okay, okay, I'll take you somewhere else, I'll take care you. Do you trust me?" I asked, pulling her arms from around my neck, so I could look into her beautiful eyes. *Fuck, she is even beautiful when she cries.*

"Yes, I do, I trust you, Kane. Get me out of here, please."

Nodding down at her, I scooped her back up in my arms. I avoided the area where everyone was still sitting around the fire having a good time. I opened the passenger's side door and set her down, but she wouldn't let go.

"Kitty, you gotta let go. I'll be right back," I said, pealing her arms from my neck. I ran around the truck and got in. She instantly took my hand as I laid it on the console between us. Gripping it for dear life, she didn't let go the whole way home, my home.

I parked my truck and got out, after tearing my hand from hers. I came around to her side and opened the door. I expected her to walk, but she hopped into my arms again. I wasn't going to complain. I set her down on the porch while I took my keys out and unlocked the door. Shoving it open, I lifted her up again, walked in, and slammed the door behind us. I headed straight for the stairs, got into my room, and closed the door behind me. I placed her in my unmade bed and cursed myself for not taking the time to make it that morning.

I stood from the bed and watched as she curled up into a ball on my pillow. I pulled the covers up and tucked her in. I went to the bathroom, tugging my shirt off as I did. I washed my face and hands, checked out the nice cut on my cheek, and then exited. I still had my swim-trunks on, so I lost those for a pair of clean boxers. I walked back to bed. When I reached to grab a pillow, a hand tightly gripped my wrist.

Caroline turned to me, fear still etched on her face. "Where are you going?" she asked though a shaky voice.

"I'm not going anywhere. Just getting a pillow. This floor is harder than you think. I don't want a stiff neck tomorrow when we play." I smiled down at her, pleased that she gave me one back.

"I don't want you to sleep on the floor."

"Well, I'm not sleeping standing up, so…"

"Lay with me? I—I don't want to feel alone, if that makes any sense." She bit her lip and gripped my hand tighter.

I sure as hell wasn't going to say no. I knew I wasn't going to be able to contain my dick. That fucker had a mind of its own, but I also didn't want to seem like a horn dog after what had just happened. *What the fuck had just happened?* It was only then that I was able to think, rationalize. The girl that I had all these feelings for was almost raped tonight, by a cop! I was getting angrier, the more I thought about it. I couldn't believe that fucker was touching her. He fucking slapped her. If he wasn't fucked up enough tonight, when the guys found out, he was going to wish he had never laid a hand on our Kitty.

How are we going to deal with this? Who do I tell? Would they even believe a guy who spent his days fixing houses and nights banging anything that walked, and a girl who worked at a bar who had a tendency to flirt, over a fucking cop. I had heard him say that that wasn't his first rodeo. That fucker had done this to other women. *He had a little sister. How could he even consider?* I felt my jaw get tight. I wanted to jump back in my truck and finish him for touching Caroline, and any other woman he might have hurt. I knew the guys would help me bury the body—

"Will you hold me?" she asked, bringing me back to my room and the gorgeous girl who was lying in my bed.

"Yeah, Kitty, I'll hold you, but I might not be able to let go," I added, letting the thought of murder slip away.

She smiled up at me and I could swear to fucking God, my heart melted.

"I don't want you to," she said, tugging me to her.

She moved over and I climbed in next to her. We moved to the middle of the bed, sharing one pillow. We didn't need any more than that. She conformed to my body and I to hers. I snaked my arm around her, resting it on her stomach, she placed hers over mine lovingly. I didn't care that her hair was tickling my face, or the fact that she butted up against my junk. I didn't care, because she was in my arms, and her warm body, finally relaxed into mine.

I woke up, feeling cold in the dark. Reaching out, I

felt the space in front of me, searching for her. It was empty. I sat up, and looked around my room for the girl who had stolen my heart without me seeing it coming. A light was glowing from the bathroom, and then I heard the water running. I relaxed back in bed, the anxiety of not knowing where she was faded as I stared at the light coming from under the bathroom door. Her shadow blocked it a few times. I then heard the familiar closing of my shower door. *Kitty, was naked and in my shower, right now.* I wanted to strip down and join her, but I didn't, after what had just happened, or almost happened. I was just glad to be, kind of in the same room. I sat in bed, picturing what was going on behind the closed door. It took a millisecond before the sheet rose from my lap. Clearly my dick wasn't as sympathetic as the rest of me.

CHAPTER 25

Caroline

I stood under the scolding water. Steam poured up and out of the shower. I pressed my body against the cool tile. I was still in shock, my mind racing. I remembered what happened, but then I didn't. It was like my mind was protecting me from itself.

I could remember lying on the ground, the itchy fabric of the blanket, the sticks under it pricking my skin. I remembered seeing Nate at my feet, his hands going up my legs. I could remember turning my head, my eyes full of tears that finally spilled over as my head rested on its side. I remembered blinking them away, trying to get my mind to think of anything other than what was currently happening. My brain took me to my bedroom, the first night I got here. It took me to the part when Kane had laid me down in my bed, his trembling hand caressing my face. When I opened my eyes back up, I thought I was still dreaming, because I could see him off in the distance.

I remembered calling his name. He came closer, faster. I called him again, louder this time. My body was still limp. I could barely move my head as I cussed out

Nate. He slapped me, but I couldn't feel it. The next thing I knew, he was off me, and Kane had him on the ground, slamming his head over and over again. He had saved me. Kane Lawson saved my life.

Turning from the cool tile, I let my face take on the scorching water. Reaching down, I grabbed a bottle of soap and tried to wash away the night. The distinct smell reminded me how tenderly Kane had carried me away from that fucking nightmare. I had made a mistake, and I had paid the price. I had pushed away feelings I had for Kane, because I was scared. I was so scared of turning into her, that it had nearly led me to a worse fate. This was going to change me, not for the better. *How was I going to face Nate in the bar tomorrow?* I knew he would be there. I knew he was going to come find me. What if he tried again? What if he went after Kane? I had truly made a mess of things.

Stepping out of the shower, I reached for a towel, drying my body. Glancing at my clothes on the floor, I winced in disgust. I was going to burn them the first chance I got. Looking around the barren bathroom, there wasn't a shirt in sight. What single man didn't at least have a shirt lying on the floor? I guessed there was something I didn't know about Kane. He was evidently a clean freak.

Drying my dripping hair in a towel, I flipped it back and saw a brush on the counter. *Perfect!* I took a moment to brush out the knots. Good thing he had such fuckable hair, otherwise, mine would be a ratty mess. Wrapping the towel tightly around my chest, I opened the door, praying that, one, Kane was still asleep and, two, that he had a shirt laying on the floor somewhere. Otherwise, I was going to have to rummage through his drawers. I didn't want to do that, because some part of me thought that he had a drawer filled with woman's underwear, some sort of sick trophy system. I didn't think I could handle that right then.

Glancing around the door, I saw that neither one of my requests would be answered because he was fully awake and there wasn't a stitch of clothing lying on the floor. *Fucking clean freak!*

"Hey," I said, clutching at the towel.

"Have a nice shower?" he asked.

It was so obvious that he had a raging hard on. The sheet was virtually levitating.

"Yeah, can I borrow a shirt and some shorts? I don't want to put my other clothes back on. It just reminds me—" I couldn't finish my thought, and thankfully, Kane didn't let me.

"I get it, you don't have to say anything else."

Getting out of the bed, he walked the few steps to his dresser, adjusting himself as he turned away from me.

I covered my face to hide my smile. I knew that, right then, I shouldn't be thinking…things. But Kane, "adjusting" himself had a way of putting a smile on my face and a heat between my legs.

"This should work," he said, turning from the dresser.

Striding over, he stood before me, the clothes between us. I looked down at them—a white under shirt and black boxers. My eyes wander up his bare chest. His blue eyes fixed on mine.

"Are you all right?" he asked.

Am I all right? I knew that, if it wasn't for him, I wouldn't be "all right." If it wasn't for him, I'd probably still be in that dark forest huddled in a ball. His hand came up between our bodies. I watched it. The back of his fingers swiped at my cheek, the cheek that Nate had slapped. I shut my eyes the moment the memory came crashing back.

"Kitty, look at me. Don't go back there, just look at me."

I will my eyes to open at his words, they follow as commanded and the image of Nate disappears.

"There you are. Keep looking at me." His voice was soothing and calming.

"You saved me." Realization hits again, as I say this to him.

He licks his lips and that fire that had started in my core burned to life again. He was in boxers, his chest, bare. My body came alive around him. It always did. I *always* knew when he was near.

I know how the night had started out and it was fucking messed up, but now, I was standing in front of Kane, a towel and boxers were the only things that separated us. I was done fighting. I was wrong to stay away, I was wrong to think that I was going to turn out like her. I had been falling for the man standing before me from the moment I saw him. I didn't want to miss out on anymore and, since I wasn't going anywhere just yet, I was going to indulge in all that I had been missing.

He had a way of making things better and, most of all, he was making me forget what had almost happened tonight. I felt safe in his arms. I was forever in his debt. So with a nervous hand, I took a breath, knowing that once I did this, things were going to be different between us. I looked into his clear blue eyes, not seeing the rock star, or asshole, just Kane. I loved when he looked at me like that, because as I was seeing all of him, I was certain he was seeing all of me.

Releasing the towel, I felt it fall to the ground, bunching at my feet, my eyes still locked on his. A cool breeze coming from the ceiling fan had me wondering if my nipples were hard from the cold or from him staring at me, completely naked.

He smiled down at me. "You dropped something."

"Did I?"

Glancing down at the ground, I saw not only the towel at my feet, but the bulge that had returned to his shorts. My eyes found his again, as I bit the inside of my cheek nervously. Yes, I was nervous as hell. This wasn't a fuck in the hallway, or a make out session in my room. This was going to be different, because I wasn't going to stop it. I wasn't going to end it. I was going to have to fight all my instincts to stop and just keep going.

Truth be told, I might have been suppressing what happened earlier, but I had also been suppressing the way I felt for Kane for over four months. If him holding me all night made *me* feel better about what had almost happened, then I was going to do it. If I would have been in his arms from the beginning, tonight wouldn't have happened. I was going to have to face what happened tomorrow.

Right now, I only wanted Kane to kiss me, make love to me, and hold me until the sun came up and shone through the windows.

"Caroline, I don't know what you're asking here but—"

Since I had moved here, he only ever used my proper name, when he was being serious and this wasn't any different.

"We don't have to—I can just hold you," he said, nerves ever present.

"Kane, I want you to do everything. I want you to hold me till I fall asleep and I want to wake up in your arms in the morning."

"And by everything you mean, get you dressed?" he asked, holding up the clothes that were still in his hand.

"No, no getting dressed," I answered back, shaking my head, my wet hair dripped down my back.

"So, by everything, you mean to say that you want me to—"

I sighed. "Kane! Shut up and kiss me."

He dropped the clothes in his hand and crashed his lips down to mine. *Finally!* My hands went up and around his neck, the same time his snaked around my waist. My body flush with his, he backed me up till we were at the edge of the bed. The back of my knees hit it hard, making them buckle. Our kiss broke, as I fell back on the bed. Scooting, I make room for him. He crawled between my legs. I could feel the slickness at my core and the throbbing of my insides, begging for release, but he stilled over me. Leaning back on his haunches, he stared down at me.

CHAPTER 26

Kane

Beautiful didn't even begin to describe the way she looked. She trusted me to take care of her. If you would have asked me four months ago, and if this would have been anyone else, I would have been running for the hills. I didn't do "more" with anyone. But fuck if I wasn't considering putting a fucking ring on her finger, so she wouldn't do "more" with anyone but me.

I didn't want to rush it. I didn't want to do it like I had done in the past. I wanted to take my time, kiss every inch of her, and know every curve of her body. I wanted to know if I grazed the dimples above her ass, if she'd moan or laugh. I wanted to know if I kissed the inside of her thigh, would she buck harder or grab my hair and put me where she wanted me. I wanted to learn all those things about her, things I never took the time to learn about anyone else.

I wanted to cherish this because if I knew my Kitty, she'd freak out and push me away. After we did it, there would be no going back to playful banter and "just friends." After this, *I* was going to want more. God fucking help me, I wanted more. She had already ruined me for anyone else and, after tonight, she was going to destroy any ideas I might have had about being the playboy rock star who banged celebrities.

"Kane?" She whimpered my name from the bed.

"Yeah, Kitty?" I answered back, my eyes still wandering over her body.

"What are you doing?" she asked, as a seductive smile spread across her face.

Leaning over her body, I pressed my hands into the mattress on either side of her face. "I'm admiring my woman, so let me admire." I smiled down at her. I brushed the back of my fingers across her cheek again. It was still a little red from that fucker.

"Fine, but only as long as you don't stop looking at me like this. I like seeing you, Kane."

"Same goes for you. Keep your wall down, so I can keep staring at you."

Her hand snaked up my chest, around the front of my neck, and finally to the back of it. Tugging me closer to her, she licked her tongue at my lips. Clutching at the back of her neck, I let my lips find hers, our tongues dancing back and forth. She was the sweetest thing I had ever tasted and I never wanted to stop. Her breasts were full and heavy in my hands, her nipples, already taunt and asking for it. I moved from her mouth, making my way down her neck. Kissing the tops of her breasts, I latched my mouth down around her, flicking my tongue over and suckling tenderly on her nipple.

Her body arched off the bed, her hands lost in my hair as she pulled me closer. I released her and headed over to my next stop. She was wiggling and moaning the whole time, and fuck if I wasn't ready to explode in my pants just from sucking her tits. I couldn't wait any longer. I stood from the bed. She followed me, sitting up herself and scooting to the edge. I yanked my boxers off as fast as I could. I stood there, as she admired the view, flexing my muscles a little. Y*eah, I did that shit*. She was licking her lips, hungry for what I had. I didn't think I had ever been that hard before. It was almost painful.

She stood from the bed, just as I was going to come back to her. Her hands found my chest, running delicately up and down my body, outlining the indents of my abs with a single finger. It gave me the chills. She then came to my V. A finger on either side, she let them move together and meet at the bottom. My friend twitched at her, begging to be touched next. Kitty didn't disappoint either. She wrapped her hand around my length, moving up and down with ease. I let her have her fun for a while, but I couldn't let her keep doing that or I'd embarrass myself.

My hand found the back of her neck, her hair still dripping wet. I ran my hand up the front of her thigh and over her core. I was hoping like hell that she couldn't tell my hand was shaking. I let a finger slide, and I mean *slide,* between her legs. It was warm and welcoming, and I couldn't wait to lay her down. So, that's exactly what I did. I pushed her back. Letting me go, she braced her arms on the bed as we lay back down. My hand still between her, she was quivering every time I ran my finger over her soft spot.

"Kane! I can't hold on any more, please," she begged through a panting breath, while trying to reach for me.

I wiggled my fingers faster, smiling against her face as I kissed her. I'd get to that, but right then, I was going to do it this way first.

"Kane! You fucking ass—ho—le," she screamed out in pleasure, gripping my back with her nails.

I swear she drew blood. Her core squeezed my fingers and I fucking loved every minute of it, until she punched my arm.

"I told you, I couldn't hold on. Why didn't you listen?" she asked, still panting and arching off the bed.

"I heard you, but I have a check list. That's just the first on the list. We got at least…I don't know…ten more to get through," I said, smiling down at her.

She shook her head and hit my arm again, smiling like the Cheshire Cat. *Yeah, she liked it.* She couldn't say a damn thing in return. We spent the next six hours checking everything off my list. I learned that, yes, she did moan when I kissed the dimples on her back. Also, like I had guessed, she pulled me by my hair and put me exactly where she wanted me when I kissed the inside of her thigh.

I had lost count of how many times I'd made her scream my name, but I knew exactly how many times I had screamed hers. Five, to be exact. Twice in bed, once on the kitchen table, once on the wall, and once in the shower.

We were getting some beers and nourishment, when she sat up on the table. I was sitting in a chair when she spread her legs around me. Her feet were resting on the arms of the chair. She moved the long shirt she had on up her thighs while I sat back in the chair and watched. I'd never be able to eat on that table again without imagining her legs spread wide while…I indulged.

The wall was like coming home. I was standing at the foot of the bed after our snack, putting my boxers back on when she ran at me full speed and jumped up in my arms, her legs wrapping around my waist. I kicked off my boxers, which were only around my ankles, and shoved her up against the wall.

The shower was our attempt to "clean up." *Yeah, that wasn't going to happen.* She was standing in front of me, her ass wet, glistening, and facing my spoiled friend. Her long hair stretched longer from the water, and it sent a trail of water that ran right down her ass. It didn't take long before her hands were splayed on the tile as I sank into her. The water falling around us made for an added bonus as I slammed into her.

That led us back to the bed, where we lay, panting and holding on to one another. The bed was wet from our hair. The only thing left on it was the sheet that I had pulled up from the floor to cover us. My room looked like a tornado had come through and I fucking loved it. I'd be happy to have it look like that from now on, as long as Kitty was here to help me keep it that way. I was usually a clean freak. I didn't like my shit all over the place. The guys always gave me crap for it, but I didn't see any ladies complaining, when they were able to fuck me on a clean pair of sheets and piss in a tidy bathroom.

Kitty's head was resting on my chest as I ran my fingers through her still-damp hair. I never wanted that moment to end. I wanted that night to last forever. I had this sick feeling that it wouldn't, that she wouldn't let me give her "more" than what we just had. It fucking scared the shit out of me, so I held her tighter as the thought passed through my mind.

There was so much to sort out once the sun came through those windows, I'd give anything to keep the moon out longer. She was going to have to deal with Nate. I, for the life of me, didn't know how to even begin that decision. I had a feeling she was going to try to block it out the same way she was blocking out her mother's existence. I couldn't let her do that. That fucker needed to pay for what he had done to her. I was going to make sure of that. Cop or not, he couldn't treat women that way, especially mine.

CHAPTER 27

Caroline

I was content to lay there forever with Kane. I was going to put Nate Rodgers out of my mind and focus everything I had on Kane. That was my plan at least. Being with Kane made me forget about what happened last night with Nate. So, logically speaking, I should keep doing it—go to my happy place, out of sight, out of mind.

Our night together was everything I had ever thought it was going to be, and more. Since I wasn't going anywhere, no job, no home, I was content to stay a while, make good use of our time together. I'd cross the bridge of fear later, but for now, I wasn't afraid of letting him in. I was more concerned with forgetting everything with Nate.

I went to sit up from his chest. My bladder couldn't hold its walls shut any longer. I needed to get to the bathroom.

"Where you going?" he asked, sitting up and grabbing my wrist.

I was up and off the bed, my legs crossed for dear life. "Let me go, Kane," I said with urgency, tugging my arm from his grip.

"No! You're not doing this again. You're not going to run from me because you're scared of turning into your mother. No fucking way, Kitty. You don't get to love me and leave me anymore. You're fucking stuck with me. I'll watch out for you, I won't let you turn into whatever it is that you're afraid of."

I was now bouncing on my tip toes to keep from peeing myself. Scrunching my face up, I bit my lip, concentrating really hard on holding it together, so I didn't pee on his floor.

"That's a very nice thing to say, but I need you to let go of my hand. Now!" I shrieked.

"No! You're not running away again," he yelled, tugging me back onto the bed.

"Kane! Let me go. I'm going to piss on your floor, if you don't let me go."

Never, had he let go of me so fast. I turned from the bed and ran on my tip toes to the bathroom, slamming the door behind me.

"For the record, I knew you weren't bolting," he yelled a few seconds later, from the bed.

I rolled my eyes as I washed my hands. "Un-huh," I called back.

It was cute, and I loved that he wasn't going to let me run, even though I had already decided not to. I was right. Things had changed between us.

I came out of the bathroom, sauntering back into bed. "Did you mean all that?" I asked, leaning over him.

I took a moment to brush the hair from his face, before I slipped my leg around his waist to straddle him. Lowering myself onto his lap, with his hands on my hips, I could feel him growing beneath me. *Again? This man is a fucking machine, like a real "fucking" machine.*

Just when I thought he couldn't possibly be ready again, bam! He was. Not that I was complaining.

"Yeah, Kitty, every word of it."

I'm not going to try to lie, but that scared the shit out of me.

He tenderly rubbed my hips with his thumbs as he spoke. "I mean it, I'm not letting go this time. You run, I'm running after you," he said, sitting up from the bed and swallowing me in his arms.

"So does this mean that Kane Lawson is giving up his playboy ways for little ole me?" I asked into his neck.

He sat back, his hands coming up to hold my face. "You better fucking believe it. This ride is shut down for everyone but you, baby," he said, raising his brows and kissing my nose.

Again, that scared the shit out of me. Him giving up the way he had always lived his life. Don't get me wrong, it was fucking hot, but I knew more than anyone that giving up a part of yourself could backfire. It was just a matter of time before it all went to shit.

But fuck if it doesn't feel good to know he'll be all mine until then.

ભ૭ભ૭

There it was, that stupid sun. It had come up, even though I was willing it not to all night. I awoke to not only the light, but to Kane's head, sleeping soundly on my bare chest, his arm slung over my stomach, his leg hitched over mine. *I could get use to this.*

I was pretty sure that, that wasn't the morning sun. I glanced around, finding a clock on the nightstand. I was right, it was almost noon. I must have stirred too much, because Kane's head of fuckable hair moved on my chest. His chin sat between my breasts as he looked up at me. Through sleepy eyes, he smiled up at me. "Morning, Kitty."

"Morning," I answered back, running my fingers through his hair.

"I don't want to, but I have to get up and piss. Don't go anywhere," he said with a wicked grin.

"I'll be here," I said, raising my eyebrows.

The moment he was out of sight and behind the door, the bubble that we had been in since he carried me away had popped. Nate came crashing back to the forefront of my mind. Me staying here and turning into my mother and killing myself because I would become so unhappy was a close second, but mainly it was Nate.

I sat farther up in the bed, pulling my legs in closer, my head resting on my knees. I sat there, reliving every disgusting moment, every kiss with him, the way he'd touch me, and of course when he had drugged me and then slapped me.

The sting on my cheek came back. My hand clasped over my cheek, I was terrified that it would happen again when I saw him.

The door to the bathroom opened and Kane walked out. The instant his eyes found mine, he rushed over to the bed and climbed in next to me. "Talk to me. Don't go there, don't build it," he begged, taking the hand at my cheek into his.

He sat with a leg on either side of me. His arms then went for my legs. Undoing my tight ball, he set them over top of his and brought me closer to him.

"He drugged me. He almost raped me last night." *Yeah, I can't handle this.*

"He didn't, baby, and he won't do it again, to anyone. I think we should tell B and he can talk to the chief. He'll believe B. You can press charges. We'll get him put away where he needs to be."

I looked at him. My deep frown must have made my eyebrows really scrunch together, because they hurt. I wasn't doing that. No one was going to know about last night but us.

"No," I said, shaking my head. "No one is going to know about this but me, you, and him. We are definitely not telling my dad."

"Kitty, you have to tell him, so that fucker can get locked up. I know you heard him say he had done it before."

I kept shaking my head, getting more upset at every word that left his mouth. "No, Kane, I'm not. You'll be with me, and I'll stay near Dad. I won't give him that chance to get close to me."

That was my plan from the beginning—out of sight and pray to God out of mind.

"Caroline."

Oh fuck, he said my name.

"I can't just sit back and let that fucker get away with touching you like that. He slapped you, or don't you remember."

"Well, you're going to *have* to sit back, and thanks, but I do remember, I remember everything and I probably will for the rest of my life." I scooted back from him, moving my legs from over his. I went to the edge of the bed, my feet barely touching the floor. I saw the white shirt, that I had on for all of fifteen minutes last night, right next to my feet. I stood from the bed and snatched up the shirt from the floor. I pulled it over my head and went in search for the boxers Kane had tried to give me.

"Caroline, come on. You can't be serious about letting him walk."

Pulling my hair out of the shirt, I turned back to him, hands on my hips. "I'm serious as a fucking heart attack. Drop it, Kane."

He stood up, grabbed a pair of shorts from the floor, and put them on.

"No, I won't drop it. You're not going to push this away like you did your mother. Not on my fucking watch. I wasn't there for that, but I am here for this. I will not let you put it out of your mind and pretend like it never happened. It did. It fucking sucks, but it happened. Now you have to do something about it. Nate cannot get away with this, and you and I are the only ones who can stop him."

I threw my hands up, my eyes burned with the promise that tears were close by. "I can't," I said with a shaky voice.

"Yes, you can. I'll be right by your side. I'm not leaving. We'll do it together."

He walked over to me, rubbing my arms. I stood before him, still shaking my head. I wasn't strong enough to do it. I didn't want to be labeled or looked at any differently.

"Can you imagine what people are going to say around this fucking small town, when they find out the daughter of the local bar owner is calling rape against a cop! No one's going to believe me." I knew Kane thought we'd have more clout with him saying he walked in on it, but he was a fucking man whore, no one was going to believe him either. They'd all take Nate's side for sure. It was a lost cause. I just had to convince Kane not to open his fucking mouth.

We stood there arguing back and forth for the next fifteen minutes. He wasn't budging and neither was I. The sound of my phone ringing from my pile of clothes in the bathroom made us both pause. I had put my phone in the cup of my bikini while we had been at the lake yesterday. When I stripped in the shower last night I placed it on top of the pile of clothes. So when it began ringing, I huffed away and went to grab it, leaving Kane standing there, fuming.

"Don't answer it. We need to figure this out, now!" he said, following me into the bathroom.

I bent over, taking the phone in my hand. I didn't recognize the number, but I'd take any excuse I could to end the conversation with him.

"Hello," I said into the phone, turning away from Kane.

"Can I speak with Caroline James?" the friendly, female voice asked.

"This is she."

"Miss James, this is Cynthia at J&K Marketing. I was wondering if you had a moment to speak with me?"

CHAPTER 28

Kane

What the fuck just happened?
I left her in the bathroom, talking on the phone.
I stalked out, pacing the length of my room. I could hear the guys down in the kitchen, their muffled voices laughing and carrying on.

My life had changed so drastically since Caroline arrived. Mostly for the better. I mean, I could honestly say she had me by the balls, and it felt damn good. When *we* were good, I loved it. I loved messing with her, I loved making her laugh, and I *fucking* loved making her scream my name. I got it all from her. I didn't need anyone else, and she was fulfilling every single desire I ever had.

She changed me. I didn't care about having sex with different women. I didn't care about competing with the guys over who had the best number, because I did. I had Kitty, and she was *my* ten. I kept pacing the room, my hands firmly on my hips. I racked my brain, trying to figure out a way to handle the whole Nate situation. It would be easy to do what she wanted—let her forget—but that jackass deserved to be locked up. A wave of anger washed over me. I thought back to how he was laying between her legs, touching her, kissing her body. I reached out and punched a hole clear through the drywall.

"Shit," I yelled, shaking my hand, which was going to fucking hurt tonight when I played. Still shaking my hand, I turned, hearing the door to the bathroom close. Kitty was leaning against it, a confused smile on her face, the obvious glimmer of a tear in her eye. *What the hell now? I can't take anymore drama.*

"Who was on the phone?" I asked, gaining her attention.

She looked up at me, her smile getting wider across her face. *Okay, smiling is good, right?* Flicking my hand one last time, I was taken off guard as she rushed to me, locking her arms around my neck, her face buried in my shirt. I hugged her tightly, one hand on the middle of her back the other just above her ass. I couldn't tell if she was laughing or crying. *Maybe I've bitten off more than I can chew.* Women were so fucking complicated. It was then I remembered why I never got in relationships with them, but Kitty was different. As good, bad, and confusing as it was, I wasn't going anywhere. I was strapped in, and ready for crazy town, so long as she was strapped in next to me.

"I got it!" she said into my neck.

"You got what?" I paused for a moment as my heart sank to my stomach. "Oh fuck, did you think you were pregnant? Tell me you got it. I can't be a dad, not now, I'm not ready."

Why isn't she saying anything? I loved the girl, but I couldn't be father. What if she was knocked up, I can't go from having a sex schedule with four different women, to falling in love and having a kid in four months, I needed time to process that shit.

I yanked her hands from my neck, grabbing her shoulders to stare at her.

Her eyes were glistening which made them look like liquid.

"Kitty, are you knocked up?" I asked urgently.

"What? Knocked up? No."

I let out an exasperated breath. "Oh, thank God."

She stood there for a second, mentally counting maybe. I didn't know how women keep track of that shit, all I knew was I didn't use a condom and I assumed she was on the pill because she didn't stop me.

"I got the job, Kane," she said, smiling up at me.

The job? The job, in New York.

"They want me to come back to J&K. They heard I had an interview with the competition. There was some huge mix up after my internship. They were going to hire me all along, but some paperwork got messed up and they told me to leave, instead of someone else. I got my dream job, Kane! They are offering me an assistant lead position on a huge account. They're going to pay my first year's rent in an upscale condo, and I get a 50,000-dollar bonus on top of my 105,000 dollar salary!"

She was jumping up and down by the end of telling me. Her pony tail was bouncing all over the place, she even squealed in excitement.

"Did you say yes?" I was happy for her, truly I was, but how could I be happy when she was going to leave me?

"Of course, I said yes! I'd have to be stupid not to!" She was laughing as she said it, but once she saw my expression falter, I think it hit her, too.

"Well, congratulations, I guess." I tried my best to smile, but fuck if I didn't want to go over and add another hole to the wall.

"Don't act like this, Kane. You knew I was going to be leaving. I told you from the beginning that I wasn't staying longer than the summer."

Taking a breath I tried to stay calm. "Shit's changed, Kitty, you know it, and I know it. You have to call them back and tell them no."

"You're kidding me, right? You honestly think I'm going to give this job up? It's what I've always wanted, Kane. It's what I've been working toward the past two years. I gave up everything for this job, friends, a social life, everything. I can't turn my back on it." She sounded, again, as if she was trying to convince herself and not me.

"So you're going to turn your back on me, the guys, and your father?" I asked challengingly.

"No—I—Kane, I told you I was leaving."

"No, you're not leaving. You're running, you're running away again. What did I tell you about that?" I asked, getting in her face.

She took a step back from me, a guilty expression on her face. She was trying really hard to act like she wasn't thinking the same fucking thing I was. *This is a big fucking mistake.*

"I don't know, Kane, but we can't—"

I cut her off because if she said she couldn't do this with me one more time, I was going to blow my fucking lid.

"I told you, if you run, I'm running after you. Now, do I have to go tell the guys that I'm leaving, or what?"

She shook her head and, for a split second, I thought that this conversation was over, and we could move onto how to deal with Nate Rodgers. I took her in my arms, needing her closeness more than ever. I needed to show her that I was serious, that I'd follow her anywhere, because I didn't want to live without her, not after last night. I didn't want to wake up another morning without her right next to me.

The room was silent, except for the muffled voices coming up through the floor boards. I took her face in my hands, my lips found hers. Soft, plush lips that I wanted to be able to kiss whenever I wanted. I pulled back, our noses almost touching.

I sighed. "I need you, Caroline."

She smiled up at me, her eyes the color of blue liquid again. She blinked and two single tears rolled down her cheeks. I swiped the tears away with my thumbs then kissed her soft lips again.

CHAPTER 29

Caroline

Why did he have to say that? I didn't want it to happen, but he had turned into my everything, and last night just proved that I should have listened to my heart, instead of my head, all along. My thoughts were so clouded with negativity, I never let myself see the good. I was so scared of becoming my mother and so hell bent on doing the opposite, I never let myself fully trust Kane, let him in, but last night I did, and it was amazing.

I didn't expect to get *the* call that morning, to be offered my dream job. To be honest, after she told me all that they were going to offer me, I didn't think twice. I hung up, jumped up and down a few times, and then slipped on the clothes that I had left on the floor. My ecstatic mood had deflated as I stared at them on the tile floor. As the woman from J&K was talking to me, I forgot about Nate and that whole fucked up situation. I knew that I had made the right choice in saying yes to the job. I had made the mistake of running away after my mother died. I shut out my father for too many years, years I wasn't going to get back, but I wasn't going to do that again. I'd call, visit, and have him visit me. I wasn't running away, just moving on with my life.

A loud bang got my attention, bringing me back to the present. Outside the door, a man who had grown on me like a weed was waiting for me. He was going to be so mad, hell I was even pissed I'd have to leave him behind. I had finally gotten all of Kane and now I was going to have to leave. He was not going to take it well.

Every part of me that believed in fairytales and happy endings was telling me to stay, but I knew I couldn't. I knew I was going to take the job, and they didn't want me to come after summer. They wanted me there in two weeks. I loved what I did, as much as Kane loved being up on the stage. I would never make him choose between his music and me, but he didn't have a problem making me choose. Sure, he might follow me, or run after me as he said, but it wouldn't last. He'd miss the guys and performing, I'd be stuck at work all the time, and we'd never be together. Simply put, it wasn't going to work.

So as he kissed my lips, I made a decision that was going to ruin us both. He was going to hate me, I was going to hate myself, but I was going to do it anyway.

"Kane," I said against his lips. "Will you drop the Nate thing?"

Holding my face in his hands he smiled down at me, nodding. "I'll drop it, if you stay."

I was fine with that, killing two birds with one stone, I put on my best smile.

☙❧☙

"Holy shit!" Reece said through a mouth full of Lucky Charms. Three other heads lifted up from their cereal bowls to look at me.

"Hey, Cuz," JJ said, spooning another bite in his

mouth, clearly not surprised that I was standing in his kitchen with Kane's shirt and boxers on.

"Is this really happening right now?" Trent asked.

"Fucking right, it's happening! I don't care what you fuckers say either. Call me whatever you want. Hell, I'll do it for you. I've been pussy whipped," Kane responded, wrapping his arms around me from behind.

His fingers wandered up under my shirt for a second before I slapped them away. Turning around I punched his arm, hard.

He winced. Rubbing his newest soon to be bruise. "What the hell?"

"No groping in front of the guys or this pussy will not be whipping you." I smiled up at him then made my way over to Reece. "Stop staring at my tits, you buffoon," I scolded him while swatting him upside the head.

"But they're right there—in a white shirt—and its cold," Reece said, almost crying in agony.

I shook my head and went to Trent, plopped down on his lap, and took a drink of his coffee. I knew things had changed with Kane and me, but I still loved sitting with Trent. He always smelled really good and he was like a big bad biker teddy bear. I didn't want things to change between any of us. I still wanted the guys to know that I loved them and this was my way, beating Kane and Reece, sitting with Trent, keeping an eye on Aiden, and hanging out with JJ.

Was I surprised when Kane had steam coming out of his ears as I sat down on Trent's lap? Not really.

"So you're really banging Kane?" Trent asked, his face hung low.

I cupped his cheek in my hand, so I could look at him. "I still love you, Trent," I said, smiling at him.

"What the hell, Kitty?" Kane asked, frustrated. "You're still telling him you love him and you can't even say it to me. That's wrong. And why the fuck are you still sitting on his lap?"

"Kane, calm down. Damn, you get jealous," I said, turning from Trent.

He walked over to us, yanking me off of Trent. "Damn right, I'm jealous. You're my woman. I've never had one before and fuck if I'm going to let my first one sit on some other guy's lap."

He held me tight around my waist, securing me to his body. His strong hand held the back of my neck as his lips met mine. I melted in his arms, as his tongue separated my lips, twisting its way in my mouth while I fought back with my own. My hands came up his bare arms and around his neck, to finally rest in the mess of his hair. His other hand made its way down my back. Finding bare skin at the back of my thigh, he hitched my leg up. *So much for not groping.* The warmness of his hand crept from the back of my thigh to my ass, and inside the loose fitting boxers. Oh God, I was putty in his hands and I had completely forgotten that we had an audience, until JJ ruined it.

"Ahem, I'm all about watching you get it on with a hot-ass girl, but I really don't want to see any more of my cousin's ass, please." Hurriedly I put my leg down and buried my face in Kane's bare chest.

"I got to...umm...I need to go," Aiden said, running from the table and up the stairs. His door slammed shut and I swear to God, I died a little from embarrassment.

"JJ, you jackass! Maybe the rest of us wanted to see her ass, you ever think of that?" Reece said, his hands resting on the top of his head, as if he was sitting back, getting ready for the next show.

I looked up at Kane, praying he would go over and punch Reece for me.

"We'll be right back," Kane said, throwing me over

his shoulder and rushing up the stairs to his room.

Kicking the door closed with his foot, he placed me on the ground, ripped the shirt off, over my head, and buried his face between my breasts. Wrapping his arms around my ass he lifted me up and carried me to the bed. I couldn't have helped the giddy laugh that escaped me if I tried.

"You have no fucking idea how good it feels to just take you to my room and have my way with you." His lips and hands were all over my body, bringing it to life. His hand slid up between my legs. I gripped the covers tightly at my sides. "On second thought, maybe you do know how good it feels," he said through a wolfish grin.

CHAPTER 30

Kane

A mane of blonde curls lay against my chest as I ran my fingers through it. Her even breathing told me she was still sound asleep. It was early in the morning, the sun had yet to make an appearance, but the promise of dawn was just around the corner. The last two weeks, had been the best fucking weeks of my life. I was able to call kitty my own, without her beating the shit out of me for it. On second thought, that wasn't completely true. She was still a violent little thing.

The night after she finally let me in, I had told her I'd drop the whole Nate thing, but the moment I saw that jackass walk into the bar, all I saw was red. I happened to be up on stage when he strode in like he owned the place. He walked over to a table in Kitty's section. It took all of my self-control not to jump off the stage and kill the bastard. I searched the room and, when I saw her cowering in the corner, I again had to control myself. She put on a brave face, but I knew the moment she was out of sight, she'd escape from the crowd and start to build that wall back up.

It was killing me, not to be holding her, to get her

through that. As soon as we were done, I jumped off the stage and ran to her, out back on the patio, wrapping her tightly in my arms.

"You all right, Kitty?" I asked.

Her face was plastered to my chest. Her small hands splayed on my sweaty back. "He's sitting there acting like nothing happened."

"I know, baby. I still think we should tell someone."

"Tell someone what?" B asked, walking up behind us.

She pushed away from me, fixing her hair as she looked up at her father.

"What's going on?" he asked, looking between us skeptically.

I took her hand in mine, only to find that she had started shaking with nerves. I should pull B aside and tell him, but I knew Caroline would never forgive me, so I improvised. "B, we want you to know that…" I looked down at Caroline. Her eyes were glimmering blue, begging me not to say anything. I squeezed her hand, smiling down at her. "B, I think I'm dating your daughter."

B stood there for a moment, then reached out and grabbed both of us in a huge hug. "Well, it's about damn time!" he said, laughing. "I knew you two were going to hit it off before you even got here. I guess this means that you're going to stay, right?"

She smiled up at him wearily.

I squeezed her hand again, pulling her out of a trance. *Was she still thinking about taking the job?* My heart sank at the thought of her leaving. She had told me she wasn't going to, but who the fuck knew with her?

"Dad, I'm here. Are you sure you're okay with this?" she asked, holding up my hand and giving me a dirty look.

"Well, I assume that you have put him in his place

and that he's changed his ways. As long as your happy, honey, then I'm happy for you." He gripped her chin, smiling down at her as only a father could do. "I'm happy to see you two finally together. I have to get back to it in there. Behave yourselves," he said before turning to leave.

I took Caroline in my arms again, her body relaxed against mine.

"Caroline, are you ignoring me?" Nate's snake like voice said from behind us.

We turned, hand in hand. His face was all bruised and he had a cut on the bridge of his nose. *Did this fucker really come back here to start shit?*

"Rodgers, what the hell are you doing back here?" I hissed.

Caroline let go of my hand and stepped between us. Nate, being the pompous ass that he was, placed his hands casually in his pockets.

"I think you should just leave," Caroline growled, low enough for only the three of us to hear here.

He chuckled to himself then looked over her head and straight into my eyes. "So, you finally got your dick in her, did ya?" he asked, still ignoring her and trying to get a rise out of me.

We were alone out here and I was seriously contemplating shoving Kitty aside so I could finish this poor excuse for a man.

"I'll take that as a yes. Was she as feisty in bed as she was when you found her last night? I never got to thank you for interrupting us." Taking a challenging step, he reached out, brushing a hand over Caroline's cheek, the one he'd slapped.

I couldn't take it anymore. I grabbed Caroline's shoulder and pushed her aside a little more forcefully than I intended to. She stumbled to the side before regaining her balance. My fist was flying through the air the moment I let her go. I went straight for that smug smile, making sure to wipe it clean, so I'd never have to see it again. I heard Caroline shriek and call my name but nothing was going to stop me. I had hit my fair share of faces, but this one felt the best.

My knuckles connected with his jaw, and I felt the crack beneath them. I knew his jaw was shattered, but that didn't stop me from making my point. I pulled back and went for the nose this time.

He blocked me and got in a lucky hit to my face, but nothing serious. Blood sprayed from his nose as I hit him again, my hand stung like a bitch from not only breaking this fucker's face, but from the wall I had punched earlier that morning.

"Kane, you just made a lethal mistake," he said, holding his nose.

"No, motherfucker, you made the mistake the minute you laid a hand on my woman."

"Your woman? You mean the skank that kept handing it out to everyone *but* you."

I rushed toward him, ready to kill the fucker. Gripping his shirt in my hands, I pushed it up under his chin, and shoved him back against the wall.

"Keep on hitting me. I'd love to put your ass away."

We were face to face against the wall. I shoved him a few more times before I spoke. "You're the one that needs to be put away, Rodgers."

Caroline's soft hand fell on my forearm, bringing me back. "Kane," she whispered. I turned my gaze from Nate's face down to hers. "Let him go," she said, tugging on my arm.

"Are you fucking kidding me? Did you hear him?"

"Yes, and so did everyone who's standing out here," she whispered again.

I glanced around and, sure , there were people milling about.

There was a warm breeze blowing and, as if on cue,
thunder roared above us. A crack of lightning lit up the
whole parking lot and the skies opened up. A downpour
of rain fell on us, as everyone ran under the covered patio.

The blood on Nate's face washed away as the rain
crashed down on us.

"Caroline, guys, get under here, there's a nasty storm
coming this way," B yelled from the cover of the patio.
He had no idea just how big a storm was coming.

"Come on, he's not worth it," Kitty said, pulling my
arm, before running for cover. I took that opportunity to
speak with Nate alone.

"Don't come near her again. She might want to let
what you did slide under the rug, but I sure as hell don't.
Come near her again, I'm going to do whatever I have to,
to make sure that your ass is locked up. You let it slip that
you've done this before. I'm sure it wouldn't take me too
long to find someone else to back our story up."

"Are you threatening an officer?" he said, standing
from the wall and getting in my face.

"No, I'm threatening, a sick fuck, who gets pleasure
in taking advantage of drugged-up girls," I said, eyeing
him up.

"You aren't going to do shit, Lawson. You think one
night with her is going to make *you* the better man.
You're just as bad as me."

I shook my head, water dripping off my hair. "Not a
chance. I'll go straight to B, who'll go straight to the
chief. They might not believe me, but they'll believe him,
and you know it."

That shut him up. He wiped his face of the blood that
was still trickling down from his nose. He pushed me

back, stalking off toward his car. He got in and drove away. I stood there in the cooling rain. Pushing my hair back and out of my face, I blew water off of my lips. Caroline was standing under the patio, dripping wet, her hair straight and weighed down by the rain. She was watching me, a look of desire on her face. I knew exactly how she felt. I needed her in my arms, and I needed her lips on mine.

Reading my mind, she ran out from under the cover of the patio and straight into my arms, I held her tightly, her legs wrapped around my waist.

"I don't know what you said to him and I don't really care. That was the sexiest thing I've ever seen, now take me upstairs before I rip your clothes off right here," she begged me.

Her warm breath on my cold skin sent a chill down my spine. I held her tighter, my lips finding her neck. I carried her past the guys, and the women that they had brought out back. Ignoring all their catcalls and hoots, I headed straight for the stairs.

I burst into her room, kicking the door closed behind me. I placed her on her feet. Our clothes and hair were dripping wet. She shivered under the turning fan. I rubbed her arms to warm her.

"Who saw? Did B see me punch him?" I asked.

"I—I don't know. I'm sure if he had, then he would have said something. Now shut up and kiss me."

Damn this woman was confusing as hell. "I think I should go tell B before he hears it from everyone."

Her hands were exploring my arms, nails raked down my skin. I kept my hands at her hips. Women had told me I had large hands, but I never thought anything of it until just then as I held her small waist between them.

"No, you're not. You're going to stay right here with me. I know I said you were never going to step foot in this room again, but now you're not allowed to leave, not until I say so."

So there it was. My knees weak, my heart as heavy as it has ever felt, I stayed in that room with her until the sun came up the next morning.

c/ɔc/ɔ

After that night, Nate didn't show his face. So now two weeks later, Kitty's head was peacefully sleeping on my chest. I knew that everything was going to be all right. Nate was out of the picture. She was free to let herself warm up to me, let me in. I did, however, catch her lost in thought from time to time. The first time she did this she was watching me undress. I had just gotten home from a construction job. Sweaty and dirt covered, I went up to her room to catch a quick shower before the guys and I practiced for the day. She was sitting on the bed staring at me, as if I might disappear if she took her eyes off me. Of course, I didn't mind, but it wasn't the usual I'm-going-to-jump-your-bones look. It was different.

The second time I caught her mind far off somewhere, we were on stage and I happened to see her leaning against the wall, her tray flat to her chest. She seemed to be taking in everything around her, committing it to memory. She'd be there one moment and off in her head the next. It scared the shit out of me, until she'd come back to the present.

Last night was the final time I saw her do it. I was deep inside her, her eyes fixed on mine. Her hand rose to my cheek. She froze under me, like all the times before, when she was somewhere else. Taking in all my features, her fingers ran over my brow, down my nose, across my jawline. My eyes closed involuntarily at her touch. Her hand made its way to my neck, over my tattooed shoulder, and down my arms. I took a chance, opening my eyes, but hers had left mine and were following her hand down my body.

I wanted to ask why? Why was she slipping away at times? But I didn't, because I didn't want to ruin it, ruin us. We were in my room, the Saturday morning sun had finally appeared through the window. She stirred on my chest, a beam of sun falling on her face. She was an angel, my angel, and I didn't plan on letting her get away, ever. I was under her spell, whipped, call it whatever you want. I was ready for everything with her. I found myself skipping practice with the guys, ending shows early, just so I could have her in my arms. I was a lovesick fool.

CHAPTER 31

Caroline

How am I going to do this? Once again I had made a huge mistake. I thought that giving myself those two weeks to pretend, to play house, would get it out of my system, get Kane out of my system. Of course, it didn't. I was a fool for thinking I could let my emotions run wild and not pay the consequences.

My flight left tonight at 10:05. The guys would be up on stage, and I would be able to sneak off. They usually didn't play on Saturday nights, but rumor had it, there were scouts in the area, looking for new talent. So the guys weren't taking any chances, they were going to play as often as they could. Kane had told me this rumor had gone around a couple times before, nothing coming from it, of course. So the guys were taking it as any other night, knowing that it could be just a rumor—or the break that they had been waiting for.

I only had to make it until tonight. I had to keep my wits about me. I couldn't let on that I'd be leaving. My plan was to tell my father the moment the guys went up on stage. I'd pull him aside and tell him everything. I'd tell him how much I loved him, and that I would call him all the time. I was going to tell him, I'd have him come visit me and that I'd come back and visit him. I planned on spending every holiday and birthday with him. I wasn't going to miss out on important stuff anymore. Those four and half months had changed me. I realized just how much I missed having him fully in my life, and I wasn't going back to my old ways.

The only problem I had walked out of the bathroom with a towel hanging low on his hips. As the water dripped from his hair onto his stone hard, tattooed chest, I was seriously reconsidering. He was going to hate me when he found out that I was on a plane, heading back to New York tonight. The only thing I could say about it was that I hoped he *did* hate me. I hoped he got so mad, that he forgot all about me, and moved on. I was saving us future arguments by leaving now. It was never going to work between the two of us. I was ending it now, while we didn't resent one another.

I had put on a good show, knowing that the two weeks following our agreement to be together, that I'd be leaving. I put my fears aside, the similarities I saw in myself and my mother. I kept them quiet because I knew I wouldn't be staying.

Nate hadn't shown his face, since the night after he drugged and attacked me. Maybe, one day, I'd be able to tell my story, make him pay for what he had done to me. I wasn't ready to face him again anytime soon. The night that he had come into the bar, like nothing had happened, scared the shit out of me. All I could remember was standing in the corner, dumbfounded that he could strut in, sit at his table, and act like he didn't try to rape me the night before. I locked eyes with Kane and prayed that he would get done singing so he could be by my side.

I'd never needed anyone the way I needed Kane in that moment. I always relied on myself. I was strong and didn't need a man to hold me up before, but I needed Kane that night, and being Kane, he didn't disappoint. He took me under his arm, fucked up Nate's face again, and then stood toe to toe with him until he ran off. I'd never be able to repay him for that.

I didn't know what he said to Nate, but I was thankful he got him to leave and, hopefully, never come back. And fuck if he didn't look sexy as hell standing in the pouring rain. I would never be able to get that image out of my mind.

When he turned back to me, spitting the rain from his lips—the way it dripped off his hair, the way it ran down his bare arms. *Yeah, that image will forever be engraved.*

"Why are you looking at me like that?" he asked from across my room.

"Like what?" I said, pulling my legs up under my chin in bed.

"I don't know. It's a mix. You're either plotting my death or deciding whether or not to jump my bones, because I'm irresistible. Preferably, I'll take the later."

Damn that smile of his. Tossing the covers off, I got out of bed and grabbed a pair of pants and my tank top from the floor. "Cocky this morning, huh?"

"Kitty, that hurts. You know I'm always cocky, especially in the morning."

I was going to miss this so much, but I had to keep moving forward. I couldn't stay there, not when my dream job was waiting for me at the end of a two-hour plane ride.

I was pulling my hair up, when Kane's still-damp arms wrapped around me from behind. His chin rested on my shoulder, drips of water ran down my own arm, a few drops making polka dots on my tank top.

"I know you," he said into my shoulder, leaving a tender kiss in the crook of my neck. "Something's different. Last night, you—talk to me. Don't shut me out." He spoke softly, almost unintelligibly.

I stilled my body. He was noticing the tension that had been building up in me over the last two weeks.

Nine hours left. I had to smile through nine hours. I had to make him see that nothing was different. He had to believe that, when he left me tonight to go up on stage, I was going to be standing in the hallway waiting for him to take me in his arms when he was done. I needed him to trust me that tomorrow I'd awake in his bed, like I had done for the past two weeks.

Breathe, I rotated in his arms. My hands rested on his bare, damp chest. I smiled up at him.

"Nothing is different, except that—" I wanted to say, except that I was leaving, that I was just committing him, all of him to memory. But I couldn't say that. "—I have to get home. I have a few things I need to take care of. I can't stay around, lying in bed all day with a worn-out, wanna-be rock star."

I tapped his chest and then lightly smacked his cheek.

"Worn-out, wanna-be rock star huh?"

"Yeah worn-out. You just lay around all day. I got places to go."

"Like where?" he asked.

Okay, I had nowhere to go. *Shit I was slowly digging myself deeper into this lie.*

"Sightseeing," I blurted out.

"Sightseeing?" he questioned me.

Fuck! This was not going the way I had foreseen.

"Yes. Now, I have to go. I'll see you in a few hours at the bar," I said, walking past him. His hand caught my upper arm before I could make my escape. He pulled me close again. "Wait up. Let me get dressed and we'll go 'sightseeing' together."

"No, it's fine. Stay here, relax for tonight. I'll be fine," I said in a hurry.

"Kitty, if you know what's good for you, you'll sit your ass on my bed and wait for me."

Frowning in frustration, I stared up at him. His blue eyes sparkled back. *Fuck, even if I wanted to, I couldn't say no.*

"Fine, hurry up." Throwing my arms up in aggravation, I rolled my eyes, sat on the bed, crossed my legs, and rested my head on my hand. Out of the corner of my eye, I watched the towel that was around his waist drop to the floor. Kane walked in front of where I sat to the other side of the room in all his naked glory. He stood there for a second then turned and walked back to the other side of the room. Pausing in front of his dresser, he stretched his arms over his head, flexing the muscles in his back. *This jackass is a piece of work.*

Shaking his arms at his sides. He turned back to me. "Forgot something," he said, before sauntering back to the other side of the room where his closet was. He stood there, looking into the neatly arranged closet. His hand reached between his legs, and that's when my head conveniently fell off its perch on my hand. He turned back to me, stroking himself. I shook my head and tried to act bored, though I was anything but. My abdomen tightened, my palms got sweaty, and I had to really concentrate on breathing evenly.

"Something wrong?" he asked while still stroking himself.

"Yeah, I said hurry up, and you're not moving fast enough."

He cocked his head to the side, and then nodded in agreement. "I think you're right," he said with a sexy grin.

My eyes went from his, down to the hand that was

currently moving faster. I bit the inside of my cheek to keep from making any embarrassing noises. He moved from the closet over to me, standing at the foot of the bed. I sat eye to crotch with him.

"This fast enough for you?" he asked, looking down at me.

"No," I said challengingly.

He took yet another step closer, his hand working even faster. His head fell back, and a hiss came from his mouth as he worked himself closer to an end. Exhaling loudly, his eyes found mine. "How about now?"

It wouldn't have taken much for me to lean forward and lick him. I couldn't stand it anymore. I closed the short distance. My hand over his, I shoved his aside and did it myself.

An hour later, we made it downstairs.

CHAPTER 32

Kane

Sightseeing, she said. I basically spent the day driving her around. There was nothing but long, winding roads, and farmland on either side of the truck. We did stop for lunch at a small diner in the next town over, the one that the guys and I always went to before shows. They had the best burgers around.

When we finally got back to BJ's, I was sitting out back of the bar. The guys were getting pumped up for the show while I sat silently.

Walking over to me, Trent asked, "Dude, why you so quiet?"

I was staring at the asphalt beneath my feet, my mind wandering down a road which, ever since Caroline had arrived, was getting very worn. It was always the same with her. She was hiding something, keeping something from me, and I had no clue what it could be.

"You and Kitty on the rocks already? That's got to be some sort of record, two weeks, right?" Aiden asked.

"No, jackass, we're fine." Looking up from the asphalt, I saw all four guys staring down at me.

"All right, I'm just going to say this," Reece announced. "I think Kitty's sweet ass is bad for you. Look at you! We're getting ready to go out and play, the place is packed, and Kara told us that there is a group of guy's that she's never seen before, and one of them is in a suit. Who goes to a bar in a suit? If they're not important, that is. You should be on cloud nine with the rest of us. This could be our night, and you're sitting in the corner sulking about your woman problems." His words hit me like a punch to the face.

"I don't have woman problems, and if you fucking talk about Kitty like that again, I'm going to punch that smug look off your mother-fucking face. You all feel this way?" I asked, inspecting each of my friends.

They didn't have to say anything. It was written clear across their faces. They thought I was changing.

Fuck, I *was* changing, but I thought it was for the better. "You all are just fucking jealous. You don't understand shit, none of you."

"Kane, we love Kitty, honestly we do," JJ said. "And we're happy for you, but come on. This could be our shot. You need to push aside whatever it is that's got you acting like this. We need you. We need Kane the ladies' man to perform his ass off." He clasped a hand on my shoulder as he spoke.

He was right—these guys were here for me long before Kitty. I had to put the doubt I had aside. *Fuck, I'm probably just being paranoid.* It still boggled my mind how I went from a cocky ladies' man to an unsure, paranoid boyfriend in a matter of a few months.

Standing, I hung an arm around JJ's neck. "You're right man. I'm sorry. Let's go do this shit!"

"Ah! Thank God, he's back!" Reece said with his hands in the air in triumph.

"It's all about us tonight, the five of us. We started this, and we're going to make it. If those guys out there are who we think they are, let's knock their fucking socks off! And maybe a few panties as well!"

We stood shoulder to shoulder, huddling together, like we had done since the first time we all went out on that stage together.

"Aw, look, Kara, they're having a moment," Kitty said from the doorway.

Our heads popped up to see the two of them huddled close and making ridiculous baby faces.

"I know. They look so cute, don't they?" Kara added.

"They do. I just want to go over there and pinch their cheeks." Kitty held her hands up, pinching the air.

"No way, we are not 'cute,'" Trent said, dropping his arms and pointing a finger at Kara.

"What do you two buzz kills want anyway?" Reece asked.

"Buzz kill?" they questioned in unison.

"Yes, buzz kill. You don't put out," Reece said, gesturing to Kara. "And you went and shacked up with the only man in the world who *doesn't* need to get laid. What about me, Kitty? What—about—me? Buzz kill!" he pleaded.

"First off, maybe I do put out, but I'd sure as hell never let your skinny ass in, don't want to break you," Kara said, placing her hands on her hips.

"Whatever, Kara," Reece said, flicking her off.

"Anyway, it's time for you guys to go and knock some socks and panties off," Kara said, before walking back inside.

Kitty stood there watching us huddle back up. I was facing her in the huddle. I could see her through JJ and Trent's shoulders. Even though we were a good twenty feet apart, it was obvious she was doing it again, committing the image to memory.

With one last pep talk, we broke apart and made our way to our stage, our fans, and hopefully our big break. Kitty stopped each of the guys, giving them a hug and kiss on the cheek, even Reece. If my curiosity and anxiousness wasn't already on high alert, it fucking was now. I went to walk past her. I needed to focus on everything but her if I was going to get through the performance as if nothing was bothering me. I needed to be present and not off in my own head. So when she grabbed my arm as I walked by, I was tempted to shove on, but I couldn't.

"Kane." The way her voice formed around my name always gave me chills. Her petite frame collided with mine, arms wrapped around my midsection, and her face rested on my chest, just above my vigorously beating heart.

"What's this all about?" I asked, running a hand over her blonde mane of hair.

"I can't hug you and wish you good luck?" she asked, looking up at me, her dark blue eye's piercing mine.

"No, you can do that, but why do you keep—" *I can't get into this right now*. I needed to stay focused on the task at hand. I couldn't blow this for the guys. "Never mind," I said, shaking my head, before I kissed her soft lips.

"I really hope that those guys out there are who we all think they are. You are so talented and the guys and you are going to be unstoppable once you get your big break."

Smiling down at her, I kissed her forehead tenderly. "Thanks, baby, that means a lot."

"Kane, I want you to know that, no matter what happens after you get up on that stage, that—I—just know—that—I"

She really was cute as fuck, stuttering in my arms, I

almost let her keep going, almost. "I love you too, Kitty," I said, cutting her incoherent babble short. I think I took her off guard, by the shocked look on her face.

Chuckling up at me, she hit my chest with her balled up fist. "Dammit, Kane, I was getting to that, if you wouldn't have interrupted me," she said, hitting me again.

I tried my hardest not to laugh and put a serious face on. "Sorry, go on. I won't say anything."

"What I was going to say was that, no matter what happens, I want you to remember that you're an asshole, a cocky, sexy, strong, endearing, asshole. Never change that about yourself. I love you." Her hand grabbed my shirt collar and tugged me down to her level. "Remember I loved you," she said softly against my lips. She held me to her, her warm tongue slipping between my lips.

Fuck she tastes good.

"Kane, let's go! The natives are restless!" JJ yelled from down the hall.

I pulled back resting my forehead to hers. "I'm going to fuck you so hard tonight. You better be right here when I get off stage."

I couldn't see it, but I felt the smile on her face. She nodded her head and then released her grip on my shirt. I backed away then turned to go through the door, a little more pep in my step. I was going to kill it tonight. I had a feeling that this was it, this was our shot and I was in the fucking *zone*, thanks to my woman.

We had one more song to get through, until I could find Kitty and take her upstairs. I was right, we had killed it. Still, with one song left, the crowd was just as rowdy as it was when we played the first one. It was so crowded that I had lost track of where kitty was early on. My mind at ease after our conversation, I knew she loved me and that put me as high as the fucking moon. In-between songs, I'd go back to our conversation, specifically the moment she said she loved me. Her words rang in my ears for the millionth time *'Remember I loved you'*—*wait a minute. She said loved? No, no way. It was love, right?*

Dread crept up from my insides, squeezing my heart. I frantically scanned the room but couldn't find her over the screaming women and rowdy men. Finally, I caught sight of B, standing in the doorway. Kara was hugging him, and he kept wiping his eyes. *Why the hell would B be crying?* It felt like a punch to the gut, the kind that takes your breath away. I wanted to drop to my knees because finally it all made sense. B was upset, Kara looked upset, and Kitty *had* said "loved." She fucking ran.

I jumped off the stage, my guitar still around my tense body. Taking the crowd by surprise, I pushed my way through the wading bodies in search of B. I found him in the back, his head hung low as Kara tried to comfort him. "What the fuck's going on, B?" I asked a few steps from him.

He grabbed my shoulders, pulling me into a tight embrace. He held the back of my neck tightly, and spoke in my ear. "She's gone, she's gone."

The loud room went silent. Things were in slow motion, I could suddenly see specks of dust clearly and the lights were moving at a snail's pace.

I pulled away from B, our height the same, his build slightly bigger than mine. I peered into his reddened eyes, shaking my head in doubt.

"She can't be gone, where the hell is she going?" I asked frantically.

"She took a job. She said it was her dream job," B said, in almost as much disbelief as me.

"She said no, she told me she turned it down." I broke away from B, shoving my hands in my hair. "I have to go. I have to get her back." I went to leave, but a

heavy hand on my shoulder stopped me. B moved, blocking my path. "Move. I'm going to bring her back, for the
both of us," I said with determination.

"I can't let you. She told me to—Kane, if she doesn't
want to be here, we can't make her stay."

"The fuck, we can't!" I yelled. The music in the bar
had started back up and someone was singing our last
song. Right then, I didn't give a fuck about anything but
getting Kitty back here where she belonged.

"Kane, she told me to tell you to move on, find
someone else."

"Fuck, no," I said, shaking my head.

"Kane, son, you have to let her go, just like I have to.
I knew she wasn't going to stay here. I just kept pretending that she was. It's her mother. She really messed her
up and unless she's willing to let us in, talk about what
happened, nothing is going to change. She's going to
keep running for the rest of her life. It's what she does.
She says she doesn't want to be like her mother, but I'm
terrified that by doing this, leaving, pushing her emotions
aside, they're going to catch up with her. It's exactly
what her mother did."

"I understand this, B! That's why I'm going to the
airport and bring her stubborn ass back here, whether she
likes it or not! She has my fucking heart and I'll be God-
damned if I'm going to let her leave!" I took the strap that
held my guitar off over my shoulder and shoved into B's
hands for him to hold. Once it was securely in his hands,
he caught me by the arm.

"Bring her back. You're the only one who can make
her stay."

I nodded once then rushed out the door.

CHAPTER 33

Caroline

If I kept taking all these deep breaths, someone was going to start thinking I was in labor. My leg was bouncing a mile a minute as I waited to be called to board the plane. I needed to get on that plane, so I wouldn't give in. I was so close to turning and running back to the bar, but I kept my ass firmly planted in the seat and kept on taking slow, deep breaths.

I was doing the right thing. Leaving was the right thing. Not only was this the job opportunity of a lifetime, but being trapped in a small town and working at a bar, was not how I wanted to spend my days, even if I had Kane by my side.

I hated how I had to leave, but I knew Kane. I knew he'd probably tie me to a chair to keep me from boarding my plane. So I had to do it while he was up on stage. He was on fire tonight, better than I had ever heard him. The gossip was true. I had the pleasure of getting drinks for the unknowns, that we all thought were scouts. Turns out, they weren't scouts but the very popular group, 4 Alliance. They were sitting with hats and were very well hidden. When I walked over after the guys' first song, I heard one of the cloaked guys say that they wanted this band on their tour.

I almost jumped up and down and raved even more about them, but I kept my cool and kept to myself. ONS was going to make it. They were going to get out of small town USA and so was I.

"Now boarding, flight 128 Baltimore to New York." *Finally!* I stood, grabbing my backpack. I stood last in line to board. My flight left at 10:05, and it was now 9:45. The guys had probably been done singing for at least twenty minutes. There was no way that Kane or anyone could make the trip from the bar to the airport in less than forty-five minutes. Still, I couldn't help but anxiously look around. If Kane showed up, I might not be strong enough to get on that plane. *Thankfully, I'll never know.* I was next. I handed the lady my ticket, adjusted my bag on my shoulder, and headed down the walkway.

"This is right. I'm doing the right thing," I said out loud to myself.

I held my arms tight around my waist. The hallway down to the waiting plane seemed longer than necessary. I reached the bottom, getting ready to make the sharp left turn, to finally step over the threshold of the plane.

"Caroline!"

The deep, demanding voice echoed off the walls. I twisted, not surprised to see Kane standing at the entrance of the walkway. He was gorgeous as always, his hair a sexy mess, his body strong and hard with muscle.

"Caroline!" he yelled again.

Deep breath, head held high. *You're doing the right thing, just—keep—walking.*

CHAPTER 34

Kane

I ran through the parking garage, after parking my truck in the first spot I saw. It might have been a handicapped spot. I wasn't really sure and, right then, I didn't give a fuck. I bought a ticket so I could get back to the gates. I was rounding the corner when I heard them announce the flight that I knew Kitty was getting on.

I got to the gate, scanning all over but it was nearly empty, the sign above the doorway that lead to the plane was flashing last call. I went to make my way down to the plane, but the ticket lady stopped me. When I looked down the walkway, there at the bottom was Caroline. The large woman still blocking my path, I called to her, "Caroline!"

"Sir, you can't go down there without a proper ticket," the pudgy woman said, taking another step forward to block me.

"I need to get down there!" I said frantically.

"I'm sorry but, no ticket, no plane."

What a bitch.

"Caroline!" I yelled, again.

Kitty stood there, a slight hesitation in the body that I

had come to know so well, staring at me. I could have sworn she was going to run back, run to me—that is, until she lifted her chin, fixed the bag on her shoulder, and walked away, taking with her what was left of my heart.

CHAPTER 35

Caroline

Nine Months Later:

S pring in the city was my favorite time of the year—
people walking the sidewalks instead of rushing for
cabs, buds on the trees, excitement all around.
Breathing in the warm, spring, afternoon air, I closed my
eyes as I sat at a small table outside of an eatery. *So why
can't I enjoy it like I used to?*

"I've been dreaming of this single slice of cheesecake for over a week. Thanks for coming down here with
me."

That was Sarah. Any excuse to get out of the office,
she took it, even if it was to cheat on her diet and get a
slice of cheesecake.

"I don't mind. It's beautiful out. Your only payment
will be a bite of that mouthwatering slice of cheesecake,"
I said, adjusting in my seat as she sat down across from
me.

"Fine. I guess I can relinquish one bite, but that's it!
You want more, get in line. It starts down there," she
said, pointing down the sidewalk, where the line ended

from out of the eatery. "Did you get everything done for the Miller project?" Sarah asked through a delicate bite of cheesecake.

"Yup, I finished last night." *Because I don't have a life, so I just work, and work, and work.*

"I don't know why you take work home with you?"

Well, it's not like I had anything else to do, and working kept my mind off things. "It's not that bad. I don't mind," I replied, shrugging my shoulders and wiggling my fingers for the fork. "I'll take that bite now."

Reluctantly she handed it over. Sarah was the first friend that I made since moving back to New York. It helped that we worked three cubicles down from one another in the beginning, until they gave me my own office. It was small and nothing to write home about, but I had worked my butt off and was rewarded greatly.

Sarah was the type of friend who took my mind off my own problems. I'd sit day after day at lunch with her as she ranted about all the men she had coming in and out of her life. The drama that came with each one was enough to keep me occupied with trying to figure out her love life, rather than dipping into mine. I had been dragged on a number of double dates with her. The guys were all nice, good-looking career men, but they weren't—

Okay, fine, I had slept with two of them. I'm human, a girl has her needs. Was it good? Hell no, it was almost torturous. I didn't want to admit it, but I had been ruined.

One hour left. I sat at the large desk, my fellow colleagues talking about the project at hand. The sounds of their voices lulled me into a daze. I found myself drifting off more and more as time went on.

"Caroline, do you have the charts?" Danny, the lead director, asked.

He was young for attaining the lead position, somewhere in his late thirties. A handsome guy with slicked back brown hair, he had a few hints of gray around his temples, which was the only thing that gave his age away. He had a sexy full beard—which was perfectly maintained so he didn't look like he just came out of the woods—dress slacks, button up shirt, dark blue tie, and thin suspenders.

Danny was the talk of the office. The women here couldn't get enough of him.

"Caroline," he said, a little more urgently.

"Yeah, I've got them right here." I stood from my chair and handed the papers to him.

His gaze held mine a little longer than necessary. He furrowed his brow. I knew he was asking if I was all right. I smiled back and then sat down in my chair again. I made sure to stay focused for the rest of the meeting, adding my input and staying alert.

Sitting at my desk, I was wrapping things up for the evening when Danny knocked.

"Can I come in?" he asked, peeking his head in the door.

"Yeah, I was just closing up for the weekend. What do you need? And I swear to God Danny, if you ask me to get you the Walker papers, I'm going to stab you with this pen."

We had a good working relationship. Mainly because I was amazing and got his ass out of trouble all the time. So in return, I was able to talk to him like that without getting fired, but if we were in a group setting, I knew my place and didn't step on his toes.

"Calm down, tiger, no need to stab me today. I was concerned about earlier. You were frozen for a little while in the meeting. Anything you want to talk about, you know I'm here for ya."

Danny was a sweet guy, under all the commanding

dress clothes and beard. He was a considerate, caring guy. I think he played up the whole badass business guy to cover up the shy sweetheart that he was.

"I'm fine, really, you don't have to worry about me," I said, unclicking my pen and putting it in my drawer.

We were small talking about an upcoming project when there was another knock at my door. Sarah came in, eyeing up Danny like the rest of the vultures in the office. Sarah had let Danny know her intentions. I thought it was a little game the two of them played. "Danny, looking good, love the suspenders," she said, licking her lips.

"So you've told me, every day that I wear them," he replied, leaning on my desk.

"What do you need Sarah?" I asked, looking around Danny's lean body.

"Umm, there's someone wondering around the office looking for you. Should I send him in?" she asked.

"Yeah why not, party in my office."

Winking at Danny, she turned and left the room.

"I still don't see why you're friends with her," Danny said, turning his head to look down at me, but still leaning against my desk.

"I think you two should just fuck and get it over with," I said, smiling up at him.

"I don't think so. You and I both know that girl's track record. I'm not trying to be a part of it. I'm in the market for normal, not psycho."

We laughed until there was another knock at my door. A tall man in a suit walked in and headed straight for my desk.

Danny stood, moving aside.

"Are you Caroline James?" the man asked.

"Yes, what can I—"

"You've been served," he said, pulling an envelope from the inside pocket of his suit.

I stood from my chair, taking the letter between my fingers.

"Have a nice weekend," he said, before turning to leave.

"Yeah, thanks." Turning the envelope over in my hands, I read the return address. Slumping down in my chair, because my legs couldn't hold me up, I stared at the letter. I had just been summoned to Nowheresille, Maryland, next week.

☙❧☙

I packed a bag and headed straight for the airport, a million scenarios running through my head. I was being summoned to testify in court. The case was Janet Hallows vs. Nathan Rodgers. I honestly hadn't thought about Nate since I moved up here. He was in my past, a past that wasn't supposed to make a reappearance.

I called my dad on the way to the airport. I had kept my promise and I talked to him almost every day. It was hard at first. He was mad at me for leaving, but our conversations got easier.

I told him about my new life, my new friends, hell I even told him I was dating. My father reciprocated by telling me the entire goings on at the bar. He hired a few new girls to take my place, and Kara was still running the bar like a well-oiled machine. He told me the guys were still playing every once in a while, but they were on tour with another band. He'd always stop there because I'd change the subject.

Kane was a big part of why I left, I was just happy to know that he was doing well. I didn't need details. It hurt too much when my father would tell me how down he was, or how he'd drink himself stupid over me leaving. We'd end up fighting over the phone, and I'd eventually hang up, but either he or I would call back the next day. After about a month or so, my father stopped bringing it up. He would tell me funny stories about the guys but never pinpointed Kane.

The only thing I knew about him now was that he was on tour, opening for 4 Alliance. I hadn't talked to him or any of the guys. I tried calling JJ once but he didn't answer. I didn't leave a message, and he didn't call back. I understood why. I had hurt his best friend, but I missed the guys, I missed seeing them in the beginning. They were such a big part of my life those four months I was there. But time went on, and it got easier—kind of.

I waited, sitting in a cab that smelt like a potpourri jar. *One ring, no answer. Two rings, nothing. Dammit.*

"Hello."

I froze on the other end; I was going to have to tell him about Nate, if he didn't already know. "Hey, Dad."

"I guess you got your letter?" he asked.

"Yeah, I got it. Do you know what it's about?"

Now, there was silence on his end and I knew without a doubt he did.

"Yes, I know. I've known since you left."

"How did you—"

"Kane," he said, cutting me off. "He told me everything."

Why am I just finding out about this? "Why didn't you tell me? And why the hell did Kane tell you? I asked him to keep it to himself."

"Well, Caroline, when you just packed up and left without giving anyone, especially Kane, time to process, I guess telling me everything was his way of getting over you."

"Dad, you knew I wasn't staying. He knew I wasn't staying. Are we really going to have this conversation again?"

"Caroline, you put us through hell by leaving. I love that boy like a son and to see him spiral downward was almost as hard as watching you leave me, again."

We had had this same conversation or some version of it at least twenty times before and, frankly, I was tired of explaining myself.

"Dad, I said I was sorry. I'm not the same girl that left you high and dry when Mom died. I've called you every day, you've come to visit me. I don't know what else you want me to do. This is my life. I grew up, moved away. I can't stay with you forever."

"I know that, I do, but dammit, Caroline, you broke that boy's heart, his spirit, by running away like you did." His voice got deeper with his impending anger.

"Dad..." I didn't know what to say to him. I knew that I had done all those things. My heart was breaking too, but people moved on. I had moved on—I had tried to move on.

CHAPTER 36

Kane

aby, what's wrong?"
A tender hand came up my arm as I lay on my
side in bed. *What was wrong with me?* I turned
over in bed, meeting a concerned face, green eyes, and
black hair. Every morning for two months, I expected to
see a mane of blonde hair, liquid blue eyes, but every
morning it wasn't, because she was gone.

"Hey," this one said, leaving a soft kiss on my lips.

The month following Caroline's untimely departure,
I was a fucking mess. I drank every night until I couldn't
see straight, I missed work. The only thing I did do, was
sing my ass off. I killed it every night on stage. Two
months after she left, I was making my way out of a
drunken haze. It helped to know that we would begin
touring with 4 Alliance in the coming weeks. They had
signed us on for a grueling seven-month tour that started
in December and went through June. At least something
good came out of that fucking horrible night.

Two nights after Caroline left, I told B everything
about Nate. If I couldn't be with her, if she didn't want to
be with me, then I needed something to occupy my time,

and putting that jackass Nate behind bars was my distraction. I was right. It didn't take me long to find a girl, then another. The problem I had was getting them to testify. That's where Caroline came in. She and Janet were the only ones who could testify, along with me. Everyone else was too drugged to remember anything.

That's why I was back in town. I was going to finish what I had started and put Nate fucking Rodgers away. Unfortunately, I didn't think this out clearly enough, because now I was going to have to see Caroline. I had made sure that our days to testify were different. Thank God, the judge's daughter loved ONS. But that could go only so far.

This was a small town with not many places to hide. I didn't know how I was going to react if I saw her.

I could deal with overhearing about her in the bar. I had moved on like she told me to do, via her father. There was a woman in my life, the one who was staring at me right now. We weren't exclusive, and she knew that. It was convenient for us. We were familiar to one another—a "sex-only relationship" we called it. Chloe and the rest of Fallen were also on tour with us—4 Alliance had gone through Baltimore first and found them, and they, in return, sent them out here to hear us.

The rest of the bands were somewhere in New Jersey. Chloe and I were going to meet back up with them tomorrow after I made an appearance in court. We were taking advantage of the night away from everyone. Fucking in a crowded tour bus, in only a twin size cubby was not ideal, for anyone. Although I thought Reece benefited, since he was across from us. His little curtain rarely stayed closed.

"Kane, you in there?" Chloe asked, grabbing my chin and turning my head, so I was forced to look at her.

"What do you want, Chloe? I'm here," I quipped.

She sat up from the bed, turning away from me. "Whatever, Kane."

I didn't mean for it to sound so harsh. So I sat up, scooting so I was behind her, engulfing her in my arms. I moved her long, sleek, black hair away, and rested my head on her shoulder. "I'm sorry," I whispered in her ear, which made her scrunch her neck up.

"Really? What's going on with you? You've been tense and just weird the past few days. This doesn't have anything to do with that girl Kitty, does it?"

My jaw clenched and my pulse jumped at the sound of her name. "Fuck no, she's a bitch," I said, annoyed.

"Uh-huh." Chloe turned in my arms, facing me. She wrapped her long Amazon legs around my waist, waiting to hear more.

I let my hand run up the pale, tattooed skin of her arm. "I mean it. I said I was done and I am."

"Good, because I like our arrangement. Not that I'm being possessive, but I really enjoy our *time* together and don't want it to end."

"Neither do I."

I wasn't lying. I really enjoyed Chloe, all of Chloe. I had moved on. Caroline wasn't going to ruin me again. I had gotten my life back. Was there a massive hole in my heart? Hell, yeah, there was, no thanks to her. Was I going to let myself fall for her or anyone ever again? Fuck no! I learned my lesson.

∽∾∾

I walked into the courtroom earlier than necessary, my hair, slicked back, parted, and off my face, thanks to Chloe's handy work. She had also helped me buy a new outfit, something more presentable for the courtroom than jeans and a T-shirt with the sleeves cut off. Chloe was not only great in bed, but damn, could she dress a guy. I looked like I stepped out of some GQ photo shoot.

We sat next to each other during the whole preceding. It was long and boring, but when it was my turn to approach, I laid it all out there, every last detail. While I explained what I had witnessed and all the women whom had told me they thought Nate had taken advantage of them, he just sat there—twenty-some odd feet away from me, with that smug look on his face. He acted like I was telling a joke, chuckling to himself. *The fucker really thinks he's untouchable.*

My hands were fisted so tightly, I was sure my nails were drawing blood in my palms. I tried to ignore him, answer the questions being asked, but the only thing I could think of, was punching him in the face. B was there for support. I told him last night when he came to the house, that I wasn't doing this for his daughter anymore. I was doing it to stop Nate from hurting other women. I had found seven in the month after Caroline left, and I had a feeling that was just the tip of the iceberg.

When it was over, when I was done saying all that I needed to, I walked by him, my fists still clenched. I needed to get out of there before I turned back and decked him. His lawyer was telling him something, and he again chuckled to himself. They had played up the fact that I was playboy, a womanizer, but I made sure to explain that I never had to drug or rape a woman to get lucky. I was a step past him when I heard, "Meeeooooow."

I turned back, lunging for him, pushing his big shot lawyer out of the way. I had been able to keep my cool through the laughing, chuckling, even the way he smiled as I explained what I walked in on in the woods. But meowing? Fuck, no. Even if I was over Caroline, that had done it. She was still B's daughter and, even though I hated her, he loved his little girl, and I wasn't going to let this fucker get away. I was an inch from his face, my hands gathered up in his shirt, when everything seemed to click. This was what he wanted. He wanted the reaction, and he wanted to rile me up. *Fuck if I was going to let that happen.*

So I released his shirt, even smoothed it down for him. I smiled in his face, tapping his chest. "I hope you like getting fucked in the ass. I heard rumors that good-looking, fit, young men like you are a high commodity. Oh and you were a cop on top of that. They are going to fuck your brains out. Keep practicing your cat call, though, it needs to be a little bit higher in pitch."

I patted his shoulder one last time then walked away. I grabbed Chloe, pulling her close under my arm.

She wound her arm around my waist as we walked away. "Are we going home? I need you to take me home. That was—Kane, I think you need to start wearing a suit more often. Oh, God, I want to rip it off with my teeth," she said as we exited the courtroom.

I stopped at the front doors of the building, took her face between my hands, and kissed her like I've never kissed her before.

CHAPTER 37

Caroline

He was kissing her like he used to kiss me. She was the same tall height as him. He held her close. Their bodies seemed to fit together perfectly, his tattoos mixing with hers. They looked like a rock star couple.

I was coming out of the restroom when I spotted them by the door. I hid behind a huge pillar a good distance away. I didn't realize that seeing him, let alone seeing him with another woman, a woman who he clearly had feelings for, would be so, confusing. I had gotten over him. I had moved on, went on dates, even slept with a few, but fuck if it wasn't hard to see him all over someone else.

They ended their "bedroom kiss." I called it that because it was the kind of kiss that usually led to having your clothes tossed all over the floor. Kane was facing away from me, so I couldn't see his face, but I saw hers and knew exactly what she was feeling and who she was. Chloe, from Baltimore, the front girl from Fallen.

I was so wrapped up in watching them, I hadn't realized someone was standing behind me. I jumped and squealed a little as a hand tapped my shoulder. I whipped around to see a girl who I also recognized immediately as Nate's younger sister Piper. I quickly turned back, praying that I hadn't called attention to myself. Thankfully, I hadn't. Kane and Chloe where already out the front door and heading for his truck.

A sigh of relief escaped me as I turned back to Piper. "Piper, holy shit, you startled me," I said, still clutching at my racing heart.

She looked older, more mature than the last time I had seen her, which coincidentally was the night her brother drugged and assaulted me. She stared at me, and I wasn't sure if she was going to punch me for ratting out her brother or start crying.

"You remember me?" she asked, surprised.

"Yeah, why wouldn't I?"

"I just thought that since Nate, and then you left that...well, I just thought you'd hate me and forget who I was," she said looking at the floor.

She definitely wasn't going to punch me. Her eyes were filled with tears as she tried to stay strong in front of me.

"Hey, hey, hey. Piper, it's not your fault. Your brother has some serious issues."

She laughed, a few of the tears ran down her cheeks. "He's only a half-brother. The only thing we have in common is my mother," she said.

"Oh, I didn't know that," I said, fully taking in the woman she was turning into.

I could remember Piper and her friend all gooey-eyed over ONS, young and seventeen. I remember her begin carefree and running along the lake, the guys running after her and her friends. That carefree girl that sat happily on JJ's lap the night that Nate drugged me. That girl wasn't standing in front of me. I felt bad that she had somehow lost her innocence, her glow. The whole mess with her brother was taking a toll on her.

She wiped the tears away and continued on. "My mother sent him here to live with his drunken bastard of a father when he was thirteen. She couldn't control him anymore. I was three when he moved away, and only a few years ago was I able to see him. I knew about him, of course, and when I was fourteen, I think, my mother let him back in my life because she thought that he had gotten his life in order—you know, becoming a cop and all. She thought it was 'safe' to spend time with him. If I had known he was doing—I just want to say that I'm sorry."

I felt bad for her. She was going to be linked to that bastard for the rest of her life, not only by blood but, in this small town where everyone knew everyone's business, it was sure to follow her.

"Piper, you don't have to be sorry for him."

"Well, he's never going to say it, so I will. I know it doesn't mean much coming from me, but you at least deserve an apology."

"Damn," I said, crossing my arms in astonishment. "You really grew up, didn't you?"

She had more class in her pinky finger, than Nate did in his whole body.

"So everyone says. I know this is a little forward but, do you still keep in touch with…" She pointed in the direction that Kane and Chloe had been standing.

I followed her hand, realizing who she was talking about, and shook my head. "Nah, not really. I only know what my father tells me, and usually that's not more than a, 'He's alive and well.'" I bit down on my lip nervously. *How the hell did this conversation end up here?*

"I'm sorry, I didn't mean to pry. What have you been doing since you left? Rumor has it you're in New York again," she asked, saving the conversation.

"I am. I got a really good job, my dream job, actually."

"That's great! I'm moving up there myself. I have no clue what I'm going to do, or where I'm going to stay, but I saved up some money and I'm going to try to start over. I need out of this town, fast."

Something I could definitely relate to. A strange feeling came over me, a feeling that I wanted to ball her up, put her in my suite case, and take her with me. I had been where she was at, needing to start over, run away from the past. *We are kindred spirits, and you know what? Fuck it.*

"Are you serious about moving to New York?" I asked, apparently taking her off guard.

She looked at me, clearly puzzled. "Yeah, as soon as this trial is over, I was planning on jumping in the car and leaving it all behind."

She was serious. I could see it in her green eyes. "Well, I have a huge place, an extra bedroom and bathroom that are just collecting dust. You're more than welcome to it until you get your own."

She stared at me in disbelief. It was obvious that her childhood hadn't been lollypops and rainbows. This was an opportunity for her to make something of her life, and if the huge smile on her face was any indication, she was going to say yes.

"Are you serious, Caroline? I don't want to put you out."

"As a heart attack. Plus I always wanted to have a little sister."

She covered her gaping mouth with her hand. "But you don't even know me. Why are you doing this?" she asked, removing her hand.

Why? Because I was her five years ago. "Piper, don't ask questions, just say yes. I'm going to get you out of this small town nightmare. Pretend I'm your fairy God sister."

She laughed at me, covering her mouth with her hands again.

"Well?" I asked, waiting for an answer.

"Yes! Yes, please take me with you."

I wrapped my arms around her, as she did the same. Yeah, this was a good idea, added bonus—she was another distraction.

I was so thankful to have met Piper in that hallway. Together she and I made our way into the courtroom. I saw where my father was sitting and went right to him. I sat down, Piper still at my side. We sat through the trial until I was called up.

"Dad, I can't do this," I said clutching at his arm.

"Yes you can. You'll be fine. Kane did great up there and I know that you will too. Just think how many women you are helping by doing this. Do it for those women who don't have a voice, who weren't as lucky as you were to have someone come and save them," he said, squeezing my arm.

My father was right. I was so lucky to have Kane there. For if he wasn't, I would have been one of the silent women cowering in the courtroom with nothing to add. I was saved and it was my job to speak for them, since they couldn't.

I smiled up at my father with added strength. As I made my way up to the stand, I clenched my hands into fists to keep them from shaking. After being sworn in, I glanced up and got my first look at Nate in almost a year. He looked the same. Not much had changed about his appearance. He snickered to himself then nodded up at me.

He was disgusting, and now I had all the ammunition I needed to tell my story.

e⁄ɔe⁄ɔ

I came home late. The condo was lit up. Every lamp was on and the music was blaring. I tossed my bag on the island in my over-the-top kitchen, in my over the top condo, the company had put me up in for a year. Glancing in the family room off the back of the kitchen, I saw Piper dancing around the room. She had been living with me for almost two months and I still couldn't help smiling when I walked in and saw her. She was just what I needed—a burst of fun in a life that had gone very stale.

Piper turned down the music and stared at me from the couch. "Caroline! You're home, before seven. Is everything okay?"

I kicked my heels off, ran to the couch, jumped over the back, and stood next her. "Well, turn the music back up. We're going out tonight and I need to get in the mood."

She looked quizzically at me. "We're going out?"

"Yup, another one of Sarah's great ideas."

Jumping off the couch, Piper pulled at her sweatshirt and PJ pants.

"I gotta get ready—and so do you!" Grabbing my hand, she pulled me off the couch and down the hall to our, I mean my closet.

e⁄ɔe⁄ɔ

Dressed and ready to leave, I sat on a stool in the kitchen, wishing that I could just stay in and catch up on sleep. Work had been crazy and I knew that Sarah thought that getting out and meeting guys was stress relieving, but it wasn't for me. Sleeping in my cozy bed, now that was stress relieving.

"Do you know what Sarah has in mind? Oh, I hope

she's taking us to Blue. I heard it's amazing and if we got the chance to meet Spencer Salvatore, I think I could die happy."

Piper was thoroughly enjoying her time in New York. She was working for a fashion magazine and, although she started out in the rack rooms, she was quickly making a name for herself with all the right people.

"I'm not sure where we're going. She said it was a small bar that had live music. So, unfortunately, I don't think you're going to meet Mr. Millionaire tonight," I said, tossing my unruly mane of hair around.

"Hey, I'm going to get into that place, you just watch."

I nodded while patting her shoulder. "I know you will."

∽∂∽

This "small" bar was anything but. Sarah had us front and center, and the band that was currently on stage was making my ears bleed.

"Can we go now?" I asked, leaning across the table.

"No, we cannot leave yet. My brother told me that we have to stay and see the next band. He thinks they're really good, and I trust my brother, plus, if he likes them, than that means they look good too. Haven't you ever fantasized about being with a rock god? I know I have and if there's a chance I can make that happen tonight, I'm *going* to make that happen."

"You don't even remember the band's name?" Piper asked.

"Details. All I needed to know was that they're hot," Sarah said, brushing Piper off.

I rolled my eyes and sat back in my chair. I had been with a "rock god", or so he called himself. Was it amazing and everything that Sarah was probably fantasying about? *Um that's a big fat yes*. Not that she would know that about me. She was usually too busy talking about herself to even ask about my past conquests. Trust me, I did not mind.

Piper on the other hand learned that lesson a day after she moved in. She asked me about Kane. I quickly put her in her place and told her never to speak of that man in my presence.

Talking about Kane was bad, but when I saw him at Nate's trial with Chloe, I nearly lost it. The flood of emotions I had been suppressing came rushing back. Then finding out that it had been him who managed to get others to speak out about what Nate had done to them, then my father giving me the whole Kane-saved-you-you-should-feel-lucky speech was icing on the cake. The stone wall I had put him behind crumbled the day of Nate's trial. Thankfully, I was safe in New York, hundreds of miles away from Kane.

"Sarah, what are you—never mind, I don't want to know."

Danny was standing behind me. The three of us turned to see his finely dressed physic. He was leaning on the back of my chair, a few fingers grazed my bare back, which sent a chill down my spine. *That's different*. I sat all the way back and looked up at him.

"You two need some alone time?" I asked, winking at Sarah.

He placed his hand on my head, pushing it down so I couldn't look up at him anymore. "Ha-ha, Caroline, that's funny."

"I don't think it's funny. I could use some alone time with hunky boss man," Sarah said, licking her lips seductively.

She was hopeless and clearly didn't have a problem

putting herself out there, even if the guy was not interested. Trust me, that didn't stop her.

"You guys care if I join you?" Danny asked. "My
friend's running late."

"Not at all, pull up a chair," I said, scooting mine
over to make room for another.

Piper elbowed me, nodding in Danny's direction.
"That's your boss?" she asked under her breath.

I nodded and laughed to myself as she leaned back in
her seat to get a better look at him.

Finally the loud, almost ear splitting music stopped,
a DJ from somewhere, jumped up on stage as the band
was leaving. "Let's hear it for Lonely Girls. Come on,
give them a hand!" the DJ yelled, clapping as he spoke.

"I'll be back. I'm going to stretch my legs," I said,
standing from the table.

As I walked away, Piper jumped into my seat and
began introducing herself to Danny.

My bad. I'm not the best at that. I shrugged the guilt
off and went in search of the restrooms. I walked down a
long corridor, passing a group of giggling girls and a
couple getting a little too familiar against the wall. Suddenly, I felt like I was back at my father's bar. Chuckling
to myself, I kept on, stopping at a room filled with furni-
ture and instruments. The sign on the door read VIP, but
there was no one to be found. I peeked my head in
searching for a bathroom, looking left then right. It was
on my glance to the right that I felt all the blood drain
from my face.

There staring at me was a guitar, red and glossy, with
black scripture all over it. I was back at my father's bar.
This was clearly a dream. I had had this dream many
times since leaving Maryland. I'd walk up to Kane's guitar, he'd come up behind me, holding me in his strong
arms.

After that, I'd usually wake up. But I was not waking up. I was still standing in the back of some bar, looking at his guitar, JJ's, Trent's base, Reece's drum sticks on the table, along with Aiden's distinct handwriting on a stack of papers. I backed away from the door, hitting the wall behind me. I had a one-track mind, I needed to get Piper and get out of there, fast.

I ran back to the table, sitting in Pipers empty seat. I looked around the bar again, noticing this time the shirts that some people were wearing. At every glance, I saw an ONS T-shirt on an excited fan. This couldn't be happening. Of all the bars, in all the places, he was here in New York, at this bar, where I happen to be sitting front and center. *How did I not see all this before?*

"Caroline, you okay? You look like you've just seen a ghost," Sarah asked from across the table.

I grabbed Pipers forearm, taking her off guard. "We need to go." The urgency in my voice made her scrunch her brows at me.

"What's going on? Are you all right?" she asked, turning to me, concern washing across her green eyes.

"She just realized that the man whose heart she broke is in the same building as her. Isn't that right, Cuz?"

I quickly, stood from my chair, to find JJ standing behind me. Scanning the area, I let out a relieved sigh when I saw that he was alone.

"You know this guy?" Danny asked standing as well.

"She's my cousin. Of course, she knows me, you hipster asshole," JJ said, getting in Danny's face.

I moved to stand between the two of them, a hand on either's chest. *This isn't happening. It can't be happening.* My old life couldn't mix with my new one. The only exception was Piper. She was the only one who knew about both.

I turned, facing Danny, JJ at my back. "Danny, I'm

sorry. My cousin doesn't get out much. He's a bit one dimensional."

"What the fuck, Kitty? One dimensional?"

JJ took my arm and spun me around, so I was forced to see his face, forced to accept that this wasn't a dream and that he was standing before me. "JJ, that's my boss. I'd appreciate it if you didn't get me fired," I said under my breath.

He pointed aggressively in Danny direction. "I don't give a fuck who he is. He clearly thinks he's going to get a piece of your ass, and I swear to God, if you let a fucking hipster weasel his way into our family, I'm going to lose it!"

"Dude, what the hell is your problem?" Danny said in his own defense.

"As long as you're not sleeping with my cousin, then I don't have a problem with you. What I do have, is a *major* problem with you," he stated, addressing me.

I walked with JJ, following him to a hallway in the back, per his request. Twisting my face in sheer frustration when we get to our destination, I considered knocking my cousin out right there. I clenched my fists and tried to rein in my temper. Just as I was un-scrunching my eyes, I saw a mess of red mohawked hair coming my way. Behind that, a tall biker looking guy, ready to kill, and a beautiful vampire with long ink colored hair, all walking my way, and all of them looking pissed off.

A wave of worry washed over me as they all surround me. I chewed on the inside of my lip, as the four, very handsome, and even angrier men enveloped me.

"Well, well, Kitty's come back to play boys," Reece said, licking his lips.

"I didn't know you guys were playing here. I swear," I said, trying to stand my ground.

"Caroline, all jokes aside, Kane doesn't need this shit

tonight. You should leave," JJ said, getting right to the point.

"Are you kidding me? Did Kane put you up to this?" I asked.

"No, he doesn't know you're here. He's been out all night, but he's on his way. Kitty, you fucked that man up beyond recognition when you left," Trent said, leaning against the wall while cracking his knuckles.

"Well, he looked okay the day at Nate's trial. Seems Chloe's been taking good care of him. Who cares if he sees me? He's obviously moved on."

I mean shit, it hurt like hell to see him that day with her, but he looked happy, and that's all I wanted for him when I left.

"Yeah, right, just like you with the hipster?" JJ stated.

"He's not a—JJ, he's my boss, I'm not screwing him. He just showed up here tonight. Aiden, come on, you can't agree with them." I watched as he nodded in agreement with the other guys. "Fine whatever, I'll leave," I said pushing through them and making my way back down the hall way.

We had made a few turns and, for the life of me, I was so angry that they were making me leave, I must have made a wrong turn. A silhouette of a couple was flush against the wall. Their moans and wet kisses echoed off the enclosed walls.

"Get a fucking room!" I yelled to them.

Their movement stopped as my heels clicked on the concrete floor while I continued down the hall. The exit out of the rat trap of a back bar was on the other side of them. The closer I got, the more I could see. Her tit was clearly hanging out from her very low cut shirt, and her hands were resting on the man's chest. I rolled my eyes as I was passing them. It was dark and the pulsating lights on the other side of them, made it impossible to put a face to the bodies, *thank God*.

"Keep it classy, guys. Small tip—find a hallway that doesn't fucking lead to the bar," I said as I walked by them.

I was just at the entrance back into the bar when something made me stop. I didn't know how to describe it. Was it a memory, a smell, the way the lights bounced off the walls? But I stopped in my tracks. I stood there, my feet glued to the floor. My heart rate accelerated, a butterfly sensation coursing through my body.

"Caroline!"

That voice, I know that voice! I spun around to see the silhouette I had just passed separated. Only one figure was standing in the darkness. I knew without a doubt who it was. Energy like that didn't radiate off of just anyone. Stepping out of the darkness and into the light, Kane stood not even five feet in front of me and fuck he looked good.

CHAPTER 38

Kane

Fuck, you smell good, baby," I moaned into Chloe's neck. She always smelled like heaven. That bitch Caroline might have fucking ruined me, but having my nose in Chloe's neck was a close second.

"Kane, you have to get back there with the guys. You're already late." Chloe tried to push me back, but I knew she couldn't say no, so I kept on, pulling her shirt and bra down to sample her. She was fucking putty in my arms.

"Don't care, I need *this* right now," I said, as I got lost in her smell again, this time, tasting the sensitive skin under her ear as well. *I needed this right now to keep my mind from wandering down a road that always left me fucking pissed.* In the beginning, it was once an hour, then it was once a day, then once a week, and finally I began to feel free again. But every once in a while I'd see someone or—like this week—remember the best fucking weeks of my life. The weeks that I let myself love like I've never done before, the weeks we finally gave in.

Chloe was my distraction. If I was with her, then I wouldn't think about *her*. I knew the guys could tell.

They'd start babying me, tiptoeing around, keeping their usually loud mouths shut. It typically lasted no more than a few days before I was back to normal, but fuck if those days weren't torture.

I had no clue where she was or what she was doing. My plan to not see her during Nate's trial had worked, and now that that fucker was put away, I could solely think about my music and how fucking rich I was going to be. I talked to B as often as I could. He'd never tell me about her and I sure as hell didn't ask, but every once in a while he'd slip up. He'd let it slip that her job was going good, or that she had a roommate. I'd never learned more than that, though. B knew, hell he saw how bad it got when she left, and I think he was trying to protect me.

What I had with Chloe was nothing like what I had with her. Chloe and I were cut from the same cloth. She didn't want more than sex and neither did I. I had pledged to myself that I wasn't going to let emotions ever come between me and a woman again. My heart had been torn out, ripped up, stepped on, and fed to the wolves. Simply put, I was fucking done with love and relationships. *It sucks*.

"Get a fucking room!"

The clicking of heels coming our way made us pause and pull apart. I couldn't see who spoiled our little moment, but it was obvious they were pissed and still coming our way.

Chloe pushed me back a little. Her hands on my chest, she watched as the person walked by, while I held on to her hips, pulling her closer, not giving a rat's ass who saw.

"Keep it classy, guys. Small tip—find a hallway that doesn't fucking lead to the bar."

Damn, that sounded—

I pulled back from Chloe as she fixed her shirt.

"Come on, let's go," she said, whispering in my ear from behind.

"Yeah, I'll be right there. I'm going to get a drink. Tell the guys I'm here?" I asked.

"Sure," she said, nibbling on my ear lobe before leaving me in the hallway.

The angry woman who had walked by us stood at the archway that led into the bar. The lights were zooming around, illuminating everything. A mane of curly blonde hair was lit up and I knew without a doubt it was *her.*

"Caroline!" I yelled down to her.

I meant only to get her attention, but fuck I was livid. This bitch showed up here, tonight of all nights, in the bar I was playing at? *Hasn't she done enough?* I walked up to her, as she turned to me.

"Kane," she said, a quiver to her voice. "How are you?"

I didn't know what to say. *Not true, I know what I want to say, but it might be borderline verbal abuse.* So I kept quiet and just stared at her. For the most part, she looked the same.

The year apart hadn't changed much. She was clearly eyeing me up as well. Where she hadn't changed, I had. My hair was shorter, I had bulked up, gotten a few more tattoos, and, thanks to Chloe, I had some fucking nice clothes. Her eyes were on my bare arms, like they always had been. The dark blue of her eyes got big as she raked over them.

"Still like what you see, huh?" I finally said, clearly taking her off guard.

Her brows scrunched and her mouth got tight. Her petite frame tensed up like it used to when we fought, her own sculpted arms went to her hips in anger.

"I see you're still a jackass."

"Hey, you told me to never change. I took that advice. Seems to be working out for me," I said, throwing her words back at her.

"Kane, don't do this. Can't we just talk?" she asked.

"Talk? Now you want to talk? A year after you leave me high and dry, a year after you tell me you love me, a fucking year after you broke my heart!" I yelled, closing the distance between us.

"I'm sorry, I didn't mean—"

"Don't, just don't," I said, holding my hand up to her. "You made up your mind the minute you got that phone call in my room. You ran from the best fucking thing in your life and now you have to live with your decision."

"I made the right choice."

There she was again, same old shit.

"Really? You did? Because you sound like you're trying to convince yourself just like you used to. I told you before, Caroline. I know you and you haven't changed at all, but I have," I said with ice on my words.

"That's rich! I don't think you've changed at all. You're still a man whore. Jesus, I found you in a hallway, with someone's tit in your mouth! Oh yeah, you've really changed," she spat back at me. Taking a calming breath, she regained her composure. "Anyway, I'm glad you're doing well for yourself. You seem so happy with Chloe and that's all I ever wanted."

Her whole demeanor changed, her body weakened, her arms dropped from their perch on her waist. She wouldn't even look at me. Her attention seemed to be on a spot at her feet.

"I am. I am happy. What about you?" I asked.

Some of me wanted to know that she had moved on and was happy too, but then, another sick part of me wanted her to be miserable. I wanted her to be as fucked up as I was.

"Me? I...umm. I'm...I'm good," she said.

Fuck another lie. Her brows scrunched together a she tried to shrug the question off.

"Kane, I—" She paused, chewing nervously on the inside of her cheek.

The same energy that had flowed between us over a year ago was still there. Her incredible smell drifted under my nose, as she messed with her hair and closed the distance between us. That smell had always driven me wild, and fuck it still did, but I knew better now.

She was the one who reached out for me. It was her shaking hand that levitated near my arm. Her trembling fingers that grazed up it. Her eyes were fixed on her own hand as it went up my arm. Did it feel good? You have no idea how good. I watched her, her body almost touching mine. It wouldn't have taken much for me to lean down and kiss her full lips as she looked up at me. I had to end it.

"What are you doing?" I asked, looking straight into her eyes, standing still as a statue.

"I'm sorry," she said quickly, taking her hand from me, taking a step back, and tucking her arm protectively around her body. "I didn't mean to—I'm—I'm sorry. Tell the guys I said bye and have a great show. Good luck with everything."

"Wait!" I didn't know why I did it. I just knew that I didn't want her to leave yet.

CHAPTER 39

Caroline

What the hell did I just do? I couldn't stop myself from touching him. It still felt like he was mine, and I could touch him whenever I wanted to, but again I was wrong. The closer I got to him, the more anxious I became. Not the bad anxious, the good kind, the kind that left your skin tingling with excitement. The moment my fingers found their way to his flesh, it took my breath away. I was entranced in him, like I used to be and, God help me, I didn't want the feeling to go away.

He smelled amazing. He looked like he had stepped out of some rock star photo shoot. His hair was shorter but, damn I still wanted to get my fingers lost in it. My breathing was heavy and I found it hard to even remember to take in air.

As I touched him, got closer to him, it was like everything finally clicked in my head. I hadn't realized it before because I tried to fight it. I told myself, hell, I *lied* to myself, using my mother as an excuse, his past—anything I could. I didn't want to admit that I could have these types of feeling for someone, and have them last.

The I'll-do-anything-go-anywhere-be-anything kind of feelings.

I destroyed a man so I wouldn't destroy myself. *News flash, it didn't work.* I was a mess. A. Hot. Fucking. Mess. It took being close to him again to realize I had been a zombie the whole year. I was going through the motions, pretending I was happy, pretending I had moved on, but I was miserable. I had been miserable since the day I left. I just pretended I wasn't.

Two minutes ago, I realized that I didn't want to move on. My fingers on his skin, my eyes locked on his, I felt alive and I wasn't pretending. I had been a fool to leave. I had ruined us and I felt like crap for it. I wanted to go back and change everything.

"What are you doing?" he asked, not moving and keeping his eyes tight on mine.

Instantly, I recoiled, knowing I had gone too far, and stepped over an invisible boundary I had put in place over a year ago. "I'm sorry." I took a steadying breath. Now that I was apart from him, I could see clearly, breath evenly. "I didn't mean to—I'm—I'm sorry. Tell the guys I said bye, have a great show. Good luck with every-thing."

I backed away from him, then turned to leave him again, because I was afraid I'd try to jump in his arms if I stayed standing there.

"Wait!"

I was a few steps from him when he called. I closed my eyes, as my heart sank a little. *Was he calling me back?* I wanted that to be true, but I also knew that I had ruined it for us and the chances of him taking me back were slim to none. I turned back to him again, wanting to run in his arms, but I just stood there.

"You fucked me up," he said, filling the hallway with his stern voice.

"Kane, I—"

"You fucked me up, but I got over you. Now you're standing here, close enough to touch, looking at me. Fuck, Caroline, you're looking at me like you want me to throw you up against that wall and pretend like this past year never happened!"

"How many times do I have to say I'm sorry? I know I hurt you, I know I fucked up. And yeah, I do want you to throw me against that wall. Is that what you want to hear? Do you want to hear that I'm miserable? Because I am. I've been on autopilot since the day I got on that plane," I yelled at him.

"Good. At least you cared a little bit," he bit back.

"Of course, I cared! I still care," I screamed at him.

Something changed in me. Maybe it was him believing that I didn't care, that I never loved him. I knew that I had to show him and the only way I could do that was to let it all go. I walked back to him, standing toe to toe. I looked into his eyes, seeing the confusion in them. I could only guess that he was thinking that I was going to punch him or smack him. Instead, I grabbed his shirt, pulled him down to me, and finally tasted his lips.

At first he held back, keeping his lips sealed, but it didn't last long. He opened up to me. His arms went around my waist, pulling me closer. For the first time in a year, I was alive, happy, excited—you name it, but the fact of the matter was, I was alive again.

So when he grabbed my arms and pushed me away, keeping me at arm's length, it was as if he slapped me across the face.

"I can't do this," he said, letting me go and fisting his hands in his hair.

"I know, I shouldn't have but—"

"Yeah, you shouldn't have," he said, taking another step back.

"Kane, listen, I know I screwed up but—"

"I can't do this with you," he growled.

"Oh, you can't do it with me, but you sure can do it with every other woman who throws themselves at you."

I regretted it the minute I said it, *Fuck my loud mouth.*

"Pretty much, Caroline. I could do this all day with anyone *but* you." He stood there another second. "I have to go. Thanks for confirming why I never let things go any farther than just sex."

With that he turned away from me. Leaving me standing there fuming.

"Wait a minute! Kane, stop!" I yelled at him.

"What do you want from me? Haven't you ruined me enough? Let me go, Caroline," he said frustrated and turning back to me. "Just let me go."

The thought of him walking away and possibly never seeing him again put a fear in me like I'd never felt before. I couldn't let him go. Fuck, I needed him. I'd pushed it down, but now it was obvious. I still loved him and I wasn't walking away. I wasn't giving into fear this time.

"I want you. I want all of you. I'm so sorry I walked away. If I could go back—" I couldn't hold in the few tears that spilled from my eyes as I told him the truth.

"Caroline, you can't go back. And did you ever think that maybe I don't want you anymore? Did you ever think that I don't want to go back?"

I shook my head at that. "You're a fucking liar," I said through gritted teeth.

"It doesn't matter if I am or not. I have to go. Chloe's waiting for me," he said with an evil grin.

I knew he said it to get me riled up, and guess what? It freaking worked. Determination was one hell of a motivator. I wiped the tears from my eyes, held my head up,

220   M. E. Gordon

and went straight for him. Pushing his chest aggressively so he was forced to move against the wall, I had him pinned there like he had done to me so many times before. And just like him, I didn't give him the chance to move.

I knew what he liked, so my hands slipped under his shirt and up his chest. My mouth inches from his, I grabbed his belt and pulled him closer to me. His hardness pressed against my abdomen. He was lying, or he was on some serious male enhancement drugs.

"I bet you haven't been this hard since the day I left," I said provokingly.

A sexy smirk appeared on his face as he chuckled down at me. "And I bet you haven't felt anything this hard since the day *you* left," he whispered back. "What are you trying to prove? That I'm still attracted to you? I can tell you that answer right fucking now. Damn right, I'm turned on at the sight of you, the smell of you, the sound of you. You got me. I haven't been this riled up since you told me you loved me."

He still wasn't touching me, and I so desperately wanted him to touch me. I needed him to touch me.

"Caroline!"

I couldn't look away from him, but I still knew who called my name. It was Danny, standing in the arch way of the hallway.

"Seems you're being paged," Kane said, cocking his head as he looked up from me to Danny.

"Kane." As if on cue, Chloe stood at the other end of the hallway. This time, I did look away from him, seeing her standing there, tall, beautiful, and beckoning Kane toward her. I felt inferior of the connection she now had with Kane.

"Caroline," Kane said, reaching for the hand that I still had clutched to his belt.

He took that hand and I reluctantly let go of his belt. I wanted him to hold my hand as tight as he could. I wanted him to squeeze it, give me a sign that he still cared, but he didn't. He just let me go.

"I'm not giving up. I made a mistake, and I'm going to make it right, I'm going to make us right again."

He leaned over, smiled, then slipped away from the wall and headed toward Chloe.

"If you run, I'm running after you," I called to him.

He stilled in front of Chloe and faced me, a genuine smile on his face. "Then make sure you have a good pair running shoes," he said, before wrapping an arm around Chloe's shoulders and leaving the hallway.

CHAPTER 40

Kane

I'm glad you stayed strong throughout all that," Chloe said as we stood outside of the room where our instruments sat.

"Yeah, me too," I said opening and holding the door for her to go through.

When we walked in, the guys were sitting around the room talking. I recalled Caroline saying to tell the guys bye for her, which meant, they knew she was here and didn't tell me.

I'm not a fucking baby. I can handle seeing her. I did handle seeing her.

"Where were you two at? Fucking in the bathroom again?" Reece asked, wiggling his eyebrows.

"I'm going to the bus. I'll see you guys later tonight," Chloe said, kissing the corner of my lips and squeezing my ass as she walked out of the room.

I waited until she was out of the room and the door was securely closed behind her, before I started in on the guys. I knew they kept it from me because they thought I was still that broken-hearted idiot that nearly drank himself under the table. *But not anymore.*

"So, I saw Caroline a little while ago," I said nonchalantly.

"You what?" JJ asked, whipping his head in my direction and spilling his beer.

"I saw Caroline." I made my words slow and even, so I knew that they had heard me clearly.

"Dude, don't even sweat it. He's a fucking hipster and who cares if he's her boss? She's probably just desperate," JJ said from across the room.

"I really wanted to go fuck that guy up when he was feeling up on her," Trent said as he cracked his knuckles.

"Yeah, I even wanted to jump in. No one who looks that ridiculous should be touching our Kitty. Fucking tight shirt, suspender-wearing, wanna-be hipster. He even had a fucking beard and slicked back hair, like he's a fucking heartthrob or something. You're way better looking, dude, I'd fuck ya. Kitty's head's fucked up, if she's had to downgrade to ass hats like that," Reece said confidently.

"She's dating that guy?" I asked, getting off track.

I didn't want to think about something like that, but fuck if it didn't bother me now that it was brought to my attention.

"Looked like it, bro. She played it off like it was just her boss, but they seemed pretty cozy, and he stood up for her when I approached her earlier," JJ said.

"Why the fuck didn't any of you fuckers tell me she was here?" I asked frustrated and feeling like a child kept in the dark about important information.

"This is why," Aiden said, flicking his hand at me.

"I don't know why you think I'm going to go back to the way I was when she left. It's been a fucking year. I'm fine!" I spat at them.

Aiden stood, throwing his hands up in the air. "See? This is why we went to her and asked her to leave, so you wouldn't act like an ass before we go on stage. Or worse when were up there performing and you see her in the crowd sucking face with that fucking hipster asshole."

JJ nodded. "Kane, we knew this might happen, that eventually you'd run into her. We were just trying to prolong the inevitable. We didn't want to see you hurt again. We care about you, man. We just—"

I cut JJ off. "No, that's not why you did it. I'm not a fucking idiot. You didn't want me to see her so that I'd be fine to perform tonight. You fuckers have such little faith in me, it's disturbing. You think I'd ruin myself again for her? I'll tell you right now, that's not fucking happening. I'm fine. She had me against a wall, hand practically down my pants, and her sweet-ass lips on mine, and I'm still here. So stop treating me like some broken-hearted kid and lets go bring the fucking house down tonight!"

My four closest friends stared at me a second.

"She really have her hand down your pants?" Reece asked.

"That's all you got out of that? For fuck's sake, Reece." He kept staring at me, waiting for an answer. I couldn't help it. A smile cracked the stern look I was trying to maintain as I shook my head in disbelief. "Yes, her hand was down my pants," I said rolling my eyes.

"And you didn't—I mean, you just—"

"I walked away," I said, confirming what he was trying to say.

"You're serious?" Trent added.

"Yes, why is that so hard to believe?" I asked the four of them.

"Are you sure it was Kitty you were talking to?" Aiden asked.

"I'm pretty sure it was her," I said.

"It couldn't have been, because Kitty looked fucking

hot as shit tonight, and no one can say no to her. There's no way," Reece challenged.

Hearing him say that made me think back to how she looked in that hallway. It was dark and even though I tried not to look, I knew exactly what they were talking about. She had looked amazing, and of course I wanted to rip her dress off, or shove it up her thighs, but I didn't. I didn't because I knew what would happen if I did. I'd go right back to a year ago. I'd go back to needing her more than air.

I had wanted to believe what she had told me tonight, but I knew better now. I had given everything I could to her and what did I get in return? A broken fucking heart. So even though she looked good enough for me to push my anger aside for her leaving, it wasn't enough for me to forget how it felt when she walked onto that fucking plane and didn't even look back. That was the reason why I walked away. I walked away because I didn't ever want to feel like that again.

"Well, it was her. She seemed to want me pretty bad, but I left her standing there. Now can we forget about all of this and move on?" I asked.

"If you're good, then we're good," JJ said, speaking for the guys.

"Just promise us that you're not going to go ape shit when you see her sucking face with someone other than you, and by that I mean, don't get pissed at me when I'm kissing those sweet, sweet lips," Reece said through a sneer.

"Whatever, dude," I said, reaching for my guitar. "Let's get out there. Chloe's waiting in the bus. I want to finish what we started earlier."

That night I had to perform with Caroline sitting front and center. She was with a group of friends, one of them looked strangely familiar, but I tried my best not to pay any attention. JJ was right. The guy who called for her in the hallway was sitting closer to her than necessary, but just like always, she didn't seem to notice. She was the kind of girl who never noticed when guys were looking at her. She didn't notice when she was tossing out mixed signals like free shots. *And right now is no different.*

When we finished up and left the stage, I hadn't seen her, figuring that she had left as the crowd clamored around the stage. I went straight to the bus, needing Chloe to take my mind off the feelings that I thought I had done a good job of suppressing.

I could deny it to the guys all day long, tell them that I was fine. I was a professional, I could get through it. I had said no to her, but I was still affected, whether I wanted to be or not.

The rest of the guys were hanging out at the bar, getting drinks and "making friends." While I hurried to the bus in the back, I was dumbfounded to see Caroline pacing by the bus. She hadn't seen me yet, so I stopped and watched as she kicked some rocks with her six-inch heels. Her hands kept nervously messing with her wild hair, and she looked like she was talking to herself.

Maybe she had changed, because the Caroline I met a year ago was a smart-mouthed, confident, piece of work. This girl looked nervous and awkward. A guy came outside from the back door, tossing some trash in the dumpster. It made a loud crash, making Caroline stop pacing and look around. Her eyes locked immediately with mine and she froze by the bus.

"What are you doing?" I asked, walking across the parking lot toward the large tour bus that I was praying Chloe was still in.

"Nothing," she said nonchalantly.

"Caroline, why are you here? You shouldn't be here.

Aren't your friends and boyfriend wondering where you are?" I asked, still making my way to the bus.

"Boyfriend? No, he's not my—I'm single, very single. I'm not seeing anyone," she said, shaking her head.

The part of me that was happy about that information was quickly ass whooped by the part that knew thinking of her as available was a bad fucking idea.

I finally made it all the way over and stood across from her. *Damn, she looks sexy in her little black dress and strappy looking heels.*

I was pretty sure they were the same ones she had on one night when we were together. I could distinctly remember those heels digging into my sides before I ripped them off.

"So, now what?" I asked, crossing my arms over my chest. Maybe I only did that because I knew she had a thing for my arms and, quite frankly, I liked seeing her squirm.

"I told you. I'm running after you. Simple as that, really."

Her posture straightened as she spoke, as if she was trying to puff herself up and look strong and stern. It was fucking adorable—and extremely dangerous.

"Well, I hate to burst your little bubble, but I'm going in that bus right there to have sex and try to forget that this—" I said, pointing between the two of us. "—ever happened. Now, if you'll excuse me, I have some things to take care of."

I summoned a charming smile and walked up to the door of the bus, which she was standing next to. My hand on the handle. I was a step and a door away from forgetting this night ever happened.

"I'm going to say this one time," Caroline said as she moved like her pet namesake, blocking the door behind her.

"What could you possibly have to say?" I asked, letting the door handle go.

"You said that you knew me. Well, I know you, too. I know that you're pissed and you're an asshole—"

What the hell is she getting at? "You know, if you're trying to be nice or if this is some sick apology, it's not working," I said, huffing in frustration.

"It's not an apology. I've already said I was sorry. This is me making a promise—"

"A promise? To what? Torture me for the rest of my life? No thanks, I'm peachy fucking keen without it."

"Will you just shut up and let me finish?" she hollered back at me. "I promise that I'll let you take whatever time you need to get over yourself. I also promise that I'll be there, waiting for you to get your fucking head out of your ass and see what's in front of you."

I couldn't help but let a haughty laugh escape me. *This is fucking ridiculous.* "You're wasting your time. I see what's in front of me and I'm pretty sure I'm over it."

"See? I don't think you are. I'll leave you to…Chloe, is it? My guess is you're not going to be able to take care of business as usual, so, maybe I'll see you back in the bar," she said snidely before patting my shoulder and walking away.

What the fuck just happened? The parking lot was empty. The only sound was her heels clicking on the asphalt, getting softer the farther away she got. I didn't know if I was pissed or turned on. *Fuck, it's a little of both.*

That night, it took a hell of a lot longer to get "ready" to spend quality time with Chloe. *Fucking Caroline ruined me again.* There was no way she was going to be able to keep her word and "run" after me. So I felt pretty confident that she wasn't going to be fucking with my head anymore.

Like I had said before, I didn't expect her to keep her word. I expected her to go back to her life, her "dream job," her friends. I sure as hell didn't expect to see her at a bar in Boston a week later. We had finished our set. Chloe was busy with some ass who managed to weasel his way into her good graces. She had texted me, saying she was going to the hotel that 4 Alliance had gotten after the show. I took the opportunity to hang out at a bar with the guys, until the stage crew had everything packed up.

It was a small town bar off the beaten track from the midsize outdoor arena we had just played at. When I pushed the doors open, I was hit with the sight of Kitty sitting on Trent's lap, the rest of the guys in chairs around the table, beers in their hands and women at their sides. I stood in the doorway and, for a split second, I wanted to stay, but then I turned around to leave. *I cannot do this tonight*.

"Kane, look who tracked us down!" Trent yelled across the small bar.

Caroline sat there on his lap, a stupid grin on her face as she tried to look innocent, but I knew she was anything but.

I nodded over, knowing that if I didn't go, I'd get shit because I had already told them I was fine and over her. The last thing I needed was them babying me again.

CHAPTER 41

Caroline

I drove all day to get to Boston by the time their show started. I was kind of appalled at how easy it was to get back stage. I had called JJ and asked him to meet me, discreetly.

"Kitty, what are you doing here? Don't you have to work or take care of your hipster boss?" he asked cheekily.

"Ha-ha, no. I'm here because I made a promise to Kane."

"You made a promise? To do what? Bug him to death?"

"No, you jerk! Listen, I know I fucked up. I fucked up big time. I know that now. I'm just sorry it took all this bullshit for me to realize it."

"So…you're here…because?" he asked, confused.

"I'm going to win him back," I said confidently.

"You're going to *what*?"

I spoke slowly. "Win him back."

"No, no, no, not happening," he said curtly, shaking his head and waving his hands in front of him.

"Listen, JJ," I said, getting in his face. "I'm here

now. I'm going to be everywhere you all go until he real-
izes how ridiculous he's being. Seeing him with Chloe,
seeing him with anyone is fucking making me want to
pull my hair out! I'm not going anywhere. I want to be
with him. I miss him and I'm going to do whatever I have
to, to make him realize it."

"Caroline—Fuck! All right, listen. I get it, you want
him back, but you broke him. He is broken and it's going
to take more than you following us around to make him
see that you're not going to leave him again. I can't
watch my friend go through that again. None of us can. I
need your word that whatever fucked up shit that was going on in your head before is done. I need to know that
I'm not going to have to watch him climb out of that
ditch again."

My cousin loved Kane like the brother he never had,
and if he was willing to give me the go ahead, I *knew* I
stood a chance to get Kane back.

"JJ, I was scared before. I was scared of loving him,
I was scared of being my mother, and I was scared of letting my life slip out of my grasp. I was terrified I'd be
like her. But I was *turning into* her. Leaving him was
slowly turning me into her. I was lost, dead. I could feel
myself drifting, but it took seeing him at Nate's trial to
wake me up and, once I was awake, I guess fate did the
rest. Running into you guys at that bar saved my life. I've
never felt more alive or determined."

"You're really serious?"

"Yes, I'm serious! God, why doesn't anyone believe
me? Piper didn't, you don't. Hell, Dad didn't even believe me."

I was getting more frustrated the longer I stood there
with my dense cousin.

"Piper? Is that—"

"Nate's little sister. I know. Don't even start with

that ass. I know Kane was behind it all and I have yet to even thank him—"

"Is she with you?" he asked, cutting me off and looking over my head.

"Who? Piper?"

"No, 'she' your father. Of course, Piper."

"No she's at home—Oh, right. She's my roommate. After Nate's trial, she moved in with me."

He paused a moment, clearly thinking something over in his head. "All right, I give you my blessing to win Kane back—on one condition."

"Are you fucking kidding me, JJ?"

"Nope," he said, making the work pop.

"Okay, what's your 'one condition'?"

"Next weekend, and every weekend after that you're trying to 'win' Kane back, you bring Piper with you," he said casually.

I stared at him, skeptically looking him over. *What the hell? Nope, not going there.* "Fine, I'll bring her with me whenever I can. She's a pretty popular girl in the fashion scene nowadays, and she might not be able to come all the time."

"Don't care. No Piper, no Kane," he said, crossing his arms defiantly.

That's it, enough of this craziness. I took hold of his ear and tugged him down to my level. Being as he was a good head taller than me, he had to bend over quite a bit.

"Now you listen here," I growled. "I'm done being nice. I said I'd try to get Piper here, so you're going to have to be okay with that. I *need* to get Kane back, and I'm tired of fucking around. Do we have an understanding?" My words cut through the air like a samurai's blade, leaving no room for a comeback.

"Yup! I got it. Can you let go of my ear please?" he begged.

"Oh, sorry," I said, releasing his ear. He rubbed it and then started laughing loudly. "What's so funny?" I asked.

"Fuck, I've missed you, Cuz," he said through a huge smile.

"I missed you too," I said as I hugged him around the neck.

So, all of that, led me here, sitting on Trent's lap waiting for Kane to walk through the door. The guys didn't take as much persuasion as I thought. Trent asked for a great big bear hug, Aiden asked me to kiss his cheek and Reece...well, Reece was Reece. I shouldn't have expected anything less from him. His one request to get in his good graces was to let him feel up my boobs. Since I loved Kane, and I was willing to do whatever I could to get him back, I let bozo the clown get to second base.

When Kane finally came into the bar, I immediately felt the tension. My body stiffened on Trent's lap.

"Kitty, you okay?" he asked, resting his head on my shoulder.

"I'm scared Trent. What if he doesn't give me a chance?"

He smiled at me. "Then he's stupid."

I turned from Trent to watch Kane. He looked like he was going to turn back around and leave, so again, I stiffened on Trent's lap.

"I won't let him leave," Trent whispered. "If he leaves then you'll leave and I don't want you to leave. None of us want you to leave."

I smiled at him and began to relax, knowing that I had him and the rest of the guys on my side. "Thanks, Trent."

"Kane, look who tracked us down!" Trent yelled across the bar, stopping Kane from leaving. "See, Kitty, he's not going anywhere," he whispered in my ear.

"Thanks."

"What is she doing here? And why is she sitting on your lap?" Kane asked, obviously refusing to talk directly to me.

"I'm willing to share tonight, if you want her to sit on your lap, bro," Trent said, before taking a sip of beer.

"You can keep her," Kane said, moving to the other end of the table.

The rest of the night, I sat talking and laughing with the guys just like we used to do. It was fascinating how easy it was to slip back into the roles we had before. Except for Kane. He just sat at the end of the table, drinking his beers and acting like he wanted to be anywhere but where he was. Three hours later, the guys all got up to go smoke again, knowing that Kane didn't, and JJ, who had been Kane's distraction, left with some girl. I knew that that was my chance to talk to him alone. He must have sensed it because, as soon as the door to the bar closed behind the guys, he stood from the table. Finishing his beer, he placed it on the table and went to leave.

I jumped up and blocked him before he could make an escape. "Where are you going?" I asked.

"Anywhere where you're not," he said, buzzed by the beer he had been downing all night.

"That's mean," I said, crossing my arms.

"Yeah, it's downright criminal. Almost as mean as leaving me standing in an airport and walking away like you don't give a fuck," he said, leaning over, getting in my face.

"Well, clearly you still have some issues," I said back at him.

"Ya fucking think?"

"I do, but your little pissy attitude isn't going to scare me away. How's your mom doing?" I asked smiling up at him.

I was grasping at straws here, but I knew the only way to get back to him was to be there, showing him I wasn't leaving, that I wasn't running anymore.

"My mom? You're that desperate that you're trying to make small talk about my mom? She's fine," he snapped back. "How's your mom—oh, right, you don't talk about her because you pretend she didn't exist. I forgot."

"Low blow, asshole." *Okay this was going to take more self-restraint than I had planned on.* I wanted to reach up and slap that smug smile off his face, and I almost did, but I reigned in my temper and took a calming breath. "Whatever, Kane, you can say what you want. I'm not going anywhere."

"I will, thanks. And more importantly, if you're not going anywhere, then I am." He moved the chair under the table to walk away.

"Where you going?" Trent asked, coming back to the table, a strong whiff of smoke following him.

"Back to the bus," Kane said.

"I can't let you do that," Trent retorted, cracking his knuckles like he always did.

"Why the fuck not?" Kane asked, just as the rest of the guys walked in and stood around the table.

"You see, me and the guys were talking outside, and we all agree that you're being a wee bit of a dick to our Kitty. She came all this way to get you back and, dude, we don't want her to leave."

"Too fucking bad. Let me remind you that not only did she leave me without notice, she left you fuckers, too. Why the sudden change of heart? Last week you were trying to keep her away from me and now, all of a sudden, she's allowed to sit on your lap," Kane said, pointing at Trent. "You two are best fucking buddies again," he said to JJ. "You're protecting her like she's your kid sister." He pointed to Reece. "And you—I don't even fucking know why you're letting her be here."

"Oh, she let me feel her tits so, we're good," Reece said with a shrug.

"Are you fucking kidding me?" Kane screeched. He glared at me. "Well, shit, if you're here to get me back, having Reece cozy up to your tits *really* makes me believe you."

"Reece, you asshole!" He was next to me, making it easy for me to punch him in the arm.

"Oh, Kitty, you have no idea how long I've waited for you to do that," Reece said, holding his arm as an adoring smile spread across his lips.

"You're a sick fuck, Reece, and you, thanks for turning my friends against me," Kane snapped at me.

"I didn't turn them against you. Stop being so dramatic, you big baby. I told them exactly what I told you."

"I'm outta here. I can't listen to this madness any longer. I'll see you guys on the bus," Kane said abruptly, walking from the table and out the door before any of us could react.

I hit Reece again before I ran after Kane. I was going to make him see that I had changed, that I was wrong before. I crashed through the door and looked left then right.

The buses were in an empty parking lot next to the bar. I caught a glimpse of a figure walking between them and knew it was him. I raced over, making it to the buses as he was opening the door to one of them.

"Kane!" I called to him.

"Fuck, Caroline! Leave me alone," he said, looking up at the sky.

"No, I will not leave you alone. I will not stop until you give me what I want," I said, crossing my arms and stamping my foot.

"And what is it that you want?" he asked, whipping around.

His eyes were wild with rage but I had to press on. "I want you. I want you to forgive me. I want you to kiss me. I want you to believe in me again."

I dropped my arms. The seriousness of what I had said made him let go of the door. The anger was gone from his face, replaced with confusion, misery, and I knew that I was the one who made him that way. I was the one who broke him, and now I had to fix him.

CHAPTER 42

Kane

Why is she pushing this? The more she talked, the more I wanted to give in and shut her out all at the same time. *Doesn't she realize that I'm fucked up now, that she fucked me up? Maybe—*

The door to the bus rattled and swung open, almost hitting me in the face. I moved out of the way as a man who could have been my twin stepped out off the bus.

"Hey, man! You're that lead singer. I love your stuff, it's really good."

My twin stood there nodding at me like an idiot. Same height, same build, same hair, same blue eyes.

"Thanks, what the fuck are you doing on my bus?" I asked.

"Oh, I thought—" He pointed nervously back to the bus. "Um, she said we could come back to the bus. I just followed directions, you know what I mean?" he said, winking so Caroline couldn't see.

Yeah, I fucking knew what he meant. When Chloe told you to do something that involved sex, you did it.

"I guess you're next up! Threesome? Totally hot, bro. Would you mind if—"

"Are you fucking kidding me?" I hollered, cutting him off.

"No, not at all. I could totally help you out," he said, taking a step to get a better look at Caroline. "You can have Chloe. This petite blonde over here is—Damn, bro, please let me help you out," he said, biting his fist while undressing Caroline with his eyes.

"Did he just..." Caroline asked, pointing at my doppelganger, but keeping her eyes on me.

For some reason, I laughed, which only seemed to piss her off more. She closed the space between her and my twin, getting right up in his face. He was taken off guard and smirked down at her.

"All right! Looks like she's in," he said, nodding over at me.

You know what? I'm just going to sit back and see how this one plays out. I took a step back and held my hands up, giving him the go ahead.

Caroline was watching as I backed away. I thought she might say something harsh, but she seemed more hurt than anything. Served her right. Her eyes shot back up to my twin. Her expression changed as she studied his face. A ping of jealousy pricked my heart as I watched the two of them have a moment. It was like I was watching our first night together, the way she was looking at him, *fuck!* Suddenly anxious, I rested my hands on my hips. I wanted to turn away. I didn't want to see her with—

"What's your name?" she asked, all breathy.

My dick twitched at the sound and the memory that came with it.

"Justin," he said, while he rested a hand on her jean clad hip.

His hair fell out of place as he looked down at her. Hers fell wild and free down her back, lightly moving in the warm breeze. Her body was flush with his, and I

fucking began to lose it. For someone who wanted to win me back and wanted me to trust her, she was out of her fucking mind. *Like I said before, she must have multiple personalities and I can't fucking keep track anymore.*

I had to turn away when she got on her tiptoes. Her lips, *the lips I was...am...obsessed with,* were centimeters from my twins. Fuck if I wasn't jealous as hell. I was looking at the ground when I heard a loud thud and a groan. The next thing I knew, my twin was lying on the ground, his hands covering his balls, and his face was red as fuck.

"Don't you ever assume that I would sleep with you, you sick fuck," she yelled over his crippled body.

"Damn, bitch, I think you broke my balls," he said, writhing on the ground.

"Good! Maybe next time you'll think twice about treating women like your personal fuck toys," she said, kicking him in the ass for added effect.

I was pretty sure my mouth was a gape. The old Caroline was here in full force. If this scene didn't remind me of our first encounter, then nothing would. Most of me wanted to forgive her, but I needed time. I still didn't believe that she had gotten over her shit and showing up for one weekend wasn't going to instantly make me change my mind.

My twin was still wincing on the ground when the door to the bus opened up again. Chloe stepped out in a rush in her underwear, which shouldn't even be called underwear because it wasn't covering anything. Her black lace bra was so tiny her tits would have fallen out if she leaned over.

"What the hell is going on out here?" she asked as she stepped onto the asphalt. "Dustin! What the hell happened?" Rushing to him, she petted his head like a dog and knelt over him in her six-inch heels.

"It's Justin," he said in a brittle voice.

"Oh sorry, Justin. What the fuck happened?" she asked, standing and looking between me and Kitty. As her eyes fell on Caroline, realization hit her and her questioning stopped. "What is *she* doing here?" she asked suspiciously.

This was way too awkward even for me. The girl I was fucking, standing next to the girl I was trying to get over, by fucking the other girl—like I said, fucked up.

"Kane, I thought we talked about this?" Chloe said, bringing me back.

"Listen, Chloe, I'm not here to step on your toes. What I'm here to do is get Kane back," Caroline said.

"Well, he doesn't want you back. So maybe you should just run along, I hear you're good at that," Chloe clipped.

Kitty's eyes turned wild as Chloe spoke and, for a second, I thought that she was going to jump on Chloe and start a cat fight—which would have been hot.

"You don't know what you're talking about," Caroline said.

"Oh, don't I?"

"No, you don't, because you have no clue what Kane and I had. You have no clue because you've never been loved by anyone the way Kane loves me—"

"Loved, past tense," Chloe corrected her.

Caroline whipped her head to me, as Chloe laughed in the background. She was looking for me to confirm out loud what she and I knew, that I did still love her, but I didn't, because I was fucking scared of telling her the truth and her breaking my heart again when she left me. So I just shrugged my shoulders.

"You're a fucking liar."

She stepped over my twin who was still in the fetal position on the ground and wrapped an arm roughly around my neck. Pulling me down, she crushed her lips to mine. I wanted to push her way, and then I wanted to pull her closer and, just as I was going to wrap my arms around her waist and take what I had dreamt of for over a year, she pulled back. Her hand cupping my cheek, she looked at me, seeing deep into my soul like I knew only she could.

"Tell me you don't still love me," she said, still peering into me.

"I—I—" I couldn't form a sentence if my life depended on it. I also couldn't take my eyes off of her.

"That's all I needed. I'll see you next weekend," she said with a promise in her voice. "Bye, Chloe. He's all yours, although I'd keep your other play toy around. I don't think Kane will be *up* for anything tonight."

Fuck, I forgot how spicy that girl could be.

I watched as she walked back across the empty parking lot toward the bar, and a little bit of my heart mended as she sauntered off. *What the fuck am I going to do now?*

"Kane, you just let her—Oh, fuck, you still love her, don't you?" Chloe said, covering her mouth in shock as she watched me watch Caroline walk away. "Don't you remember what she did to you? She left you, Kane! She fucking left you," Chloe shouted.

"I know she did, Chloe, I was fucking there. But shit, she's here trying to—"

"Nope, you can't let her back in. Who gives a fuck if she's here? She's leaving tomorrow to go back to her 'dream job,' remember? Hell she left just now!" Chloe was in front of me now, pulling on my jacket and rubbing my chest with her hands. "You did everything for her, Kane, and she still left you," she said, caressing my face.

"I got it, Chloe," I said, stilling her hand on my face by placing mine over it.

"Good, now let's go work her out of your system."

She kissed the corner of my lips then turned and pulled me along with her. "Thanks for the shag, Dustin, I'll text you next time I'm in town," she said, walking over his body.

"It's Justin!" he moaned from the ground.

"Oh, sorry," she said before going up the stairs, with me in tow.

CↃCↃ

I could strangle Caroline right now. We'd been at it for more than an hour and—nothing, absolutely nothing!

"I know a guy," Chloe said, coming up for air.

"*What*?" I asked frustrated that my dick had betrayed me, again.

"A guy. I can get some viag—"

"Fuck that! I don't need fucking Viagra!" I sat up, pulling a stray cover over my traitor of a dick.

"Well—"

"Chloe, just shut up," I said, hitting my head against the back of my cubby.

She looked at me through hooded eyes. "Okay, okay. I have that guy's number, maybe he can bring a girl and we can, ya know, get you inspired."

"I don't think so. It's freaky enough that guy looks just like me. I can't go there." I moved from the cubby and pulled my pants on. "I'm just going to go for a walk. I'll be back."

"Kane, don't. Stay with me." She was up and tugging on the waist band of my jeans the moment I had them fastened. "Let me prove her wrong. She's wrong. It's not because of her you have this...issue."

Maybe Chloe was right. Maybe it was all in my head. I needed to prove that I was over kitty, that she didn't affect me.

But hell, how am I supposed to do that? I'd be lying my ass off.

Teeth nibbled on my ear lobe as soft fingers slipped down my pants. I guess my dick decided to wave the white flag, because as her finger teased the tip, it jerked to life.

"See? I told you," she said triumphantly.

"I'm still taking that walk, and you should shower, you smell like my doppelganger."

She sat back down on the bed. "Fuck you, Kane!" she spat.

"When I get back," I said, pulling a shirt on.

She didn't need to know that as her fingers caressed me, I was thinking about blonde curls and liquid blue eyes. All that mattered was that it worked. If I had to imagine Caroline to fuck Chloe to get all the tension out of me, then that was what I was going to do.

ഗ്രെ

My traitorous friends had been in contact with Caroline now, more than when we all lived in the same town. Any given night on the bus, I'd find at least one of them talking to her on the phone. When they'd ask if I wanted to talk to her, I gave them the finger and walked away. They might have been able to forgive and forget, but I hadn't. I hated that they were all getting along. They were my friends, and they were supposed to be on my side not hers. The abandonment had fueled the fire during the week, so that when she would show up, I'd be good and pissed.

The second weekend that Caroline tracked us down, I still gave her the cold shoulder. I wasn't able to joke or even talk to her yet, and I refused to call her Kitty, but fuck if it didn't put a smile on my face, for a second that is, when I saw her sitting on Trent's lap before we pre-formed.

Now, four weeks in, here she is again. Somewhere in North Carolina at a large festival, I walked around the bus to find everyone sitting in lawn chairs around a fire pit. I did a double take. A pretty girl with long black hair and bright green eye's sat on JJ's lap and I swore it was Chloe, but the girl didn't have any tattoos or look like an Amazon warrior princess. I looked again and matched her up to the friend that was sitting with kitty the night we had our reunion.

She had looked familiar even then, but I pushed it out of my mind. Now that she was here I was going to figure out who she was. If anything, it was going to take my mind off kitty, and these days I was desperate.

"Kane, there you are! We were starting to think that those girls ate you alive," Aiden said laughing.

"Close, but I got out before they ripped my shirt all the way off," I gesturing to the tear on the collar of my shirt. I had just gotten done with a "meet and greet" with the 4 Alliance guys, before either of us went on stage later tonight.

The manager of the tour insisted that we sit with them during their meet and greet, because so many fans were asking for us, so the guys and I took turns and tonight happened to be my night.

For once, Caroline wasn't on Trent's lap. She was in her own chair on the other side of the fire pit. Her usual wild hair was pulled back, giving a clear sight of her long neck and toned shoulders. She had a simple, tight T-shirt on and jean shorts that should be illegal. I didn't want to be around if she stood up because I knew the bottom of her ass would be peeking out.

She never dressed up when she showed up every weekend. She didn't have to and, fuck, that bothered me.

"I see someone let the cat back in," I said, gesturing to her. She smiled across at me, shoving her middle finger up in the air. "One of you should really think twice before letting her back here. She's messing with your game."

Reece adjusted himself in his chair, "No, dude, she's messing with your game, not ours,"

"I got a ripped shirt, and a hundred screaming women that say otherwise."

"Yet, none of them are here, are they?" Reece said, looking around for those hundreds of screaming women I just referenced.

Sitting back in his seat after craning his neck, he held up a hand. Caroline's hand met his as a sexy grin spread across her face while she high fived Reece.

"Whatever." I grabbed an extra chair and placed it next to JJ. Caroline was still across from me. The fire made it hard to see her clearly and I was grateful. If it was hard to see her, then, hopefully, it was hard to see me, I didn't want it to be obvious that I was staring at her every two seconds.

"Who's this?" I asked, looking at JJ and the girl on his lap.

"This is Piper," the girl said, turning to get a look at me.

"Piper? Wait a minute, you're—"

"Nate's little sister. You got it," she said, wiggling on JJ's lap a little.

"Oh, why are you here?" I asked curiously.

Was this some sort of sick joke from Nate, to have his little sister flaunt around and remind me of that jackass?

"It's nice to meet you too," she said with an attitude that usually lead to me getting slapped.

"Dude, chill the fuck out. She's here for me," JJ said,

finally speaking up and holding Piper a little tighter around her waist.

Piper scrunched her brows together, looking confused and a little pissed all at the same time. "No, I'm not. I'm here with Caroline, mini vacation."

"Eh, tomato, tamato. You're here and on my lap. You're happy, I'm hopeful. Why argue?" JJ said, sitting up to kiss her blushing cheek.

I remembered her from the bonfire at the lake. She was glued to JJ that night and it seemed he was pretty fucking hung up on her now.

I shook my head and sipped on my beer, but then I caught a glimpse of Caroline on the other side of the fire. *Fuck she was hot.* She shouldn't have that much fucking pull over me. My dick twitched every time I looked at her.

"Bro, just give in already," JJ said, leaning behind Piper to whisper to me.

I adjusted myself in the chair, praying I hadn't just got caught staring through the fire to where Kitty sat, legs crossed under her as she sipped on a beer.

"Give in to what?"

"What else does she have to do? I'm fucking tired of watching you watch her like you're deciding which part of her you're going to lick first. It's disturbing, dude. I know your escapades with Chloe are…well, you haven't fucked her all week and that's a record for you two," JJ said.

"First off, I don't trust her. Second…" I had a second, I did, but my attention got pulled as the fire popped loudly.

I turned from JJ to make sure I wasn't on fire as sparks flew all over the place, that's when I saw it. Kitty jumped out of her chair, hopping up and down and brushing her hands over body. She yelped loudly, swiping at the ashes that landed in her lap. Facing her chair she bent over and wiped away the ashes that had landed on the flammable fabric.

Fuck, I was right, those shorts should definitely be banned. There was no fucking way she had underwear on. One move to the side and I was positive I was going to see everything.

"Are you fucking kidding me!? This is my only shirt!" she hollered, turning back around.

There was a bunch of little holes in her T-shirt. Along with the holes, it was black from the ashes she had wiped off. She looked over the fire at Piper then at me. A sneaky smile pulled at the corner of her lips and I knew I was fucked.

She reached for the bottom of the shirt and I swear it was in slow motion. Her stomach contoured as she pulled up, her tits bounced, when she hit them with her hands. And when she tossed the ruined shirt at Reece, he stared at it like it was the first time he'd ever seen a naked woman. Once he turned his eyes from the shirt, he reached out to touch her. I heard a chuckle come from my right. Piper was trying hard to keep it together, then she buried her head in JJ's chest.

"Go get me a shirt," Kitty demanded, hitting Reece's hand away.

His eyes were zeroed in on her tits. "Fuck that, I don't have any. You're going to have to rough it, Kitty."

"Here, Kitty," Trent said, pulling the shirt off his own back off and tossing it to her.

"Thanks, Trent," she said, holding it. Taking it under her nose, she inhaled deeply. "Why do you always smell so good?" she asked with a dreamy look on her face.

"Blessed."

He stood from his seat. She walked over to him, her hands resting on his chest. Trent was even taller than me.

He had broad shoulders littered with tattoos, a shaved head, and a chiseled face. Kitty looked even smaller standing before him. I had to look away as she hugged him and left a soft kiss on his cheek. Her breasts flattened on his chest, her bare stomach met up with his.

"Fucking ridiculous," I mumbled under my breath.

"You say something?" JJ asked.

"No," I mumbled, taking a drink of my beer.

"Hey, you guys have about half an hour till you're on," Dave, the stage manager said.

His headset on and clipboard in hand, he stopped in his tracks the minute he saw Caroline. He moved the headset from his ear and stationed the clipboard to cover his junk. He openly gaped at her, the shirt Trent had given her was still in her hand. So there she stood in her lacey bra and shorts for everyone to see.

"Dave, put your fucking eyeballs back in your head," Trent said demandingly over Kitty's head.

"What the fuck, Dave?" Reece asked. "Don't look at our Kitty that way. Only we can do that. When's the last time you got laid, man?"

He bit down on his lip, "Sorry, it's just—I can't take my eyes off her."

The urge to get up and punch him for looking at her like...like a piece of perfectly cooked meat that he was going to devour...was messing with my head more than usual.

I didn't know what the fuck came over me. Maybe it was the fact I could see his dick pushing against the clipboard from where I sat, or maybe it was the way he was licking his lips, but I fucking lost it. I stood and got in his face. "I think you should leave," I said, looking down at him.

He adjusted his headset with one hand, keeping the clipboard securely over his dick.

He shook his head. "You fuckers always get the good pussy."

"That's because we're rock stars, benefit of the job."

He turned his head and looked at Caroline again as she started to put on the shirt that Trent had given her. I followed his gaze and we both watched as she grabbed her shirt from Reece. She stood in front of her chair, staring across at Dave and me.

"I thought you were done with her," he said, eyeing me up.

"Get the fuck out of here, Dave. We need to get ready. We'll see you back stage in thirty."

I followed his gaze again to Caroline, who was still attentively watching.

With a cocky air about him, Dave made in intentions clear. "Fine, but while you're up on stage, I'll make my move, since you're done with her and all. She's free game now."

The guys who worked on the tour were known for picking up scraps or promising girls things, and Dave, manager and all, was no exception.

"You can try, but that girl is fucking hard for my dick and my dick alone. Good luck, though," I said, clasping his shoulder. "Oh and you might want to wear a cup if you're going to try anything while we're on stage," I said before leaving Dave, the guys, and Caroline and heading for the stage.

I got around the busses and out of sight. Leaning against one, I rested my head and stared up at the darkening sky. Hands in my hair, I wanted to punch the bus behind me, get the frustration out. I didn't want to admit it, but I was falling under her fucking spell again. I shouldn't have cared that Dave or anyone was interested in Caroline. She wasn't mine any more. *I don't want her…I don't want her…fuck, I want her!*

CHAPTER 43

Caroline

Thursday, eight o'clock at night, and I was stuck in the office again. The large table in the conference room was filled with stacks of papers. Hours-old Chinese containers and coffee cups sat atop the span of papers.

Ever since I got home from last weekend's adventures to win Kane back, I couldn't stop smiling. He had stood up for me and, damn, if I didn't want to jump over the fire and do all sorts of naughty things to him. My plan to get him back was working, slowly, but it was working. He was on his way back to me. I had one weekend left before their tour was over.

JJ and the guys were keeping me informed of all their moves so I could be with them. It didn't surprise me that once the tour was over they were headed to LA to work on an album. They were going to sign with the same record label as 4 Alliance and they were through-the-roof happy. It was happening for them. They'd be playing those big arenas Kane had always known they were destined to play in.

Their last stop put them in central Maryland, home

field advantage. All I had to do was make it through all the papers in front of me, and I'd be free to head home—

"Caroline, you okay?" I looked up from the file, that I had been reading and re-reading for the past twenty minutes, to find Danny looking at me.

"Yeah, I'm good. Why you ask?"

"I don't know. You've been frozen in that position for, like, a half hour, and you're smiling at the files. No one smiles at files, especially these," he said, holding one up.

"Oh, sorry, I didn't mean to get side tracked. I just had a really good weekend and can't stop thinking about it."

"That weekend have anything to do with that guy I saw you with at the bar a couple months back?" he asked, raising a brow.

"How do you—"

"Sarah busted you. I got stuck in the elevator with her, and she told me everything," he said.

"What do you mean everything?" I asked, sitting up in my chair.

"She told me you were trying to win the guy back or something. Caroline, can I give you some advice." I nodded for him to go on. He sighed. "Don't you think you're wasting your time? I mean, you've been going to see him every weekend and then coming back here to work. Listen, I heard that the ups were going to offer you a senior position and a team to work under you. If you keep running after this guy and acting all starry eyed, they're going to give it to someone else."

That information hit me like a freight train—a senior position, a team of my own.

I slumped back in my chair, "Are you sure?"

"Yeah, I am. They called me in a week ago to give an evaluation. Caroline, I saw you with that guy. He didn't seem interested. I know that sucks, but I also know men who *are* interested."

Okay, this conversation just took a sharp left. "What are you trying to say, Danny?"

"I'm saying why the hell run after that asshole when you have someone here who's going to—I mean—"

"Danny," I said cutting him off before it was too late "Don't do it, please don't."

"Caroline, I like you. I mean, I like you as more than a coworker."

Fuck, he went there. You know, when it rains, it fucking pours.

It took me all night to get it through Danny's head that there was never going to be an "us," that I was in love with Kane, and I'd stop at nothing to get him back. I meant it too, and I would do what I had to. The opportunity to run my own team would be amazing, but I'd take Kane over it. I didn't before. I left him, thinking this was what I wanted, and I was wrong.

The coming weekend was my last chance to get him back. He was leaving for LA. I had this job opportunity. If he didn't want me after this weekend, I'd have to take the promotion, put Kane on the back burner till I came up with another way to get him back.

c⁊ɔc⁊ɔ

I was late getting there. Crowds of people clamored around the gates that led to where the busses sat. Fitting that it was the biggest stage the guys had played on. That I had seen at least.

The gate was guarded by a guy who worked for the stadium and he wasn't letting me through. I called all the guys, but no one answered. It was my last chance, and I couldn't even get back to see him. *Fucking, pouring rain.*

I thought that I'd have to leave and find another way, until the door to the bus the guys rode on, opened up. I stood straighter to see who was coming out of the bus. The sight of Kane always made my heart pump a little faster and my knees get wobbly and, even after a year, time hadn't changed the way I reacted to him. A bunch of girls who were standing next to me started screaming and pushing on the gate once he was in sight. He turned at the screams and waved over to them—us.

"Kane," I yelled over them, gaining his attention.

He took another look in the crowd and took a few steps toward the gate. The moment his eyes landed on me, he shook his head in disbelief.

"Kane, tell him to let me in," I said, not having to yell as much because he was closer.

"Do you know this girl? Should I let her in, she keeps saying she's family," the guard asked from the other side of the fence.

I saw it in his eyes, that little snicker and evil grin. "No, I've never seen her before."

"Are you kidding me, Kane?" I yelled at him.

"Yeah, man, I've never seen her, better keep her locked out. She looks like the kind of girl that'd claw her way through that gate. I'd also keep you're balls away from her knees if I were you." Winking at the guard, he nodded my way, waved, and kept on walking to the back stage area.

"You're an asshole, Kane! You're just going to leave me here!" I screamed.

He stopped mid step and looked back at me. Straightened his body, held his head up, and continued walking. *Fuck, he wasn't over it.* Here I was thinking I was closer to getting him back and he just walked away, leaving me, like I left him.

The door to the bus opened again and a skinny, red-mohawked man came sauntering out. Again the girls next to me went wild. Unlike Kane, Reece walked over to the gate, grabbing hands and signing autographs. When he got to my hand, I pulled him tightly against the fence. His face was plastered to the gate in a painful looking position as girls pulled on his clothes through the rails.

Reece loved the attention but when he saw it was me his smile fell. "Kitty? What the fuck are you doing over there?" He flipped his hand around and held mine tighter as the girls around me tried to push me out of the way so they could get a hold of Reece.

"Please, just get me out of here," I begged, holding his hand for dear life.

Reece turned to the guard, asking him to open the gate so I could get on the other side.

The guard shook his head, "I'm sorry, I can't do that. Kane gave strict instructions not to let her back here."

"Well Kane isn't fucking Prince Ali. I said let her in and I mean it," Reece said, still holding on to my hand.

"Me too!"

"Please let me in!"

"I need you, Reece!"

"I want in too!"

Shouts like these, were flying all over the place as Reece argued with the guard to let me in.

A few minutes later, he let me through after he called another guard to help hold back the masses so there wouldn't be a stampede. Safely on the other side, I walked with Reece to the back stage area.

"Why the hell didn't he just let you back here?" Reece asked.

We stood outside the doors that lead backstage. "I don't fucking know. He was trying to prove a point I guess. Where the hell is he? I'm going to beat the shit out of him for that,"

I followed Reece in and down the winding hallways. "He's probably getting ready to do the meet and greet. We all are actually. Last show, they want all of us to sign autographs and meet fans."

We'd made it to the room where the meet and greet was going to take place. I sent Reece in there and told him to send Kane out without letting him know it was me. I stood against a wall, a hallway away from the signing. Kane's footsteps were getting closer. As he came around the corner, I stepped out of the darkened doorway I was hiding in. I stood in the middle of the hallway, his only option was to turn around, but he must have known I'd just run after him.

So, he stopped in his tracks.

I smiled up at him, "Hi, Kane."

"Jesus Christ, how did you get back here?" he demanded.

"Wow, Kane, it's great to see you too," I said, taking a step closer.

He crossed his arms defensively, "What do you want, Caroline?"

"I just want to talk to you," I said, dropping the annoyed act. This was my chance to make him see I still loved him. He gestured for me to get on with it. "Can't you see that I—Kane, I've said it before and I'm going to sound like a fucking broken record but, I made a mistake leaving."

He nodded in agreement, the hard exterior he always seemed to have up when I was around dropped as he leaned against the wall. *Was I finally getting through to him? Was he finally hearing me, instead of reminding himself of the past?*

"You want me to, what? Forgive you?" he asked, looking over at me.

"Yes," I sighed.

Silence was all around us, even the screams from the arena were muted as I waited to hear what he was going to say.

"I want to forgive you," he said, breaking that silence.

Unfolding his arms, he pushed himself off the wall to come closer to me. His hand moved, so he was almost touching my cheek. I'd never felt power like and he wasn't even touching me. My eyes closed of their own accord, as I took in the energy coming off his hand. I wanted to lean into it, to feel his touch against my skin. I craved it more than air.

With my eyes still closed, I whispered, "Then forgive me."

When I opened them, I expected to see his beautiful blue eyes, but he'd closed them, and I knew that was him trying to keep me out. Our bodies were pulling us together, without us even knowing. His cool blue eyes finally opened. I could see him and the struggle he was having.

"Caroline, I—Damn, you're beautiful," he said, finally running the tips of his fingers across my cheek.

I felt hopeful and terrified at the same time. Terrified that this would be the last time he'd touch me, hopeful that it was just the first of many more.

"You're not going to stop, are you?" he asked, moving his hand from my cheek and down to his side. "Well, I'll make it easy on you. You can stop. Stop running after me. I'm letting you off the hook. I forgive you, so you can go back to your life in New York, go back to your dream job and whatever else you have to go back to."

Is he kidding me with that! "All right, Kane, enough with the bullshit!" I was livid that he still wasn't getting it. "I've been here every weekend, waiting for you to get your head out of your ass. Can't you see that I'm crazy about you? Open your eyes, Kane. I'm here, and I'm not going anywhere!" I was up in his face, trying desperately to make him see me, see that I was here for him.

"Fine, you're here right now, but tomorrow you'll be gone. You'll leave to go back to your other life in New York."

"You're right. I could go back tomorrow to my job. They offered me a position that I'd be stupid to turn down," I snapped at him.

He's being so fucking stubborn!

Cleary disgusted, he took a step back from me and tossed his hands up. "And there it is, right back to the beginning—you leaving!"

"Then make me stay, Kane! Make me believe you want me, make me believe you could love me again, make me believe you give a shit, and I'll stay!" My voice echoed off the walls all around us. I took a breath, gathered my thoughts, and spoke softly this time. "Make me stay, so I'll never leave you again."

He stood there, a foot or two from me, staring at me, fighting a battle in his own head, a battle I could see clearly through his eyes. If this was it, if this was the end, I wanted to burn his image into my mind, catalog his smell, and remember how he tasted. If this was the end, I knew that I'd never make it without him, but maybe having these memories could keep me alive.

So I studied his face, his strong jaw, the stubble that grew on it, the sparkle in his cool blue eyes, and the warmth of his shaggy brown hair. The way the muscles in his arms flexed as he moved them. I took in everything, before I wasn't able to anymore.

I never thought about the force a man could have when he had been deprived of what he really wanted for so long. I knew now that it was rough and sensual all twisted together into something that couldn't be put into words.

Everything happened so fast, my back slammed against the concert wall. I braced my hands against it as his body pressed into mine. He cupped my face in his hands and I watched as he let himself go. Lips, plush and wet, crashed down over mine. The moment his mouth touched mine, I found myself falling down a kaleidoscope of colors and shapes.

Those strong hands drifted down my neck as he kissed me. He wrapped them around the back of my neck. My head slid down the wall as he tugged at my hair. My lips were forced away from his. I tried my best to get them back where I wanted them, but he was reacquainting himself with my neck and didn't care what I wanted. The moans, groans, and growls coming from the two of us bounced off the walls, giving a soundtrack to a long awaited kiss, a kiss where neither of us held back. A kiss where we let go of the past and simply focused on what was right in front of us. I ripped my hands from the wall and held onto him for dear life. My hands wrapped around the shirt at his waist. I wasn't about to let go. I wasn't ever letting go.

CHAPTER 44

Kane

I was on my way to the signing, our last one, since it was the last show on the tour. Our next stop was LA, to work on recording an album. The contracts were signed at the beginning of the tour and our home away from home in LA was waiting for us. As soon as that was finished, we were right back on the road to promote the album.

I was feeling good about everything that was happening in my life, that is, until last weekend's slip up with Caroline. I thought that I had her under control. I thought that I was doing well. That is, until I nearly beat a man for looking at her. I had to refocus. I had to get back on track.

So when I saw her standing on the other side of the gate when I walked off the bus, I thought to myself, *self, this is your opportunity to put her in her place.* I informed the guard not to let her in, no matter what she was saying. When she started begging, it made it so much sweeter. The cherry on top, was when she asked if I was just going to walk away and leave her there. *Bam, bitch! Yes, I am!*

And I walked away from her, just like she walked away from me.

When Reece arrived in the signing room and informed me that John, the manager for 4 Alliance was looking for me, I didn't waste any time. I left the room and headed down the hall and around the corner to where Reece said he was waiting for me in our dressing room.

"Hi, Kane," Caroline said, jumping out a dark hallway and scaring me half to death.

"Jesus Christ, how did you get back here?" I demanded.

"Wow, Kane, it's great to see you too," she said, taking a step closer to me.

Crossing my arms I asked, "What do you want, Caroline?"

"I just want to talk to you," she said, dropping her little attitude. I tried to interrupt her but couldn't. "Can't you see that I—Kane, I've said it before and I'm going to sound like a fucking broken record but, I made a mistake leaving."

Can't argue with that. I also couldn't help but feel my heart warm up to her, like it always did. I moved to the wall and tried to put my thoughts in some sort of order. "You want me to, what? Forgive you?"

I was desperate for her to just leave me alone and move on. *This shit is hurting too much now, seeing her is hurting too much.*

"Yes," she said on a shaky breath.

Wouldn't that just be easy? Forgive her and forget, but how do you forget the worst fucking year of your life? How do you forget the way it felt when the only person you've ever loved left you with no explanation, no warning?

"I want to forgive you," I said, breaking the silence that had grown between us.

I pushed myself off the wall. I got in her face, her beautiful face that always seemed to be right behind my eyelids whenever I closed them. I couldn't help myself. My hand came to her cheek but didn't touch it. I was afraid that, if I touched her, I'd be done. That soft delicate skin of hers was going to crack me, and I needed to stay strong, sane.

Her eyes closed as she waited for me to just do it, just touch her, and she begged, "Then forgive me."

Shit, she opened them, the liquid blue in them was pulling me in, and I couldn't look away from her. I was stuck in a trance. I didn't want to be affected by her, but I sure as hell didn't want to stop looking at her either.

"Caroline, I—Damn, you're beautiful," I said, clearly not thinking sanely anymore.

When her face lit up with a smile, it was like a punch to the gut. My heart hit against my chest, demanding for me to get it over with and finally touch that soft delicate skin on her cheek.

I moved my hand away from her cheek before I gave in and touched her. "You're not going to stop, are you?" Thankfully, my brain had kicked in and put a stop to my fucking heart. "Well, I'll make it easy on you. You can stop. Stop running after me. I'm letting you off the hook. I forgive you, so you can go back to your life in New York, go back to your dream job and whatever else you have to go back to."

There, fuck, I hope that's the end of this because I can't hold out any longer. That was my last hope at getting her to move on. I simply didn't know what else to do.

"All right Kane, enough with the bullshit!" she seethed.

Fuck me, she was pissed. That's good, right?

"I've been here every weekend, waiting for you to

get your head out of your ass. Can't you see that I'm crazy about you? Open your eyes, Kane. I'm here, and I'm not going anywhere!"

She was up in my face, and, as her words hit home, I lost it. "Fine!" I yelled, "You're here right now, but tomorrow you'll be gone. You'll leave to go back to your other life in New York."

"You're right. I could go back tomorrow to my job. They offered me a position that I'd be stupid to turn down," she snapped at me.

Is she fucking serious? That's not the way to win the guy you left stranded for a job back. I was beyond frustrated and quite frankly disgusted. "And there it is. Right back to the beginning—you leaving!"

At least she had the balls to tell me this time. I took a step away from her, needing some space. Tossing my hands in the air, I let them land and run through my hair.

"Then make me stay, Kane! Make me believe you want me. Make me believe you could love me again. Make me believe you give a shit, and I'll stay!" Her voice echoed off the walls all around us. I watched as she took a breath, gathered her thoughts, and spoke softly. "Make me stay, so I'll never leave you again."

I stood there, a foot or two from her, staring at her, fighting the fucked up battle between my head and my heart. Honestly, I didn't know what to fucking say. I wanted to turn around and leave her. I wanted to hold her in my arms and never let go. But all I could do was stare at her.

Caroline had the perfect skin color, tan but not overly dark. Her body was made for my hands. I knew she fit perfectly between them. That wild mane of blonde curls atop her head reminded me of how feisty and stubborn she could be. Her eyes had a way of drawing me in, even if I tried to resist them. Her lips, fuck, her lips—

I was done. I was done fighting. *I won't deny myself anymore*. I rushed to her, grabbed her face between my hands and slammed her against the wall. There was nothing soft or kind about that kiss. I had been fucking dreaming of kissing her like that for over a year. I lost it. I lost myself in it, not caring about the consequences and only caring about how it made me feel to have her again. I took what I wanted, what I needed in that kiss. I was selfish. I didn't give a fuck about anything else as I kissed her. When I finally came up for air, I held her hostage against the wall, my face buried in her neck as I caught the breath that the kiss had taken away from me.

"God, you ruin me, woman," I breathed into her neck. "I miss you too fucking much to be mad anymore."

Having her close to me, my lips on her flesh, it was as if I could breathe again, like the whole year I was only getting little gasps of air, but at last I had taken a deep, fulfilling breath.

"Take me home?" she asked, her fingers still clutched in my shirt.

Those words hit me and I was back to a year ago. I was back to the lake, holding her in my arms while she was shaking and begging me to get her away from the nightmare we had just been a part of.

I hadn't planned on giving in, I hadn't planned on taking her back, and I sure as hell didn't plan on kissing her. When she kissed me before it wasn't like this. This hit me hard. It hit me right in the fucking chest, and I was done.

I stared into those liquid blue eyes, stunned that after all that had happened—after a whole year apart—we still managed to come back together. "Take me home," she had asked me. But where the hell was that? New York? The bus? The bar?

Right then, my home was a bus full of rowdy musicians, looking for their big break. Her home was in New York in some luxury apartment.

I started to think back, recalling all that she had once said. All the times that she pushed me away, held me at arm's length. *How was this going to work? There was no way I was giving up my dream, and she made it perfectly clear before that she wasn't giving up hers. Fuck! Maybe she was right all along.*

She must have sensed the change in me, seen the drop of my smile as I realized what she had been trying to tell me all along.

"Kane, what's the matter?" she asked, taking my hands in hers.

I stood there shell-shocked. "You're right. You've always been right."

Even though I had finally admitted that I still loved her, and that she still had a fucking hold over me, nothing had changed. *We'll never make it together.*

"What are you talking about? Kane, look at me!" she demanded, squeezing my hands tightly.

"No matter what we do, no matter how much I love you or you love me, it won't work. I won't take your dream job away, and I won't let you take mine from me like I tried to take yours. Kitty—"

It was the first time I had called her that since she left. I avoided calling her Kitty for fear it would make me weak, but *now,* now I didn't care. What had started out as a way to get on her nerves backfired, big time. She was my Kitty and saying it out loud made me as vulnerable as I had let myself be since the day she left me.

"I told you I'd leave it. I'd leave it all behind, as long as I'm with you. It's not worth it, nothing is. Nothing is worth leaving you again," she pleaded.

"Kitty—aw, fuck."

I couldn't think straight when she said shit like that

and looked as hot as she did. I grabbed her neck and pulled her up so her lips met mine again. Seemed we had come full circle, making out in a hallway, pushing each other away. *What the fuck is wrong with us?*

"I'm going to be late for the meet n greet," I said softly against her lips, palming her cheeks. "Can we finish this after?"

"Yeah, I'll meet you back at the busses. I guess I need to put my two weeks' notice in," she said, giddy and smiling.

She reached up and left a gentle kiss on my lips then turned to head back to where the busses were parked. The image of her leaving on the plane flashed across my eyes and I fucking panicked. That feeling of dread returned. The thought of never seeing her again, that she was going to bolt on me, pulled a heavy cloud of darkness over me, and fuck if I was going to let that happen. I grabbed her arm, spinning her back to crash into my chest.

"Kane, don't you have to go?" she asked, tilting her head back in delight as I left kisses along her neck.

"Fuck, yeah, I have to go and so do you." She looked up at me, her brows scrunched in confusion. I grinned down at her. "You're not leaving my sight, ever. You can put your two weeks' notice in later."

Taking her hand in mine, I interlocked my fingers through hers. Pulling them up, I kissed the back of her hand, then headed back to where the meet n greet was with Kitty by my side.

Just as we were going to walk through the door, she held me back, pulling at my arm. I moved to the side of the door and she held my hand tighter. Her eyes, fixed on mine. I waited for it. I knew it was coming, this was Kitty, after all. The same old I-can't-do-this-it's-a-mistake Kitty.

"Kane, I need you to know that I'm in this. Before

we go in that room where your—our—friends are, your colleagues, your boss, I need you to realize that I'm not leaving you again, no matter what. Because right now, I can feel you tensing up. I can feel you wanting to shut me out again. I know I've told you in the past that I couldn't do this for one reason or another."

I nodded down at her, agreeing with everything she said.

"But that's over. The positives outweigh the negatives. They always have. I just tried to ignore it. Kane, this is your last chance, because once we walk in there, I'm claiming you as mine, and I don't ever plan on changing that," she said, staring into my eyes, into my soul.

I grinned back. "Ditto."

She gave a relieved sigh. "Good. I didn't want to have to beat you up on our first day back together."

"All right, so I guess you're my number-one groupie now. I think you should start and head up my official fan club—Ouch! What the hell? What happened to not beating me up on our first day back together?" I said, rubbing my sore arm.

"Kane Lawson, I am not one of your groupies. I'm your girlfriend and you better never fucking forget that," she seethed, hitting my arm again for added effect.

I cringed, holding my arms up to block her next attack. "Whoa, whoa, whoa, put the claws away. I get it—girlfriend, not groupie."

"Good! We can go in now," she said cheerily.

Hand in hand, we walked in that room, knowing that it was going to be hard and wonderful all rolled up into one. With her hand in mine, we entered the room and all eyes fell on us. John, the manager of the tour, stopped us a few steps past the door. "Kane, who's this?" he asked rather rudely, which instantly put me on the defensive.

"What's it matter to you?" I said back.

I caught Chloe shaking her head, and a few of the other guys adverting their eyes from the scene. *What the hell is going on to make everyone on edge?*

"Did you even read the contract?" John asked.

What the fuck was he talking about? Of course, I read the contract, kind of. I mean, I skimmed it. It was a lot of lawyer garbage. Who the fuck could even read that shit, anyway? I read a few things about them putting us up in a house while we recorded, something about the label having a say in advertising. I didn't fucking know what he was talking about. All I focused on was the number 3 with a bunch of zeros behind it.

He shook his head, "You didn't read it, did you?" He pointed to Kitty. "She can't be here."

It took a few seconds for that to sink in, and when it did, I found it rather hard to contain myself. "The *fuck* she can't," I yelled for all the room to hear.

"Okay, I get it, you're upset. You want your lady friend to be here, but you signed a contract stating that any public signing or appearances, you would be alone. No flavors of the week, women of the night, no 'friends.' Is any of this ringing a bell?" he asked.

"Yeah you're ringing a bell, John. First off, Kitty isn't any of those things. Second off, I don't remember reading anything about that. And third, she's the fucking love of my life, and I hate to break it to you, but she's not leaving my side. So now what? Am I in breach of contract? You need to call the big wigs? Because she's not leaving, and if you make her leave, then I'm leaving too," I said as serious as I've ever been.

"Kane, its fine. I can go wait by the busses," Kitty said, wrapping her hand around my arm and bringing my skyrocketing temper down slightly.

She knew how long I'd dreamed of being a rock star,

but fuck if she was going to sit in the back row while it happened. I wanted her right by my side for the whole ride.

"You should listen to her. You'll be done in half hour and we can forget this ever happened," John said charmingly.

"No, we won't forget this ever happened, because she's going to be with me for every one of these. Don't girlfriends get privileges?" I asked, not dropping or giving in at all.

"No, they don't, Kane. We can't be liable for her or anyone unless it's legal," he said, standing his ground.

"Legal?" I questioned

"Yeah, legal, like legally married," he said, like I should have known all along.

Well, maybe I would have if I had actually read the contract. I knew that a few of the guys from 4 Alliance always had the same girl with them. I assumed it was a girlfriend, but I was wrong. When I turned toward where they sat, two of them held up their hands displaying silver bands around their fourth finger.

"Married, huh?" I asked, looking back at John, who nodded in agreement. "Fine." I turned to Kitty, took both her hands in mine, and held them in front of us.

Reece yelled from across the room, "No fucking way!"

We all turned in his direction. He stood there gawking at Kitty and me.

"Oh, come on, someone back me up here," he said, looking to either side of him where his fellow bandmates gave him dirty looks. "Fine, continue," he said dramatically, sitting back down.

I don't think it hit her, until I knelt down.

"Kane, what are you doing?" she asked frantically as she tried to pull me back up.

I stared up into her blue eyes and asked, "Do you love me?"

"Kane, I can wait at the bus, really, it's okay."

"Answer the question. Do you love me?"

She stood there staring at me in disbelief.

"Kitty, this is when you say yes," Trent piped up from beside us.

She turned to him, obviously shocked. Aiden was nodding along with Trent as he spoke.

"Come on, Cuz, you can do it," JJ added.

"For the record, I say no. I still have faith she loves me," Reece added nonchalantly.

"Well?" I asked, gaining her attention back.

A few times she looked like she was going to speak but the words weren't coming out. For a split second I thought that I'd fucked up again, that she was going to run, that is until—

"Yes, I love you, but—"

"Then marry me," I said, grinning up at her.

"Marry you? Just so I can be in this room with you?" she asked, shaking her head at the insanity of it all.

"No, so you can be with me forever."

She smiled down at me. "Kane, are you serious? We just got back together like ten minutes ago. Don't you think this is a little fast?"

"Considering I said I was going to marry you the first day I saw you, I'd say no. So, what do you think?"

"I think you're crazy!" she said, throwing her head back and laughing. "And—I—this is—" She laughed again but the smile on her face grew. "Oh, fuck it! I want to marry you."

I've never seen her face light up as much as it did when she said those five words. The only time it ever came close was when she had Reece in a head lock and a pair of scissors in her hand.

I stood up as fast as I could, taking her in my arms. I held her tightly, lifting her off the floor with ease. I spun us around then placed her back on the ground. I took her face between my hands and kissed her. I kissed her lips, her cheeks, her nose, everywhere.

It was the happiest that I'd ever been, and having her by my side, I'd never have to be anything but.

"Jesus, Kitty, you're killing me," Reece called out as I kissed my fiancée. "Oh, come on, guys, you don't have to fucking rub it in," he said again. I made sure to rub, squeeze, and slap her ass just so Reece had to watch. He slammed his head on the table. "All right, all right, we fucking get it."

I felt a smile spread across Kitty's face. I felt her heart beat against my chest. All the shit we put ourselves through, even though it fucking sucked, I don't think I'd change it for anything. "Well, John, looks like my fiancée is here to stay," I said, draping an arm around Kitty.

"Whatever, I don't have time to deal with your love life. Get it down on paper, get it legal," John said.

"Are we really getting married?" Kitty asked from under my arm.

"Fucking right, we're getting married. Not every day you get to marry your number-one groupie," I said, smirking down at her. Then I immediately grabbed the side she'd just punched. "Damn, baby! That's spousal abuse!"

"Hit him once for me. That fucker deserves everything he gets for taking you off the market," Reece said, sulking in his chair.

"Looks like you're going to have to deal with only getting to second base," Kitty said, winking over at him.

"Yeah, that's never happening again, for any of you. I got my eye on you Trent," I said, making sure that everyone in the room heard me.

Kitty hit my chest. "Stop being so mean."

"What? No one, not even your little chair over there is getting away with that shit anymore."

"I resent that, but I'm happy for you guys," Trent said with a smile.

"Congrats, bro," Aiden said from his chair.

"On behalf of Kitty's family, I approve of this, and I'm so fucking stoked to actually call you family!" JJ added.

"Okay, are we done with all this sappy love shit?" a female voice piped up over all the male voices. Chloe stood from her chair, her arms crossed and a pissed off look on her face.

"Chloe, come on—"

Rolling her eyes, Chloe let everyone know exactly how she felt. "Save it, Kane, you're a traitor. Can we just get this signing over with so I can get the hell out of here?"

"Yeah, all right," I said, giving in.

I knew she was pissed at me. She might try to hide the fact, say that I meant nothing to her, but it was written all over her pissed-off face that I did. *What can I say? I'm a heart breaker, but as long as I don't break Kitty's heart, I think I can live with myself.*

I took Kitty's hand in mine and walked to my seat. She sat in a seat behind me, but I never let go of her hand.

CHAPTER 45

Us

I'm Kane "Whipped as a Motherfucker" Lawson. I'm in love with my wife. I trust her with my heart, I trust her not to break it, again. I never thought that I'd be a one-woman kind of man, but fuck, if a petite, foul-mouthed, punching machine, wild-haired, blue-eyed beauty didn't put me right in my place. I'm so fucking happy that she ran after this asshole, because he is the luckiest bastard in the world. *I* am the luckiest bastard in the world.

છ૩૯૩

I'm Caroline "Kitty" Lawson, I'm in love with my husband. I'm not afraid of anything anymore. I'm not afraid to see my future when I kiss him. I'm not afraid of the day-in-day-out because with us, it's never boring. I'm not afraid of becoming my mother, because I know my husband will fight for me. I know he has faith in me, and I *know* he'll Make Me Stay.

CHAPTER 46

JJ

Okay, enough is enough. It's been two, fucking weeks! I pulled the pillow over my head, praying that it would at least muffle the noises coming from the room above me. Hearing my cousin and best friend screaming each other's names in ecstasy, isn't how I wanted to start or finish my day, but here we are—day fourteen.

About the Author

M.E. Gordon, was born and raised in Maryland, where she still resides with her husband. She is a stay at home mom to four children, three boys and one very, spoiled, little girl, all under the age of five. Growing up Gordon was an avid journal writer. She wrote her first romance novel at the age of fourteen, and it was pretty bad, but over the years and through all the kids, she honed her craft. When Gordon doesn't have her Mom hat on, you can find her reading, working on her next story, or watching guilty-pleasure television.